Khara Bennet-Vengeance

By Elliot M. Rubin

The sequel to

Hot Cash/Cold Bodies

Acknowledgements

I would like to thank my father, Herman S. Rubin for his inspiration and encouragement to write.

He wrote essays, prayers, and poetry his whole life, and his writings are treasured by those who have read them.

Also, I would like to thank my beloved grandmother, Bessie Greenberg, for giving me the gift of creativity and imagination. Her lunchtime stories of Moishe Kapoya when I was a child stirred my creative mind to picture the story, and mentally be in the scene.

And finally I want to thank my dear wife Laura who is an avid reader, and whose encouragement to write is most appreciated so I stay out of her hair.

Other novels by Elliot M. Rubin are:

* Hot Cash/Cold Bodies

* People Stories in 600 words -
    as told by a raconteur

* Romance and Murder in Bensonhurst

* Wilted Minds -
    Stories of Sex, Addiction, and Lost Love

* The Phartick Chronicles -
    Yiddle Stories of Satire and Humor

* The Writings of Herman S. Rubin -
    Edited by Elliot and Bradley Rubin

    www.CreativeFiction.net

Copyright September 2, 2016

United States Library of Congress

ISBN # 978-0-9913060-9-1

Chapter One

"Nine One One operator, where is the emergency?"

"224 Hightley Street. Help me, my husband is gonna kill me."

"The police are on their way, what is your name? Where are you now?"

"I'm hiding upstairs. I can't speak any louder, hurry."

The phone goes dead, and there is silence on the line.

A dispatcher broadcasts the incident. Detectives Khara Bennet and Matt McMann are driving back to their precinct from an earlier investigation when they hear this on their police radio. Matt responds they will take the call since the address is only one block from their current location.

By luck Khara is sitting behind the wheel, she flips the siren on, the gas pedal smashes to the floor, and the tires screech as she turns a corner onto a tree-lined residential street in the Borough of Richmond. The second home on the left they discover the front door is wide open, and the house number is correct.

The doors slam shut on the unmarked car as they bolt inside the home through the open door, aware this is a domestic violence call which can be dangerous and deadly. Both of them are in street clothes with their gold badge hanging on a chain around their necks.

Once they enter the main hallway Khara is surprised to find a large man standing in the rear kitchen of the house. The room is about twenty feet away, and she observes beads of sweat running down his face. With hair and clothing disheveled he appears to her to be perturbed and unbalanced.

The suspected husband is sized up by her, and she figures he is well over six feet tall. A huge beer belly protrudes beneath his plaid flannel shirt, tribal tattoos on his neck are showing through the front of his unzipped army fatigue jacket, and yet Khara is unfazed.

The expression on his face tells her he is upset as they enter the home. This huge man explodes with unfiltered verbal rage towards them.

"Where is my wife? I will rip her hair out of her head when I find her. Husbands come home and expect a hot meal on the table, no excuses. My piece of human garbage wife is going to regret not cooking for me tonight. The bible says a woman must obey her husband!"

Khara signals to Matt pointing to the steps leading up to the second floor.

"Matt go up there, and try to find where she is hiding, I'll handle him myself."

Aware of Khara's martial arts ability he leaves her, bounds up the stairs shouting to the hidden wife hoping she will hear his voice and come to him for protection

The husband is approached with measured steps. Khara is not taking her eyes off him for a second. With not so much as a blink Khara stares at his face as he shrieks curses to her at an unrelenting pace. The words are ignored as her arms are outstretched from her body only a few inches, palms upwards. Confident in her skill in Krav Mega, not showing him any intimidation due to his immense size and displeasure she continues to advance into the kitchen.

The distance to him is getting smaller as she goes forward at a snail's pace almost to where he is standing. The stove is now next to her as she speaks to him in a commanding voice. Fearless Khara is composed in the face of danger.

"I am Detective Bennet. Calm down, and sit on the chair behind you."

"Screw you bitch, where's my wife, I want her now, I'm going to beat her, and you ain't going to stop me."

The man begins to move forward toward her as she enters deeper into the room. Not flinching and continuing to stare straight at his eyes Khara is ready for action.

At this point, she is standing by the stove and using her peripheral vision she grabs a steel pot sitting on the top of the gas burners with her right hand. With no hesitation, she flings it across the room away from her and hits a glass door on the wooden cabinets resulting in a loud crashing sound.

Shards of sharp glass shatter all over the room including on the granite countertops. The husband turns his head following the thrown pot, and the shattering sounds of glass give Khara the split second needed for her to sprint forward kicking him in the groin.

In an instant, he drops to his knees holding his genitals. Now in front of him, she takes her hand and strikes him with force in the throat. From the hard strike, he reels backward while grabbing his neck. The back of his head hits the edge of the dinette table behind him flipping it over as he falls down. The sharp tip of the laminate table slashes his head, and blood begins to run down the rear of his shirt.

Stunned for a second when he lands on the ground there is enough time for her to leap over his immense body, and grab his hand to put him into a wrist lock. With a violent twist on his arm, she turns him over face down on the kitchen floor. Not wasting any time Khara hurries to handcuff his wrists. Once he is secured she grabs a handful of his thick black hair, and with determination yanks his head upwards sitting him upright with his back leaning against the wall.

"Think you saved my lazy piece of shit wife? Wait till I get out of these handcuffs, and I'll teach both of you bitches a lesson."

"Think you're a tough guy?"

"Screw you too, you black bitch."

Upon hearing what he said Khara leaned over and picked up the metal pot she had thrown before. With her arm raised over her head, and with the flat side of the pot, she slams him with all her strength in the middle of his face.

"It is illegal to threaten a police officer, sir."

Blood pours profusely out of his nose after the metal pan flattens and breaks it. Stunned he opens his eyes and is trying to say something. He is sputtering bright red blood as it runs down his upper lip while he tries to speak.

"Bitch now I'm going to murder you and my asshole wife too."

Again Khara holds the handle and raises her arm, and pounds him in the face with the pot once more breaking additional teeth. More blood is now pouring out of his face, and congealing on the floor. Two of his teeth chipped off and falls on his lap.

The husband stares at her, attempting to mutter something to Khara but it is garbled and unintelligible.

There is still fury in his voice. With a lot of difficulty she cannot understand what he is saying but it does not matter. His unbridled anger is understood.

For a third time, the pot thunders into his face sending his eyes rolling back into his head. The forceful impact of the metal hitting bone on his forehead sent vibrations up Khara's forearm. Dazed he rolls over on his side and is now unconscious.

Matt is coming down the stairs with the wife after spending time calming her down, and assuring her she is safe. The smallish woman is holding a handful of tissues drying her eyes, and sobbing with deep breaths.

The petite woman enters the kitchen, stops, stands next to Detective McMann, and spots her husband lying motionless in a pool of his blood with Khara perched over him.

"Officer, what happened to him?"

"Resisted arrest and threatened a police officer with bodily harm; he had to be subdued," she said.

Without saying a word the wife steps in front of him as he is sprawled out unconscious and bleeding, and kicks him in the groin. "This is for the beat downs you gave me, asshole. Detectives I want to pack my bags and leave after you take him to jail. Can you watch him while I put my clothes into a suitcase?"

"Yes no problem at all, Matt can you go with her to help if you can?"

A call goes in for backup, and an ambulance to take the perp to the hospital for medical care. The directory in Khara's cell phone gives her the information the woman asked for. The wife jots down on a piece of paper the number and address of a hotline for abused women on Staten Island.

There is one question Khara asked the wife who is still shaking from nerves.

"Was he always abusive to you?"

"My husband has anger issues, but he never hit me until a few weeks ago. Now he is seeing a doctor about it, but there is no change in him."

"Do you know who it is, and where is his office?"

"Yes, it is a woman psychologist, not a man. Here is her card, he keeps it on the refrigerator, and this is where she has her patients come for sessions. The office is located in Eltingville on the Island somewhere."

"Thank you, I'll visit her next week as part of this investigation."

The EMT's brought the husband out to a waiting ambulance, and transfers him to the emergency room, leaving the premises.

Upstairs Matt lets the woman pack her clothes while he searches around wondering if there are any guns in the house. There are none found.

After helping her out to her vehicle the wife leaves in her car, and the detectives return to their office to file the event report.

In a cubicle at the precinct, Khara is sitting at her desk and receives a personal call on her cell phone from one of her boyfriends.

"Hey, it's me, Al. I'm in Brooklyn at your apartment house in Brighton Beach with Olga. After you leave work stop by the dance club, I need to speak to you."

"What time is good for you Al?"

"Does not matter, I'll be back at the club in about thirty minutes, and I'll wait until you arrive."

The computer on her desk is whizzing as she hurries to finish her reports, and tells Matt she'll be back in the morning. The rear stairway goes downstairs to the lobby as she leaves the building, and hops into a new black BMW M3 Al purchased for her. Before he gave it to her he installed flashing lights on the rear interior deck and on the front grill for her. The round custom manual shifter is shoved into first gear as she starts to drive to the dance club he owns off the back

440 highway. The business is run as a front for money laundering, and other organized criminal activities.

An adrenalin junkie Khara punches the gas pedal to the floor, and shifts into second with the car lurching forward at speed as she pulls on the freeway passing slower cars to her right. The visceral roar of the engine combined with the thrust of the powerful V8's torque slams her into the back of her leather bucket seat. This is an endorphin high for her, and she is enjoying it to the fullest.

With little traffic on the road, she drives to the building, stops at the valet awning, and flips her key fob to the waiting attendant. The young man parks her car next to Al's red Cadillac in the front of the building. Fancy and expensive luxury automobiles are parked near the entrance for appearances.

There is no rush so she takes her time going up the entry path where Big Boy is standing, he smiles and pulls the engraved glass doors open for her.

"Thanks, Biggie, courteous of you to hold the door for me."

"Good to see you Khara. Play nice please."

"Of course, when don't I?"

Big Boy smirked knowing her better than most from past dealings.

Upon her entering the lobby a hostess in a short skimpy sequined outfit approaches, and asks Khara "please follow me the boss is expecting you."

The dance floor is crowded as she follows the girl through the club to the glass-enclosed elevator in the rear of the building. Always alert to everything going on around her she misses very little. Going up Khara eyeballs him, and he is waiting for her on the balcony. After a quick kiss and embrace, he takes her hand and leads her to a secluded booth where they sit overlooking the dance floor below. The music is loud, the beat is constant, but upstairs it is somewhat muted so they can talk in private.

"Haven't seen you in a while Khara, what's doing at the precinct?"

"Same shit, just more of it, I'm getting tired of Staten Island. Not enough action for me. Now the Mexican Ecru Cartel is finished I'm thinking of asking for a transfer back to Manhattan. Too quiet here. I'm bored and need something real happening. This borough is too dead for me; nothing exciting is going on here."

"I can understand what you are saying, and before you put in for a request I wanted to tell you what is going on with our mutual friend Olga. Alejandro was brought back to Brooklyn after she shot him in Beach Channel Queens, and one of her Ukrainian doctors worked on his shoulder. In the firefight, her bullet hit him and shattered bones, and his right arm is now useless. The doctor, on her orders, severed some nerves on purpose when he went in to take out the bullet and bone fragments. Now he only uses his left arm."

"Good, he's an asshole. Screw him; it serves him right for trying to kill me and blowing up my home. Did she obtain any good information out of him regarding his drug operations in Mexico?"

"Yes, and her retired Russian FSB men helped him decide to fully cooperate with her. Too bad I was not there when they questioned him, but Olga told me he is now circumcised. The procedure was done without any painkillers."

"Wow it must have hurt," Khara said.

"Yes, I'm sure it did. She found out the picture Big Boy's men took of the presidential candidate with the naked underage Mexican girl in Laredo, is the real brains behind the cartel and drug smuggling. Alejandro was the muscle of the organization operating out of Mexico. The congressman will be in Manhattan soon campaigning, and fundraising. We need to decide how we want to approach him and finish him off."

Thinking for a moment Khara responded. "To get close enough to attack is going to be very hard to do. The Secret Service is now guarding him all the time after he won a few primary state elections. Someone with a security clearance is needed to even get within ten feet of him now."

"In the back of my mind, I figured something like this is going to happen if he stayed in the race long enough. Try to transfer into the terrorism bureau at the police department so you might be able to be close enough to him. Once you are in there I think you'll learn about his travel schedule. Also if you could it would enable Olga to make arrangements with her Russian Special Forces guys to take care of this new problem."

"Maybe, let me see what I can do," Khara said.

With a satisfied look on his face due to her answer, he is sitting at her side smiling. It didn't start out this way, but over time she found herself being dragged deeper and deeper into the black pit of organized crime.

"By the way Khara, how is the M3 I had acquired for you?"

"Love it, it's great. Thank you."

"Yer it is the least I can do after your last one was blown up. Listen, I appreciate your helping me out in Queens last year."

"This car must have cost you a lot of money Al, BMW I know is an expensive car, and the new M3 you gave me is not cheap."

"No Khara it didn't cost me a penny. This guy I know needed help with a few problems he had importing stuff into Port Newark. The car was bought for you as a thank you to me, and I'm glad you like it."

"How can I show you my gratitude, Al?"

"Later you can, come on we're going for dinner, and we'll relax a bit at my place in Bay Ridge after we finish eating."

Standing he helps her out of the booth as they go back downstairs. The elevator doors close as she presses her body against his while beginning to kiss him. She gyrates in a slow up and down motion as the all-glass enclosed elevator descends to ground level.

The doorman opens the front door as they walk out to the overhanging awning, and the valet brings Al's red Cadillac to the carpeted entry for him. After both sit in the car, he says he is taking her to a small cafe he invested in. The place is located in Bensonhurst and is off Bay Parkway near 85th Street in a private home.

"How did you start a restaurant in someone's home, can you do something like this in the city?"

"The owners are friends of a friend Khara, and I know them for many years. The house only has four tables in their dining room and five in their living room. Every dish is fresh, made when ordered, and you need to know someone to even enter the home. All my associates go there for good home cooked food. This is real Italian cooking, not like the garbage you find in the chain restaurants or in the malls."

"The restaurant makes enough money from only nine tables?"

"Yer and it's not cheap. Without making a reservation you can't get in. The place is sold out every night of the week. To make it work I had to buy real commercial ovens and stoves for them, I want you to know the food is out of this world. In their basement, I put two big restaurant refrigerators so they can store whatever supplies they might need."

"Do they offer a set menu?"

"No, it changes daily depending on what they feel like making. There is no choice from a big menu. The chef makes two new dishes every day, one meat and one fish. At the time you make your reservation you tell them which one you would like so they buy the amount they will need for the night."

"Did you preorder for us?"

"Yes, when I spoke to you earlier I made our reservation, and ordered both dishes in case you wanted the other one."

The Cadillac is passing over the Verrazano Bridge during the early evening rush hour as Khara sits back in the tan leather seat and glances out at New York Harbor below. The small whitecaps are churning as birds are having a tough time flying against the wind. The car turns onto the Belt Parkway heading east to Kennedy Airport, and he gets off at the Bay Parkway exit. The restaurant is only a few minutes away.

After parking, they stroll two short blocks to a nondescript two family brick house situated on a corner. In no apparent rush, they walk in the driveway on the side of the building. Al knocks on the wooden door; a young man opens it and greets them in fluent Italian.

The young host asks them to follow him to the first floor as they enter a baroque styled room with round tables which seat four people at each one. The interior of the room is designed with tons of brass and crystal on the chandelier, and hand-painted murals of the Northern Italy countryside on the walls. Two tables are full with patrons, the third one is reserved for him and Khara, and at the fourth table the people are finishing their meal and getting ready to leave.

The men at the other three tables stand when they enter the room, acknowledge Al with a slight bow of the head, and a wave hello. A few of the men come over to shake his hand. Smiles are flowing all around the room. Soft violin music is playing in the background over speakers placed in the ceiling.

The owner is an older man who leaves the kitchen when he is told his silent partner is present. He comes out to greet him with a handshake and a hug asking if they would like some complimentary wine. The young host who also serves as a waiter brings over a carafe of a fine imported dry white vintage to their table. Pursuing his lips, Al sips a little from a glass and approves of the choice he tasted.

The fish sounds interesting so Khara decides on the baked halibut steak with Italian style vegetables and feta cheese. The beef Braciole is ordered by him. The dish consists of thin steaks rolled around a tasty stuffing of raisins, freshly made Parmesan, and cooked in homemade chunky tomato gravy.

Dinner is finished and an aperitif is served. After drinking it he saunters into the kitchen to thank the chef in person, for a delicious meal. The waiter escorts them out of the house and holds the door open as they leave the home entering the side driveway.

The area is dark as they walk back to the Cadillac with Khara continuing to scan the neighborhood as she is holding his hand in hers.

"Thanks for a wonderful evening Al. We must come back here again. The fish entree I ate tonight was fantastic."

"Yer the fish is fresh. The chef goes daily to a charter boat in Sheepshead Bay, and purchases the day's catch late every afternoon when the fishing boats come back to the dock."

The key fob clicks the doors open as he holds Khara's door for her, and once they are seated he drives back to his condo in Bay Ridge to spend the rest of the night together.

***

The large Cadillac maneuvers through the basement garage entrance as he inputs his pin number to lift the steel gates, parks in his reserved space, again in the center of the three parking spots he owns. They leave the car and walk to the elevator arm in arm. In the corner of her eye, as she is holding onto him, Khara now sees someone suspicious in the shadows. Without saying anything she unlocks her holster and places her free hand on her pistol grip. One more time before going in she glances back into the garage but does not see anyone sneaking around. Upstairs in his condo, he asks her "why did you reach for your gun?"

"I thought someone is lurking between the cars downstairs, but I didn't see him again before we entered the elevator. I could be mistaken, but I doubt it."

A glance at Al tells her he did not seem too concerned about it. Once the doors close he double locks the deadbolts.

"In the morning I want to bring you back to your apartment building in Brighton Beach before driving to Staten Island to pick up your car.

"Why go there first?"

"Olga and I arranged a meeting with her Russian organization to work out how we are going to handle this presidential candidate issue. He is the real brains behind the cartel. Also, you can meet with Alejandro too.

Once inside Khara goes to the bathroom, undresses, and turns the shower on full force.

"Hey, Al I see you bought my favorite coconut body wash. Oh, and my number one fragrance Chanel No.5 is on the medicine cabinet shelf in here also. I'm so glad you thought of me."

"Why not, you're my girl, aren't you?"

Khara recognizes a BS line when she hears one and tries to seem happy for him, smiling; she is not going to bite the hand which is very good to her.

"Stop talking, and get undressed. Come join me in the shower, I'm waiting for you."

"Not yet, I have something else here for you. Come out and see it."

Without clothes, Khara walks into his bedroom and seeing him standing next to the bed holding a large square box, and she wonders what is in it for her. The box is placed in her hands as she grasps the cover and peeks inside. Khara's jaw drops as she looks at a woman's gold Rolex set with diamonds all around the face. The expensive timepiece is engraved on the underside with her first name.

"This watch is unbelievable; you shouldn't have bought me this Rolex. It's gorgeous; I don't know what to say. Thank you."

"I'm not finished yet. The envelope on the bed is also for you, here open it."

A large manila envelope is placed into her hands as she feels it is thick with papers inside.

"Open it Khara, go ahead."

The twine unties, and she takes out a stack of untraceable bearer bonds.

"What is this?"

"In the envelope are tax-free municipal bonds, you clip the attached coupons, and get the money. It's my way of saying thank you for what you did for me last month in Far Rockaway. The bonds are worth one hundred thousand dollars, plus the interest. Put them in your safe deposit box in the bank, for your eventual retirement. Olga and I, with her lover Viktor, now run the cartel's operations in the states."

"I never met him yet," Khara said.

"Viktor was her boss in the KGB, and the FSB when they changed the organization's name in Russia. They are lovers, and when he came here he brought her along. Viktor knows some amazing contacts worldwide."

"Come on Al, enough talking, let's shower. Don't you want me to show you my gratitude?"

Chapter Two

The Russian crime syndicate in New York is centered in Brighton Beach Brooklyn. Olga Levinsky, and her boss and lover Viktor are ex-KGB/FSB operatives. Herself an accomplished international assassin with a lot of experience she is in charge when he is away. Their brick apartment house is not only their residence but in the thick-walled concrete basement is the headquarters for their national and foreign operations.

Olga is tall and thin and wears long flowing skirts which hide the holster she straps on her leg. The .45 is never far from her reach. Viktor is often out of the country on covert business.

Since Al is based in Staten Island and Brooklyn he occasionally does a few joint operations with them. Arrangements are made by him for Khara to secure an apartment in their building after the Mexican Ecru

Cartel blew up her home in Staten Island. The brick multi-unit dwelling is guarded twenty-four hours a day by Russian ex-secret police and Special Ops soldiers. Nobody gets admitted without the proper credentials and lives long enough to talk about it.

The next morning after waking, and showering with her favorite coconut body wash, Khara strolls naked into Al's kitchen for breakfast. She sits opposite him at the clear glass table ready to eat. His housekeeper comes in early and makes fresh pancakes for them. Every morning when he wakes up, as is his custom, he reads the morning paper in depth and doesn't acknowledge her when she unfurls her cloth napkin with the fork and knife wrapped inside.

"Please pass the maple syrup Al."

"Oh, I'm sorry Khara; I didn't hear you walk in. You're light on your feet without shoes or clothes. The newspaper printed some interesting articles about the presidential primaries and the different candidates."

"Not a problem, thank you," she said.

With gusto, she poured the delicious Vermont gourmet syrup on her plate as she proceeds to cut the pancakes and begin to devour them. The Italian coffee cup he imported from Venice she places to her right on the clear plastic table mat.

"Listen to this Khara. The paper reports the Texan who is running for president is asking for donations to his campaign. The media reported one of his big donors is Pablo Gonzales, the champion boxer, and philanthropist who is assumed to be dead after his home blew up due to a suspected gas explosion in Laredo Texas. We know better though. I'm surprised they didn't do a DNA analysis of his body parts from the Reis Park episode."

"What a shame Al, too bad for him. All pedophiles deserve a painful death. These pancakes are delicious by the way."

"Yer I know they are. Good thing you and Olga took care of Pablo. Pretty soon she, Viktor, and I will be running the Ecru Cartel operation internationally along with the Mexican Secret Police. There are still a few loose ends to tie up first."

"Tomorrow I'll put my papers into transfer to Manhattan. Hopefully, this should get me closer to the candidate when he arrives in the city for the big fundraiser you mentioned yesterday."

"Let's finish here and get dressed, I need to do a lot today. At ten o'clock I must meet with Olga in her office" Al said.

After breakfast they both dress, and Khara picks up the envelope full of bonds, finishes re-arming, and now they are ready to leave.

With his eye placed close to the door, he peeks out of the one hundred and eighty-degree peephole of his solid steel reinforced front door to ascertain no one is waiting for him. The door to his condo is unbolted, and they take the elevator down to the basement garage.

The sliding door opens, Khara again unlocks her holster and places her palm on her pistol grip in case trouble erupts. Positive she saw someone lurking around last night, she didn't want to alarm him unnecessarily.

With a sudden move she puts her arm out to block Al as he walks out, and she goes out first. Her eyes dash around looking for motion. Nothing is moving so they continue to his red Cadillac.

"Why did you hold on to your gun in your jacket a moment ago?"

"Force of habit I suppose. Ever since the shootout in the Brooklyn project, I always check out the area before I leave an elevator."

"Makes sense to me. I understand, let's go."

Once in the Cadillac, he backs out of his parking space and heads for the exit ramp in the garage which leads to the street. The window on the driver's side rolls down, and he presses in his pin. The heavy steel gate lifts up allowing him to drive out. Neither of them spots a plain brown rental car parked across the road with two men, waiting, and watching them. Al drives to the Belt Parkway as the brown car is discretely following them while keeping a safe distance behind.

Traffic is light as he cruises on the Parkway and gets off at the Coney Island Avenue exit going to Brighton to Khara's building. The painted yellow line in front of the brick apartment house is reserved for valet parking. The attendant catches the key fob as Al flips it to him after stopping, and he heads for the entrance with her at his side.

The Ukrainian doorman recognizes them, smiles, and greets them as he pulls open the heavily acid etched art deco glass entry door so they can enter. Behind the tall marble concierge desk, another Russian security person calls Olga to inform her the expected visitors arrived. With a flick of his wrist, he waves to some men sitting nearby on a sofa, and one of them stands to say hello to Al and Khara by their first names. The guard realizes she lives upstairs in the building but escorts them both down to the basement. In the bowels of the cellar are the interrogation rooms, and holding cells for prisoners.

The elevator stops, and Olga is waiting for them in a small vestibule with three of her men standing behind her. She waves for them to follow her in the subbasement as they go through two more inner doors before entering the room Alejandro is located in. He appears to be bored sitting up on his bed watching Telemundo when they enter. The room is made of cinder block walls with no window. For sunlight, a special fixture is installed to provide the needed daylight for him. His ankle is chained to the footboard with only enough links to allow him to either sit at a table and chair nearby, or use the toilet next to the bed.

They follow as Olga enters first. "Here is the woman you wanted to kill Alejandro," she said.

With his legs in chains, he glances up at Khara and spits at her. It misses and lands on the floor. Slowly Khara speaks to him in Spanish choosing each word carefully before saying it to him so he understands exactly what she is trying to convey to him.

"The last time your brother Pablo did that to me I killed him. The same thing can happen to you."

He coughs up some phlegm, and this time when he spits at her it settles on her unsoiled polished boot. Incensed Khara steps back two paces, and turns to Olga.

"Do you need him anymore?

"No. We are finished with him."

"First I want to see his left wrist if a small red cross is on the underside with four drops of blood dropping off. He's the big cartel boss if they are tattooed on, and he will know everything about their operation" Khara said.

Olga moves a little closer to him, and he remains motionless. The prisoner, a ruthless killer, is in fear of her after she personally circumcised him without anesthesia. With a sudden move, she grabs his arm and twists his wrist over for Khara to stare at his tattoo.

Unfortunately for him, only three droplets are present, not four.

"He's not the top man of the drug operation Olga. The real boss tattooed four teardrops falling off the small cross. Did you get all the information you wanted from him?"

"I'm finished with him. He's all yours Khara."

Again she speaks in Spanish to Alejandro.

"You made my life miserable. You kidnapped innocent young girls, and you sold them into prostitution. You blew up where I lived twice, tried to kill me, and I carry on me the bullet scars on my scalp and thigh to prove it. Now it is payback time asshole."

With defiance in his eyes, he stares at her.

"Vete a la puta" [Screw you bitch]

"Khara, what did he say?" Al asked.

Without answering she retreats back a few feet, takes out her snub nose revolver from her leather jacket pocket, and aims at Alejandro's head. The .38 is her personal weapon, not a service gun, and she uses it when she does not want a firearm traced back to her. The police department's Sig Sauer is in her left shoulder holster, and secure.

The echo of the gunshot in the small subbasement room bounces off the walls and is deafening.

Alejandro's brain matter smacks against the cinderblock wall behind him. Fragments from the back of his skull bounced off the wall, and land at Khara's feet. The body crumbles and tumbles over in bed, and is motionless.

"Olga, can one of your men bring down a large plastic garbage bag? I want his head cut off and frozen; it may come in handy in the future."

In Russian, she orders her men to do as Khara requested.

***

With their visit to Alejandro done all three of them turn and leave the room, and start to go upstairs to Olga's penthouse apartment for something to eat. In the elevator, a conversation takes place regarding where to go to for lunch.

"Anything particular you would like? We can order in, and my men will pick it up for us" Olga said.

Before anyone can say anything Khara speaks up and makes a suggestion. "Did you ever eat at the kosher deli down the street? Recently I went, and the sandwiches are unusually good."

"No ... It never crossed my mind. Never knew the place existed. I only go to the Russian restaurants in the area for my meals. Let's go to the delicatessen I would like to try it" Olga said.

They walk to the apartment building's main lobby where Olga tells the concierge where they are going to lunch. Two of her men hustle to stay in the lead while three follow slightly behind them, and one is on the other side of the street walking parallel to them as they stroll to the kosher restaurant on Brighton Beach Avenue under the elevated trains.

The place is small, and only fifteen feet wide. The aroma of steaming pastrami and corn beef floats out to the busy sidewalk through the open door of the delicatessen. Pedestrians walking by begin to salivate from the enticing smells of the steamed meats wafting by their nose. The meat counter is in the front and a dozen or so tables are in the rear. The group comes in and the counterman recognizes Khara from her previous visit and smiles at her.

"Glad to see you again Miss. You and your friends can be seated anywhere in the back, we're empty at the moment. The waitress will be with you in a second."

Everyone strolls to the back where they spread out amongst the tables with the three of them taking the rearmost table. The women sit with their backs to the wall facing the entry door. Al probably doesn't feel the need to face the entrance as he is having lunch at the moment with two of the most deadly killers in New York City.

The elderly white-haired waitress who is working there for almost thirty years comes over to Olga's table first and speaks to Khara. "Hey, I remember you, welcome back sweetie, and make yourselves comfortable. What will you ladies and gentlemen like today?"

"If it doesn't bother anyone I'll order the food. We would all like a hot corn beef on rye with mustard, and a homemade round potato knish for everyone to eat. Also please bring us an assortment of different flavors of Dr. Brown's soda, it is good stuff" Khara said.

"Honey, give me a few minutes. I'll carry everything out for you, also the pickles. The real sour ones are highly recommended by our customers. The half sour isn't tasty enough for me, not enough of a bite for my taste. I like them sour like my dead husband."

"Thanks. Believe it or not, I can appreciate your statement more than you know. Once I had a sour husband too" Khara said.

The two countermen in the front take the hot meats out of the steamer and start to trim off the fat. The corned beef is dangling on the end of a long fork as they place it on the slicer. With years of experience, they begin piling the tasty ethnic meat high on a piece of fresh brick oven baked rye bread, and using his knife schmears spicy deli mustard on the top slice of rye, and cuts the sandwich in half. Two plates at a time the waitress starts to bring out the food and serves it to all the tables with the steam still rising from the meat.

The World Series is on a television overhanging where they are seated, and while they are eating everyone is watching the baseball game. The new shortstop for the Mets, the Levy kid from Brooklyn hit a double, and he is on second. The score is tied, and it's the beginning of the fifth. The next player up hits the ball, and Levy rounds third base racing for home plate. The Yankee's experienced second baseman Lawsky catches it on one bounce and throws it to first getting the second out of the inning. Levy did not see the throw to first and he slides into home scoring a run.

Being a Mets fan, she smiles from ear to ear as Al turned away from the television and stares at Khara's face.

"So you are a big Mets fanatic Khara? Somehow I did not know that about you. How long have you been following them?"

"Many years ago I started to watch them when I grew up in foster homes. School is not a place I enjoyed so I would go to Shea Stadium begging for someone to buy me a ticket. It usually turned out alright, and I would sit in the cheap seats in the bleachers and enjoy the game. No one molested me there, only when I returned to the foster home. The stadium was a safe haven for me as a kid."

"That sucks Khara, you never told about your background. I'm glad things worked out."

"Thanks, Al."

After answering him she turns to Olga who is sitting next to her at the table. "Hey, how'd you like your kosher corn beef sandwich?"

"Good Khara, very good, I enjoyed the sandwich. I'll take their phone number on the way out. Next time I'll order in from them."

The elderly waitress ambles over to Khara. "Is there anything else you folks might like? Today we made some freshly baked strawberry Danish and Columbian coffee if anyone would like some. We brew it fresh every hour."

"No, everything is delicious," Al said.

With a dull pencil in her hand, she opens her order pad, pulls out a check, and leaves it in front of Al. The bill is picked up as he stands, and he puts his hand in his left pants pocket. With a nonchalance attitude, he takes out a roll of hundred dollar bills peeling off four. The waitress is standing next to him as he places them in her hand. "Keep the change Honey, you earned it today."

"Thank you darling, and come back soon."

Everybody is ready to leave, and they start walking to the door. The first of Olga's security team to leave takes a bag from the counterman with a sandwich in it on the way out. The food is for the one man left outside, across the avenue, watching the delicatessen while Olga is inside eating. This hot sandwich is for him.

The security guard carrying the doggy bag is wearing a light blue windbreaker which is similar to the one Al wears as he steps out onto the sidewalk. At the same time, he leaves the deli the brown rental car which previously is following the red Cadillac starts to drive along Brighton Beach Avenue, under the elevated tracks.

It appears to be a normal quiet day in Brooklyn. Everyone is unaware of what is going to happen next.

At a slow pace the brown car cruises alongside the curb as they are exiting the deli, and comes to a full stop. A dark tinted window on the back passenger side rolls down. Gunshots are fired into the men leaving by the deli's front door squarely hitting the man with the blue jacket in the chest.

More gunshots are fired in rapid succession and strike a second security man as he steps out onto the concrete pavement. Both men drop to the floor mortally wounded.

The Russian security man who is stationed across the street draws his gun ignoring the crowded sidewalk. With utmost care, he takes aim at the driver. The tinted windows prevent anyone from seeing who is inside.

The front windows are clear, and he doesn't want to shoot past the vehicle, and hit his boss. With one shot he hits the driver in the left side of the head above his earlobe. The bullet jolts the driver toward the other side of the car by the passenger window. Only his seatbelt keeps him in place, and the car jerks forward into two parked cars about thirty feet beyond the deli entrance.

The shooter in the rear seat jumps out of the back passenger side door with a pistol in each hand. Heedless of the danger he charges toward the deli firing his guns as he runs. Pedestrians who get in his way are either shot and fall with gaping bullet wounds to the sidewalk with profuse bleeding.

After hearing the gunshots, and seeing two of Olga's men in front of her fall to the pavement Khara whips out her Sig Sauer. With no hesitation, she jumps over the two security men who are lying in the doorway while managing to land on the sidewalk standing straight. She turns to face the assassin raising her gun and firing at him. Olga lifts her skirt, pulls out her .45 and she too leaps over the bodies to stand next to Khara engaging in the gunfight. With her pistol ready to start shooting Olga quickly aims, and fires at the running gunman. The three remaining men who are stuck behind in the store cannot get out in front. The doorway is now blocked.

The lone gunman is caught in the crossfire of bullets between the two women who are standing defiantly facing him, and Olga's man running across the road toward him taking many shots also. Bullets are going everywhere. A busy commercial street is now the scene of a gunfight with innocent men, women, and children being shot. In less than ten seconds it is over.

The would-be killer is sprawled out on the pavement in front of a children's shoe store, having been hit multiple times. Khara runs over to him placing her first two fingers on his neck to take his pulse, and he opens his eyes looking directly at her. A question needs to be answered, and she begins to ask it before he should die.

"Who sent you here?"

It seems to her he is struggling to speak, but no sounds come out of his mouth. The multiple bullet wounds he sustained cause his blood to ooze out almost everywhere on his body. With a lot of effort, he raises his hand, makes a fist at her, and raises his middle finger.

What he signaled pissed Khara off to no end. With her anger unchecked she lifts her right foot, and with her boot heel stomps on his throat with all her weight. His body shakes violently and stops moving after a few seconds.

Olga comes over to the dead shooter and stares at his face. "Who the hell is this?"

Al scurries over and also takes a hard look at his face. "I don't recognize him either."

Now Khara picks up his left wrist, and there is no tattoo on it. "Damn it. Don't know who this asshole is, or who's he working for. This guy's not from the Ecru Cartel because there is no small red cross on his forearm. They all wear it, and he doesn't. Plus he's white, and not Latino."

The rental car is smoking by the engine. Khara hustles to the vehicle, grabs the door handle on the driver's side door, and peers inside searching for a clue, but it is clean. A national rental car sticker is spotted on the windshield. Now she has a starting point to find out who they are with. Only two coffee cups and one large empty donut box are in the front seat leaving it for the lab guys to bag and tag.

Bent over she reaches under the dash and pops the trunk, and walks to the rear of the vehicle. The back lid is unlocked now, and she opens it. The space is clear with nothing in it of value. Below the trunk, she observes the automobile is sporting a Texas license plate. In her front pocket is her cell phone. With her right hand, she takes it out and snaps a picture of the number, and sends it to Matt at the precinct in Staten Island. The text over the picture asks him to search whose name the rental car is registered to in Texas.

Meanwhile, Olga and Al, with the remaining members of her security team hustle back to the apartment building at a brisk pace. She does not want to be questioned about the shooting incident by the police. If no one says they saw her then she is not there. As a recognized Russian organized crime figure in the neighborhood, no sane person is going to rat her out for being there. Since two of her men are shot and killed supposedly as innocent bystanders people do not want to be involved with Olga in any way.

Not leaving with the others Khara remains at the scene for the emergency services to show up. Sirens are blaring as police squad cars and ambulances arrive at the block where the gunfire took place.

The district commander on duty comes over to Khara after seeing her badge hanging out on a chain, and she identifies herself to him. Upon inspecting her identification he remembers her from the Times Square shootout a year or so ago, where dozens of pedestrians and cops were either wounded or killed. Khara's name and reputation in the New York Police Department is well known and notorious although her face is not.

"Jesus Christ Detective Bennet look at this carnage. Holy Mother of God I can't believe the body count. Is there a death cloud following you?"

"Don't know Commander, I was sitting in the back of the deli, and when I left the asshole laying on the sidewalk over there with the two guns at his side started to shoot. Who he is, and why he started shooting I have no idea."

The officer walks away to further inspect the crime scene when Khara's phone rings. The call is from Matt.

"The computer is able to trace the license plate you sent to me. It is a leased car, by a private foundation, from a car dealer in Austin."

"What's the foundation's name?"

"Texas for Texans is the registered name, I never heard of it."

"When I was in Laredo months ago I did. They were on the news and reported to be a local hate group centered in Southern Texas. Talk to you later Matt, thanks for the information."

Chapter Three

After the usual interrogation and investigation, Khara is allowed to return home. Not waiting around Al and Olga left after the gunfire ended, and is not reported to be present. Later in the evening one of the buildings valets came to Staten Island and drove Khara's M3 back to Brooklyn for her.

Why is the question on her mind as she is walking back to her building? She is thinking about the hate group from Texas coming all the way up here to kill her. What is the reason they are here? With complete knowledge of the incident in the pizza parlor fight in Laredo, she is positive they never knew it was her. The racist group's leader's huge daughter deserved to be sent to the hospital in a coma. How did they end up here in Brighton Beach? Upon reaching her apartment she enters, double locks the door, and tries to think this out.

The problem kept bothering her, and she could not relax while it churned around in her head.

The duty pistol is placed on the nightstand as she pulls out the clip, and reloads it replacing the spent bullets from the deli shooting. The bottom drawer of her dresser is opened, and she takes out her gun cleaning kit. With care, she spreads newspapers on the kitchen table and proceeds to clean her Sig Sauer and .38 snub nose pistols. Mindless busywork sometimes eases her stress mode.

The thought of calling her other suitor, FBI Special Agent Don Weber, who is on their terrorism task force, came to mind. The cleaning and oiling of all her weapons are finished, they are put back on top of the cabinet, and she takes out her phone and calls him.

"Hello Don, Khara."

"Hi, I'm so glad you called. How've you been? This past week I was away on assignment, and I'm flying in from Washington D.C. about seven o'clock tonight to LaGuardia. How about having a late dinner with me?"

"Sounds like fun, let me tell the doorman you're coming."

"How are things going while I was away, quiet?"

"Yes, why ask?"

"Because I know you, and I'll talk to you when I arrive. Bye."

"Alright smart ass, I'll see you soon."

After finishing her conversation she now dials Olga. Remembering the mouthwatering meal she had with her at a Russian restaurant in Brighton she is inquiring for recommendations for dinner. Experienced and knowing better than to speak on the phone about the afternoon's attempted assassination she did not mention it.

"Hi Olga, later I'm going out for dinner with a friend to the place we had lunch on the avenue. What do you think we should order?"

"Sure, I'm happy to recommend a few dishes. Start with the pan seared veal liver with onions it is a good appetizer. For the main entree, I like Poperechka."

"Poppa what? Never heard of it."

"Poperechka is beef short ribs Russian style with fried potatoes on the side. It is tasty, you'll like it. Tell the maître d I sent you."

"Thanks, Olga, I appreciate the help."

"No problem. Enjoy your dinner."

Before she changes for the evening a phone call is put into her psychiatrist in Manhattan to try and see her the next day. The phone rings and Eloise's answering service picks up the incoming call.

"Is there an opening for tomorrow because I would like to make an appointment with her if possible? Can you tell her Khara Bennet is calling?"

"We will inform her of your request Ms. Bennet. Can you give me your number please?"

"Not necessary it's in her personal phone book. Thank you."

Finished with the conversation she hangs up and starts to take off her shoulder holster, but again checks to make sure her apartment door is double locked. The throwing knife is taken out of her right boot and placed on the top of the chest of drawers next to the .38 snub nose pistol. The small pocketbook with the long leather strap is hung on a kitchen chair after she opens it and removes a leftover hand grenade she's been carrying since the Far Rockaway gunfight with Alejandro, and his men.

Now unarmed she strolls to her small closet, snatches a blue cotton blouse, tan polished slacks, and places them on her bed. A pair of brown dress boots is withdrawn from her shoe rack as she bends her knees and she reaches into the back under her skirts. A chest drawer is opened and she lifts out a pink thong, and one of the LaCharita bras Eloise had purchased for her a few years ago. This is her custom made high-end bra with her name embroidered on the straps, and her clothes are lying on the bed waiting for her to dress.

After undressing and getting ready to take a quick shower her phone alerts her to a call. The caller ID number she recognizes as Eloise. This she must take. The cleansing will be shorter as time is wasting away.

"Khara my service informed me you called. Is everything alright with you?"

"There's something bugging me. Can I stop by about noon when I'm off because I can't talk about it on the phone?"

"I'll clear my appointments for the afternoon, and expect you here about lunchtime."

"I appreciate it, Eloise, I'll see you then."

Done with the call she hops into the glass enclosed shower grabbing her coconut body wash when stepping into the stall.

After showering she dresses, and rearms herself. Now she is ready for her date when he arrives. To pass some time she puts on the sports channel to find out the result of the ball game. The Mets beat the Yankees in the twelfth inning with a single to right field by that new second baseman from Brooklyn they drafted right out of high school, the Levy kid.

Happy the Mets won she pulls out the door to her refrigerator and takes out a cold Amstel Light beer to celebrate. Now she prefers the light beers for the calories she saves in contrast to her old habits of a full hearty amber brew. It's not too long until her doorbell rings.

"Hey Khara, missed you."

"Come in Don I missed you too" as they embrace and kiss.

"A delicious Russian restaurant is nearby, and I made a reservation for dinner. Let's go so we aren't late. There is a lot I must talk to you about."

The brisk salt air greets them as they leave the building turning right making their way to Brighton Beach Avenue. In apparent affection, they are walking arm in arm on the sidewalk as he hesitates but decides to ask her a question or two anyway.

"Listen I doubt you will tell me everything about the shootings in Nuevo Laredo Mexico. Washington is going nuts about the killing, and the explosions in Far Rockaway a few months ago. The Bureau feels certain the Ecru Cartel is responsible for it. The news reported bodies of Mexicans were littered all over the peninsula's streets. Strong doubt exists in my mind, and I feel I need to tell you, I think you were also somehow complicit in the deaths, but I can't prove it" he said.

"The FBI, through their informer network, is aware you were brought to the border crossing at Laredo by the Mexican Secret Police. On occasion, we do confer with them about numerous things of concern. When we put all the facts together it gives us answers we might have knowledge of, but are not quite certain about. Somehow you are the link to everything going on with the drug cartel since Alejandro Gonzales went missing, and presumed deceased. Do you know anything about these killings I might want to be informed of?"

"No, I don't. In all honesty, I can tell you I did not kill Alejandro in Mexico, or even in Laredo. The truth is I am happy if he is dead, but I was knee-deep in a major shooting this afternoon only a few blocks from here by those racist Texas for Texans."

"The national news didn't cover it yet so I didn't learn about the event because I was traveling. Are you sure it is that foundation? We've been tracking them for a while" Don said.

"Positive it is them. Matt tracked the license plate, and it led back to those bigots."

"The FBI intelligence sources tell me they did find out the foreign secret police took over a lot of the Ecru Cartels business since Alejandro disappeared and is missing. There is a partner in the states I heard they want to eliminate. The head of their operation in Nuevo Laredo would like to operate the drug distribution like the cartel did."

"Don, did you discover who their associate is in the States?"

"No, not yet. But we did obtain the information it is run by an organized crime syndicate in an alliance with them."

Now she realizes the Mexican Secret Police made a deal with the Texans who dispatched the shooters to New York. It is Al they want to kill, and not her. Breathing a sigh of relief for the moment, it is more important than ever she speaks to Eloise to help figure out how to handle this intelligence. The different options are churning over in her mind, and she needs her assistance to sort things out in a clear manner which she can then act on.

"Khara you seem to be somewhere else. Is something the matter?"

"No Don, I am daydreaming a little, sorry, everything is fine. The place where we will eat is only a few stores down from here. Let's go enjoy a delicious dinner."

Almost to the restaurant Don glances down the avenue and sees multi-colored lights flashing only a handful of blocks from where they are. "Is this where the gunfire happened today?"

"Yes, come on let's go inside, I'm hungry."

The hostess looks up the reservation Khara called in earlier, and she mentions Olga's name as a referral when she is greeted at the door. Upon hearing the name the woman smiles and realizes Khara is someone special.

With their hands entwined they follow the woman and are led to a semi-enclosed private area in the rear of the dining room away from the door, and the kitchen. The hustle and noise of the bustling eatery are muted at their table.

Once at the booth she slides in first and sits in a spot where she is facing out. Anybody approaching the table can be noticed, and then he moves in after her.

A waiter brings over the menus after the pair is settled, and Don asks what is good tonight. The food Olga recommended is mentioned, and after a short conversation, they decide to order it.

"So how is Staten Island doing? Anything exciting going on, or is it quiet?"

"The thought crossed my mind of transferring back to Manhattan to the department's Counterterrorism Bureau. If I can swing the transfer it would be good for my career and for my well-being also because I miss the action a lot."

"Don't you think being in a shootout today is enough excitement for you?"

"What happened this afternoon is a fluke event; I need more everyday stuff to keep me on track. A few years ago when I was in undercover narcotics I loved it. My adrenaline flowed through my body, and I was up for it every day."

"Well, I will be at a meeting tomorrow with the city's Deputy Police Commissioner for the Joint Terrorism Taskforce, and the FBI. Would you like me to ask her about a transfer for you?"

"Honestly yes, I think it would be helpful if you did. Here comes our food. We'll talk about it later back at my place."

The hostess walks over to them after the meal is served, and inquires if everything is satisfactory. Assured it is she tells them if there is anything they need please tell her.

The offer of coffee and dessert is refused when they finish eating, and both decide to brew it back at Khara's apartment. Don asks for the check, and he is told by the waitress it is taken care of by Olga and Viktor.

"No Khara, I don't know those people who are offering to pay for our meal. An FBI agent can't accept this gratuity because I can get in a lot of trouble if I let someone I don't know pay for my date with you."

Schussing him she places her hand on his forearm. Then she glances up at the woman and tells her "I am thankful for what they offered to do, but my friend would rather take care of the bill himself. Tomorrow I'll thank both of them myself."

Satisfied he now pays, and they are ready to leave.

They walk out of the restaurant to the sidewalk as Khara turns to peek up the block where the deli is located. The police are still conducting their investigation of the incident, but she obtained the information she needs from Matt earlier in the day.

Once back in her apartment she flips on the television for him while she takes out two cold beers from the kitchen refrigerator.

"Come here quick Khara I want you to see this. The evening reports are on, and the Texas racists are being talked about again."

"Is it about the shooting I was in today?"

"No the presidential candidate from Texas announced he is hiring them as security. The Congressman said since the champion Pablo Gonzales is presumed dead because of a reported gas explosion at his home he is now hiring the Texans to safeguard him. The boxer was to be his personal guardian before he died."

'You're kidding, right? That slime bucket is now having racists protect him?"

"Sure seems that way."

"Congressman Ted Ferry is also a pedophile," Khara said.

"No, I didn't know about his being sexually active with children. How do you know about it?"

There is no way she is going to tell him about her adventure in Laredo, and the nude pictures Big Boy's men took of the candidate with a naked young Latina girl.

"The FBI are not the only people with confidential sources. Come on, let's shower and go to bed. Tomorrow I must go to Manhattan for an appointment with my psychiatrist."

***

Early the next morning Don gets up, showers, dresses, and makes a cup of coffee before going to work. After walking into the bedroom he bends over her, kisses her goodbye, and leaves the apartment going downstairs to the valet to retrieve his rental car.

She is sitting up in bed reflecting about the Texas for Texans situation again. The news is starting to go on and she turns on television flipping to a right-wing cable station to learn what is going on with the ultra-conservative nuts in America. The presidential candidate, Congressman Ted Ferry, is being shown making a speech to a gathering of his supporters. The volume is turned up as she listens to him speaking, and concentrating on every word he says.

The congressman is talking about family values, the protection of young boys and girls from transgender predators, and government creating jobs while cutting spending by half.

The cameras show him taking off his horn-rimmed black glasses as he promises to deport all people who are not citizens, including parents with or without their children. All illegal immigrants and non-Christians are to be rounded up and deported out of the country. Fed up with hearing enough of his southern accent she turns the television off and gets ready to go to the city.

The elevator down is slow and she enters the lobby on her way out. The doorman pulls open the front door for her. The elevated train station is only two or three blocks away, and the short walk is enjoyable as she takes in deep breaths of the ocean breeze, and the salt air.

The stairs up to the tracks are steep and is situated high over Brighton Beach Avenue. There is no choice but to wait for the BMT Q express to Manhattan instead of the local which stops at every station. The wind from the Atlantic sends a slight chill through her body while standing on the three-story tall platform. The Brighton stop is only two end streets from the ocean. Other people are standing with her. By ten in the morning, most of the daily commuters had left for the city. A handful of women are waiting, and some young teens cutting school are chilling out and standing nearby for the next express with her.

The train is empty except for a person or two when she gets on.

Rather than sit she prefers to stand by the end of the car with her back to the door. This enables her to observe everyone on the subway car with her. At the

Fulton Street station in downtown Brooklyn a lot more people get on, and the train is almost full as it pulls out, and heads to the Manhattan Bridge going uptown. The subway car is packed solid, and two men who appear to be in their early twenties are standing eye to eye in front of her.

The train is rocketing along the tracks over the East River as it rattles from left to right shifting people as they stand. The young men are not holding onto the handles hanging down from the ceiling, and they begin to sway with the train's movements.

Both of them smile at her exposing their brown decayed teeth, with a few missing. The jeans they are wearing are way below their hips with their boxer shorts halfway exposed. Young men sometimes think they are invincible, but they are making a fatal mistake when they start to smart talk to her.

"Hey, you're a beautiful woman, how's you do-in?"

Khara can't ignore them because they are right in front of her. Again one of them speaks to her projecting his terrible breath at her face.

"Sista you look-in to party?"

Not flinching, she stares them in the eye with a serious and deadly look on her face.

"No, step back away from me before you regret it."

The men ignore the warning as they laugh to themselves at what she said. "You go-in to hurt us, I don't think so pretty woman."

Shaking from side to side the train lurches forward throwing them into her. One young man grabs her breasts to hold on as the subway car shakes on the tracks, and the other man snatches at her crotch.

With the first two fingers of each hand and her thumb, she thrusts out with lightning speed seizing their necks with a vice-like death grip. The dirtbags windpipes are squeezed as hard as she can while waiting for them to close and cut off their airways. Desperate they are flaying at her forearm trying to release her hands from their throats.

A few times a week Khara goes to the gym working out and strengthening her grasp which makes them deathly strong. The men's faces begin to turn blue, and their legs get soft and weaken. Other passengers, who paid attention to what is happening, start to cheer her on and yell she should not let them breathe.

With their knees touching the floor of the subway car, and their strength further weakening Khara continues to tighten her grip.

Both lowlifes are now uttering a gurgling noise and attempting to loosen her hold to no avail as their eyes start to glaze over and tear.

The train pulls into the Canal Street station, and as people scurry to leave she releases her grasp on them. The two young men fall down sprawled out as other people step over them. A gold detectives badge on a chain is pulled out of her blouse so it is hanging in front of her for all to view.

A young woman who is standing by the door is ordered by Khara to stay in the path of the door for a moment. The throttling of their necks is relaxed as the men are starting to catch their breath. Now desperate the two see the doors are open. Khara yanks them by the scruff of their shirts dragging them to the unobstructed door. They stumble out on all fours as they rush out of the subway car. The doors close and the train jerks forward leaving the concrete platform.

Again she leant back against the rear door between the rolling cars and begins to inhale in a controlled manner. The men and women on her car are applauding her actions.

The subway stops at 57th Street station, she goes upstairs to the street level and begins walking across town to Eloise's. After many years of going to for therapy as she approaches the building the doorman recognizes her and smiles hello. Giving her standard smirk in reply she enters the lobby. After almost two decades of seeing her shrink she can walk blindfolded to where the office is. The concierge calls ahead to inform Eloise her patient is here and allows her to enter the hallway by waving her in.

Impatiently Eloise waits at the front door to welcome her favorite client, and occasional lover, with a passionate kiss on the lips. The smooch is reciprocated, but as expected not with the same intensity. A few of Khara's regular weekly sessions were canceled supposedly due to her work schedule changing at the precinct. Truth be told it appears Eloise emotionally desired her more than the money she would have earned.

"Where have you been Khara? I miss talking to you."

"Been chilling out at home, and hustling a lot at work. The Ecru Cartel shootings in Far Rockaway forced me to keep a low profile."

"So you were the one responsible for all those carcasses all over the road? The carnage was all over the news media for days on end. There were dozens of dead Mexicans blown up, shot, and body parts found at Reis Park's parking lot. My God you were a busy girl."

45

"Yes, you know how it goes. Once it starts I need to finish it. Even my car was destroyed by those assholes."

"So you don't own a car now?"

No, I do because Al bought me a new BMW M3 from a friend of his at the docks. Well, let's say he arranged for me to have the car."

"I'm glad you are safe, I had a sick feeling you were participating in the mayhem in the Rockaways. What's happening to you today that you needed to see me in such a hurry?"

"Did you hear the late news last night? All the local stations reported about a gunfight in Brighton Beach. Did you hear about it yet?"

"Are you going to tell me you were embroiled in that one also?"

"That's why I wanted to speak to you. As my shrink what I say is confidential, and I need you to think this through with me. Your opinion is important."

"Tell me what's going on Khara."

"Yesterday I found out the Texan running for president, Congressman Ferry, is the real head of the Ecru Cartel distributing drugs out of Mexico. The old south of the border leaders are all dead thanks to me, and now the Mexican police are handling the cartel's operations with Al and Olga. The FBI did not yet obtain information Ted Ferry is working with the foreign secret police to eliminate Al and Olga. The candidate hired a racist group for his own protection, Those Texas for Texans guys are killers and racists. Remember when I was in Laredo a few months ago and I sent the leader of the group's daughter to the hospital in a coma? There are no regrets on my part the fat filthy mouth bitch of his was taught a lesson."

"Sounds to me like a lot of intrigues, and you are involved in most of it."

"Oh, and I forgot to mention Al wants me to transfer to Manhattan to the Counter Terrorism Bureau of the NYPD. He thinks I would be able to get closer to the congressman when he comes to New York for a big fundraiser, and either I or Olga will kill him."

"Does Don Weber know about any of this Khara?"

"No, he's too much of a goody two shoes. Innocently he told me some stuff which I did not know, but he doesn't realize how mixed up I am in this shit. There is the possibility he may have his doubts about me, I think, and I feel he's not telling me everything about the candidate either. The reason I think he stays with me is that the sex is good."

"Let me think about this for a moment or two Khara, sit back and relax on the sofa."

Eloise is sitting back in her plush office chair as she swivels around to face a wall. For a minute nobody talks, then she turns back to face Khara.

"This is what I would do if I were you. First do not tell Al yet, you can always do it later. Fortunately, you are not the target of the Mexicans for the time being. The Ecru Cartel leaders are dead, and their family vendetta against you is over. The candidate now is going to deal with Al, and try to murder him. The Congressman thinks he is his enemy due to the corrupt foreign law enforcement agency working with him. The Texas congressman is still the big boss of what is left of the drug operation, and the Mexican Secret Police are backing him for the moment. Ted Ferry, of course, is aware of you, but his thoughts and business interests are elsewhere. Go along with what Al suggested, and you'll have to play this one as it pans out."

"Guess you are right, I am thinking the same thing, but I'm still not one hundred present sure what I should do now. I trust your judgment, Eloise."

"Believe it or not I still have time before my next patient comes in this afternoon. How about going upstairs to my apartment for a quick bite to eat, and we can have little relaxing fun too?"

"Yes it is early enough, and I don't have to be at work until later today. Let's go."

Chapter Four

After leaving Manhattan Khara drives back to Staten Island where her precinct is located. A call comes in to investigate a murder at a residence. The location is not far from where they are, and when they arrive two marked squad cars are present. An ambulance is pulling up behind them as they double park in the street.

The dispatcher said the perp is already arrested so they are in no rush to enter the house. The first officer they find informs them a young woman killed her mother, and the girl is in custody inside the mother's home.

The officer points for them to go upstairs to the daughter's apartment. At the head of the stairs the door is open, and lying in the center of the room is a middle-aged woman. A large carving knife is next to the body covered in dark red blood. Behind the dead woman, about ten feet away is the daughter who is sitting on a small wooden chair. Upon entering the kitchen both step over the woman's body, and walk to the disheveled girl to talk to her. The policeman who arrested her is standing next to the teenage girl. The steel handcuffs are already the daughter as Khara speaks softly, and introduces herself.

"We are detectives Bennet and McMann. Can you tell me what occurred here?"

"Not sure, I don't exactly remember what happened. There was a discussion about money, and I guess things got heated. All I remember is seeing her on the floor with the knife beside her, and I called 911 for help."

The young woman is dressed in a tee shirt and jeans. After having previously been in undercover narcotics for a number of years Khara automatically inspects the girl's arms for track marks. The telltale signs of drug use are up and down her forearm, and now she understands who she is dealing with.

"You had an argument with your mother over money, correct?" Khara said.

"Yes and no."

"My thought is mom didn't want to give you cash for a fix, right?"

"No, I earn a living dancing at a strip club in the city at night. Mom didn't want me to continue seeing my doctor who is treating me for anger issues. The sessions are expensive, and she told me to stop going to her because they are not helping."

"Guess we can agree with her the doctor is not successful. Do you have an address handy?"

"The doctor's business card is on my kitchen counter... by the blue toaster. The office is in Eltingville."

Examining it carefully Khara thinks it is strange in two days two murder calls came in from people using the same doctor.

"Matt we need to visit this quack and find out what is going on."

The girl is escorted out of the house by the uniformed officers. When the medical examiner arrives and takes the mother's body away for a perfunctory felony cause of death exam Khara is ready to leave.

"We're finished here. Let's go back, and write up the report."

On the way to the precinct, Khara suggested they stop for an early food break. The BMW slows down and she pulls off the back highway and heads for the club.

The restaurant is located in the back of the building and grills burgers on an open flame. The food critic for the local paper wrote they are delicious in an unbiased column, although the critic is the chef's first cousin. Only prime Black Angus meat is purchased and served in the restaurant. The cafe also installed big screen televisions on the walls with all the major sports events playing. It is a popular place to eat lunch or dinner. Plenty of people go to the club for meals, and to also watch the young girls dancing.

"The lunch crowd should be finished by now Matt."

Khara drives up to the building and Big Boy is not standing by the acid etched glass doors, and there are few cars placed in the highly visible parking spaces in the front lot. By this time of day, dozens of vehicles should also be parked on the side lot, and there are none.

The unmarked squad car stops at the valet sign by the front awning, and to Khara's surprise, the attendant is not wearing the club's standard tan and brown uniform. "I come here too many times a week, and in my bones, I sense something is wrong. Matt something is definitely not right here."

With the inexperienced confidence of a younger man, the new valet approaches the driver's side of the car as Khara is standing beside her open door waiting for him to come to her for the car key.

"I'm sorry Miss, but the place is closed today for renovations. You'll have to come back tomorrow."

Not talking with a New York accent also arouses her suspicions, but she can't place the accent at the moment. Matt gets out of the passenger door and stands looking at the entrance.

With a quick glance over to Al's red Cadillac, she observes two nondescript silver Chevrolet sedans parked next to it on either side. The vehicles are all missing front license plates which are required in New York State. Khara's gut tells her something is not right. The valets are given strict orders to park only fancy expensive cars by the main entryway, not silver Chevy Impala four-door rental types, and she knows this for a fact.

Aware what he said is not true she is standing face to face with him. With one step forward she grabs the valet by the front of his shirt while placing her right leg behind him, and throws the young man to the ground. In a trained maneuver she twists his arm behind his back pushing it upwards towards his head while inflicting tremendous pain as his face is rubbed against the gritty concrete driveway. In an almost reflex motion, she reaches down to her boot and withdraws her knife placing the point into the soft flesh of his throat so he can feel it.

"Tell me what is going on here, or I'll slice you up for stew."

"The rest of the men are searching for the owner because we were brought here to shoot him."

"Who sent you? Tell me, or you're dead."

"Don't know who sent us here, my orders are to tell people the building is closed, and if they don't leave I am told to kill them."

Quickly patting him down with one hand she finds a pistol by his waist. A .38 mm automatic is pulled out of his pants waistband and slid on the gravel next to her car. Now it is urgent Khara get inside before they shoot Al, Big Boy, and probably some other people inside as well. With no time to waste with this wannabe killer, she grasps his head in her two hands and twists it violently snapping his neck. Reaching over to pick up his gun she leaves him motionless on the cold asphalt, and hidden by the low-slung hedges facing the highway's service road.

With their guns drawn they proceed to run up the entry steps in haste. Matt opens the front entrance door, and they enter looking for the hired killers. The main dance floor is deserted, no one is around, and the music is blaring with colored lights swirling all over the room. There must be people inside Khara thought because somebody is always in the building. A sudden movement coming from the rear of the empty floor by the restaurant catches her eye.

The office is well-hidden downstairs and is deep below ground level. Also, she knows video cameras are all over the place with multiple feeds in the hallway going down. Khara thinks to herself "if Al glances up at his screen he will be aware of what is going on here, hopefully, he isn't reading the newspaper getting absorbed into it as he usually does."

In silence, using hand motions, she tells Matt to go on the left side of the dance floor while she hugs the wall on the right. The goal is to head to the back where they can view what is going on.

At the same moment they both spot some people huddled together. The two progress cautiously when they see three men with guns in the dining area. A cluster of employees is sitting on the black and white marble tiles, including Big Boy. They approach ever closer to the group of hostages, and Khara can listen to a man with a deep voice yelling "where is the owner?"

Without making any noise she continues to hug the outer wall inching her way towards the dining room entryway. The parquet oak dancing area is barren as she peers across it, and can see Matt is also getting near the hostess stand. The beat of the loudspeakers is pumping adrenalin throughout her body, and she is starting to think she is invincible having the valet's pistol in her left hand, and her Sig Sauer .45 in her right one. Only one or two more small steps and she will be in the restaurant with the assassins. Now she is close enough to listen to what is going on inside the café. One gunman is screaming orders to the employees who are held captive on the floor.

"You girlie with the short skirt... get up."

A husky man walked briskly over to her and forced the barrel of his weapon into her mouth. One of the gunmen is yelling at the other hostages demanding "tell me where the boss is, or I'm going to blow her head off."

With hand motions Khara signals they are to enter the café together. Both are walking as quietly as they can to surprise the hitmen. They walk on the carpeted entry without notice when Khara's cell phone starts to ring. The killers spin around to see two detectives with their badges hanging down on a chain around their necks at the entryway.

Not being able to wait both detectives start shooting at the gunmen and a firefight ensues.

The employees who are sitting on the floor scramble to try to lay as flat as possible. With careful aim, her gun points to the man who an instant before had placed his pistol in the mouth of the cocktail waitress. With both guns, blazing Khara shoots him multiple times. The gunman falls backward over his intended victim knocking her to the floor. The gunman's blood is oozing out of his wounds, and flowing on her bright sparkling costume. The assassin fell on top of her, and the young waitress becomes hysterical and cries out at the top of her lungs due to uncontrollable terror. The gunshots echo off the walls in the enclosed space, and the noise is deafening.

The second man and Matt fire at each other at almost the same time. Matt's bullets hit its target in the chest area flinging the second assassin backward. The gunman shoots at him as he falls, and grazes the flesh on the side of his throat tearing away skin while the bullet flies a little under his ear, and lands in the painted red wall behind him. With blood streaming down his neck Matt feels its warmth as it begins to slither down the back of his shirt.

The third gunman, standing in front of Big Boy who is lying on the floor, is kicked by him in the back of the knee causing him to fall ending in a kneeling position. His reaction to the kick is a quick pull of the trigger causing the bullet to go upwards into the ceiling.

Now turning her attention to this new target Khara pumps numerous shots into him from both guns. His head jerks back and hits the ground landing beside Big Boy. The man is trying to breathe and is taking deep gasps of air. Big Boy rolls over next to him and places his huge right hand on the man's neck choking him until his chest stops moving. Satisfied the assassin is dead he raises his head and stares at Khara.

"What took you so long?"

"I wanted to see you sweat a little Biggie. Where is Al?"

"He's in his office, and two other guys are still in there somewhere looking for him."

A gunshot rings out from the balcony as a bullet hits Big Boy spinning him over onto his side as he grabs his massive thigh.

Matt and Khara glance at the mezzanine and begin shooting. The flashing klieg lights from above blind them for a few seconds but they aim where they thought the shot came from. Another round is fired, and it strikes the ground in front of Khara's feet. Both point their weapons at the second muzzle flash from the mezzanine and start firing at it. The blind shooting continues as they press the release on their guns, and empty clips fall to the floor. With no hesitation, they slam another full clip into their weapons as they continue blasting into the upper balcony near the blinding bright bulbs.

A semi-automatic rifle drops from the mezzanine with a loud crash as it settles on the wooden planking of the dance floor. In the sudden silence, they hear a soft thud as the gunman upstairs falls back into a booth probably severely injured. Beams of daylight are now shining through tiny holes in the blacked out roof their bullets pierced.

"I'll call for an ambulance for Biggie and you, he's wounded in the thigh," Khara said.

Big Boy catches what she said, and yells out to her "no don't. The boss will handle this his way, I am sure he wouldn't want any police coming here."

A muffled gunshot is heard as Khara and Big Boy face each other. They both realize it came from downstairs in Al's private office. In a hurry and with her

Sig Sauer in her hand, she runs to the hidden door which leads down to the club's basement. The door to the office hallway is wide open.

The steep stairs don't faze her as she races down them to his inner sanctum where a steel door is open, and she calls out to him.

"Al, are you alright? It's Khara."

"Yes, come in, you'll need to step over this body though."

"Upstairs Biggie and my partner are wounded, and they need an ambulance."

"No don't call them. I'll make arrangements for my men to come with a van to take both of them to Brooklyn.

Olga's Russian outpatient surgery center will take care of everything. There cannot be any publicity about this shooting, it is bad for business. I don't want any news of this getting out."

"What are you going to do with the dead bodies?"

"Tonight they'll be placed on my boat, weighed down, and dumped out at sea with the trash from the garbage barges docked at the landfill on Richmond Avenue. The fish will finish them off."

"What about the staff upstairs who witnessed everything?"

"Not a problem. The employees are all with me for years. A couple thousand cash bonus and nobody will ever find out what happened here today, you'll see."

"Yes, I understand but I'm taking my partner in my car because I don't want to wait."

***

The time to warn Al about the conspiracy to kill him passed. It is not foremost in her thoughts at the moment as she is driving into Brooklyn to Olga's private doctor, with Matt in the back seat.

After the heat of battle, it didn't come to mind to inform Al of the double cross by the Mexican Secret Police. The decision is now made for her, and when she gets back to Staten Island after this medical emergency is settled she will finally fill him in on all the details.

With a flesh wound by his throat, Matt is holding a compress to stem the bleeding. Another inch or so to the left, and he would die.

Any doctor, she imagines, can handle the neck wound with ease so she's not too worried about him. There is no way she can take him to a regular physician because a report of a gunshot injury must be reported to the authorities. Ten thousand dollars in cash in an envelope as a thank you gift is slipped to Matt by Al before they left the club thus ensuring his silence. Once he put the money in his pocket Al owned him too.

Khara speeds over the Verrazano Bridge with the colored lights flashing and siren blasting. Upon reaching Cropsey Avenue the M3 turns off the highway as she pulls behind the outpatient surgery center to park near the rear exit. Olga is waiting for her with two stocky Ukrainian female nurses at her side to help him out of the car, and take him into an inner office.

The doctor allows her to follow him in as she glances on the wall where dozens of diplomas and awards are hung from floor to ceiling, but they are all in Russian. Not one English diploma is to be seen.

"Hey Olga, is he licensed to practice medicine here?"

"No, not here, but he is an experienced battlefield surgeon in Afghanistan with the Soviet Army. After he retired he came here when Viktor and I did. The doctor only practices on Russian patients.

Your partner is in good hands. Plus it is only a deep flesh wound. A good cleaning, a few stitches, antibiotic pills, and he'll be better than new."

"Do you know when Big Boy is coming? The truck did not arrive yet at the club to bring him here when I left" Khara asked.

"The van carrying him will be here shortly. Al called me they are leaving with him. Go out and move your car to the side of the building where it will not be in the way."

About twenty minutes later a large white van pulls into the back lot, and a stretcher is rolled out for Big Boy. Surgery is required to remove the bullet. He is wheeled past Khara and gives her a big thumbs up wave. The experienced battle tested nurses' wheel him into an auxiliary room, cut off his clothing, and prep him for the operating room. An x-ray is taken to locate the bullet, but the surgeon doesn't need it. Because of the many years of field hardened experience, and also hundreds of times of finding bullets without the help of an x-ray he operates mainly by sight. Big Boy is put to sleep by a Russian speaking anesthesiologist while the doctor finishes up with Matt. The field doctor scrubs up and takes a cursory inspection at the film before going into the operating room. Assured Biggie will be fine Khara drives Matt back to Staten Island where they plan to finish up the day at their desks.

Matt walks into the precinct and the desk sergeant asks "what happened to you? A large gauze pad is taped to the side of his neck. A spare jacket which he keeps in his personal car afforded him the chance to take off his blood-soaked one, and change to a clean looking windbreaker.

"Cut myself shaving this morning Sarge, I'm switching back to an electric shaver."

"Smart move, Matt, do it before you slice your own throat."

***

Finally settling in at her desk Khara starts to write up her report on the mother-daughter episode from earlier in the day. Suddenly she remembers her phone had rung at a most importune time. She was about to be in a shooting situation when it went off. Now it is quiet, and in her cubicle, she pulled up the unknown number from her cell memory. Out of curiosity, she dialed the number, and a voice message responded.

"Thank you for calling our Family Tree and Relative Finders Foundation. Please dial extension three for assistance if you were contacted. The Foundation found a lost relative of yours, and they would like to contact you. Please press three now."

Not thinking it is real, and a scam, Khara hung up. To her knowledge, she is an only child with no living relatives. To be sure it is a not a fake foundation she sent a text message to Eloise asking her to call her when she is finished with her patients for the day. Hopefully, she might have some information on this foundation.

A call came into the precinct as she is sitting at her desk. There is a shooting and a standoff in a major department store at the mall. Matt clocked out early and went home to recuperate. With no one else to pick up the call, she answered the phone and drove to the situation alone. Many patrol units are also called in, and a few ambulances too.

By the time Khara arrived the squadron commander is already present at the scene. Crowds of people are huddled around outside as she walks in, and can hear a bullhorn emanating from the floors above through the escalator opening. A uniformed officer standing at the bottom of the up escalator told her the shooter is barricaded in the home furnishings department of the end cap department store.

The SWAT team is present in force so she decided not to take out her Sig Sauer from her shoulder holster, and hold it in her hand, as she rode the escalator up to the third floor. Gathered at the top policemen are with the officer-in-charge who is speaking to them. Upon reaching the furniture level she stepped off when the commander catches her walking onto the scene, and calls Khara over.

"Thank you for responding Detective Bennet, but this situation is under control. The department doesn't need any more dead bodies to carry out. You can wait downstairs."

Khara is known in the department as a deadly force when she is confronted, and they are not happy with her being at the standoff. The police brass could never pin anything illegal on her in the past, but the commanders, amongst themselves, are aware she is lethal. Sometimes deep down in their hearts, they wish she is at some of their crime scenes, but they would never verbalize it publicly. The bad guys would never live to stand trial if she were involved.

After turning around she calls over a policeman she knew, and before leaving asked if he could tell her what is going on.

"The guy laying on the floor in the furniture department came in with his wife. She wanted one thing and he liked something else. The salesperson put his two cents into the conversation, and the woman went ballistic when he interfered. I was told she had a handgun in her pocketbook. The story is the salesman was hit first, and her husband second."

"Thanks, I must speak to the captain on duty."

A group of officers is still standing in a circle surrounding the commander as she squirrels between a bunch of them to try and break through.

"Captain I'm sorry to barge in again, but I might be able to help you calm the situation down a bit. In the last two days, I went on two domestic calls, and the people had anger management issues. Both of the perps saw a doctor in Eltingville. It is a gamble she may be one of the doctor's patients. Ask her if she would like to talk to her doctor on the phone. The psychologist might be able to defuse the situation. This is the doctor's card. I am going to visit her next week with my partner after my time off."

The Captain took the business card, examined it, and stepped to the front of the uniformed officers. In a timid manner he is peeking out from the safety of a wall as he faced the woman who ensconced herself behind a large sofa, and through the bullhorn spoke to her.

Holding the speaker he mentioned the doctor's name, and she seemed to settle down a little, and raises her arms in the air, still gripping the pistol in her hand. The wife is now standing straight with both of her hands elevated yet she refuses to let go of her gun. The Captain continues to converse in a calm and casual manner.

The woman is adamant and will not drop her Saturday night special.

The only female policewoman on the third floor is Khara. The captain now thought a woman's voice might sooth the wife's nerves enough to convince her to disarm. The bullhorn is given by the captain to her to speak to the woman.

"Miss, my name is Khara Bennet, and I am a detective. In the last two days, I came across people like you who went to an anger management doctor in Eltingville. Can I walk to you, and talk privately, if you will allow me too. I am placing my arms outwards so you can see I am not holding a weapon. Here are my two hands."

Her hands are placed outside the protection of the plasterboard wall divider. Slowly she stepped out from behind it, and clearly saw the woman about forty feet or so away. The commander is yelling for her to get back behind the wall, but she ignores him. The woman has tears streaming down her cheeks as she sees Khara standing out in the open looking at her.

"I don't know why I shot them, I am so sorry, I am so sorry."

Hysterical and sobbing she turns her head to the floor where her dead husband is lying on the floor. She lifts her chin up and begins to stare directly at Khara. The woman's right arm is lowered from over her head as she places the barrel of the gun to the side of her temple above her ear.

The anguished woman pulls the trigger.

Chapter Five

The two days off coming up seems like an eternity to her as she drives back to the precinct at breakneck speed to retrieve the M3 and head home.

How this anger management doctor is involved with these events is churning in her mind. She does not understand how, but in her heart, she thinks the doctor is responsible somehow.

The unmarked police car is parked head first in front of the station house as she walks upstairs to her cubicle to finish her paperwork for the day. Now sitting at her desk staring at her blank computer screen her cell phone rings, and the phone's ID tells her Eloise is calling back.

"Hi Khara, what's going on, you called me?"

'Oh yer, I forgot. A call came in earlier from a foundation named Family Tree and Relative Finders. The message left on my phone said a long lost family member wants to contact me. Listen, Eloise, I'm an only child. My mother never said anything to me about other relatives, and neither did my physically abusive drunken father before he was killed. How can this be possible? Can this be a scam or something? Are they legit?"

"Listen one of my patients told me about them previously. They are legitimate, and you could discover a relation you did not realize existed, it happens all the time. Why don't you call them tomorrow after a good night's restful sleep, and are refreshed? Never know you might be pleasantly surprised to find a cousin or aunt."

"Good idea, I'll think about it some more. Maybe in the morning, I'll phone them. Thanks, Eloise, appreciate the advice."

The desk chair Khara is sitting in is tilted back for a moment while she tries to remember when she was a young child. Her mother never mentioned to her about any cousins, and when both of her parents died no one offered to take her in because there was no living relative known to her. That is when she entered into the city's foster care system. Nothing comes to mind so she calls it a day, and heads back to Brighton Beach.

The evening begins with her driving over the Verrazano Bridge to Brooklyn. Downshifting the M3 into third to slow down she follows the ramp to the Belt

Parkway. When she arrives home she stops at the yellow line in front of her building, flips the key fob to the young Russian valet, and walks to the entrance.

The elevator music is kind of lame, but she does not mind it as the melodies playing relaxes her nerves, although it is a short ride upstairs. The calming sound is appreciated as a retreat from the chaos she endures during her day. The lock to her apartment opens as she turns the key in her door, and enters as her phone starts to ring, and it is Don calling her.

"Listen I am running late. The meeting in the city went into overtime, and I couldn't leave early. How about grabbing a bite later tonight with me?"

"Not a problem for me. Down the block is a fantastic little appetizing food store. Give me a few minutes and I'll go pick up some bagels and stuff, and we can eat in. Is it all right with you, I'm too tired to go out late tonight?"

"Sounds good, I'll see you in a little while."

The leather jacket is slipped on again, and she leaves her apartment to walk on the avenue. Only a block or two away she goes in the small specialty shop and lifts out a few everything bagels from the baskets where they are stacked high. In the cream cheese section, all sorts of different types are on display. The dairy case is full as she inspects the labels, and picks up a few enticing containers of homemade cream cheese, vegetable laced cream cheese, a plain low-fat cream cheese, and one with scallions.

At the cash register, she spots a chocolate cake like the one she had purchased before from the store. With her eyes focused on the different cakes, her taste buds start to salivate. "I'll take the chocolate Bobka also please, and a six-pack of Dr. Browns Black Cherry soda?"

"Did you ever try my hand cut lox?" The balding manager asked when he saw how many cream kinds of cheese are on his counter.

"No, I never had lox. What is it?"

"Pieces of smoked salmon sliced by hand almost transparently thin, and it is a Jewish delicacy I think you might like."

"Sounds good let me try some."

The clerk continues to tell her about a few different types, but he is going to cut some Nova Lox for her. Picking up a long slender knife he slices off a small almost transparent piece, and she tries it. A smile lights across her face.

"Some people call it Jewish sushi," he tells her. "Five ounces should be enough for the bagels in the bag, and don't forget to tell me how you liked it with the cream cheese."

"Thanks, I will."

After paying for the groceries Khara heads back to her apartment. Now it is evening, and almost pitch black under the elevated tracks, and she is walking back home with her groceries in plastic bags holding one in each hand. She approaches the corner and a husky young man in a dark blue hoodie is standing on the corner. The man spots her and turns to face the approaching woman with her hands full of groceries.

"Excuse me, Miss, can you help me out, I lost my wallet. Can you loan me five dollars so I can take the train home? My mother is ill, and I need to take her to a doctor."

The man is standing in front of the intersection crosswalk blocking her from crossing the street. Not looking perturbed she places both bags filled with food in her left hand, and with her right hand, she places it on the handle of her .45 Sig Sauer inside her jacket.

With a free thumb, she pulls the corner of her jacket back a little from the bottom exposing her pistol, and a detective's shield attached to her belt.

"Screw you asshole now get out of my face before you regret ever meeting me. Tonight I don't have the patience for your stupid little hustle."

With a stern voice, she gives him an authoritative command. Upon seeing a gold badge and the large black gun in her holster he steps back, and to the side.

"Sorry, never mind," he said.

Brushing by him with a brusque attitude of defiance she starts across the avenue when she turns her head to make sure he is not following her while mumbling to herself as she continues walking to her building.

"Son of a bitch tried to scam me for money, and I'm too tired for his bullshit."

The burly doorman nods his head hello as she reaches the front of her building, and opens the door for her to enter the lobby. The young man in the hoodie is walking at a distance behind her, as he follows her with his eyes noticing where she is going.

Upon reaching her apartment house he starts to go in the alleyway at the side of the building and tries to break in the apartment house surreptitiously. Instantly the motion sensors attached to the brick walls in the alley pick him up.

The security officer in the subbasement observes him and dispatches two Russian retired special ops men to persuade him to walk off the premises. They confront him as he is trying to pry open the basement door to the building. The security guards do not recognize him and are secure in the knowledge he does not live in the building. The young man is told to leave and to help him remember they only break his nose.

**

About nine at night her suitor walks into the building's lobby, and the concierge calls upstairs to inform Khara her guest, Don Weber, is here to visit her.

"Thanks please send him up."

The elevator takes him to her floors, and he walks to Khara's apartment after the double doors open letting him out on her level. The hall is carpeted. The walls are papered in small floral patterns in shades of lavender and pink. The doorbell rings, she opens the door for him, and as he enters puts his arms around her waist, pulls her into him, and kisses her.

"I'm glad you came tonight Don, I enjoy how you say hello."

"Be assured it is my pleasure. Let's eat, I'm starving."

After cutting the bagels, trying the different cream cheeses with the lox, and drinking some black cherry soda with it they decide to sit in her living room and talk a bit.

"Good news Khara. Today I attended a meeting with the city's police commissioner and his first deputy. They came to the Federal building for a small informal conference on terrorism. After we finished I privately asked the deputy about you transferring to the terrorism bureau because I remember you asking me about it the other day."

"What was the answer, Don?"

"She read about you in the police personnel files due to the Times Square shooting last year. At the mention of your name she recalls you killed some terrorists, and also the Staten Island explosion when they blew up your home too. Yes, she remembers you quite well. Seems you made a good impression. Tomorrow you are to be in her Manhattan office in Police Plaza at noon, obviously, she liked the information she found."

"Let's shower Don, and I'll show you my gratitude in a little while, it is wonderful news."

***

The next morning Khara woke early and made bacon and eggs for breakfast. Don had his with coffee, and she drank water from the faucet with a few ice cubes thrown in the glass to chill the water.

"Many people don't know it is a proven fact New York water is one of the finest in the country. Never buy bottled water in the city, and only drink tap water. It is excellent tasting water" Khara said.

"No kidding Khara. I never knew anything about the city's water. This morning I need to go to Kennedy Airport. The Bureau is told of a shipment coming in on a commercial flight with cartons marked as electronics. We are informed by the ATF bomb-making equipment and explosives are in the boxes. ATF is coordinating the operation with us, and I'm leaving soon for the airport. If I can I'll let you know if I'm free tonight."

"Fine, call me. I'll be going into Manhattan later today to see the deputy commissioner about a terrorism appointment. Hopefully, I'll get it."

"I'm pretty sure you will, I told her I'm dating you, and I thought you are capable of doing the job. She seemed receptive to the idea when I mentioned it."

"Sounds good to me, phone me later. At the moment I need to dress" Khara said.

"Don't worry I will. I'll get ready now also."

After Don left the apartment she hurries, takes a quick shower, and when she is dressed decides to stop for a minute. She picks up her phone and calls the foundation. In the end, her curiosity won out. She's no idea who could be looking for her.

The cell phone's memory brings up the foundation's number, and she presses the send button when it appears, and automatically dials it for her. The automated operator answers at the foundation, informs her all conversations are recorded, and Khara pushes three as requested. For a few seconds of elevator music, she listens while wondering, and holds on until a live person answers the phone.

"Good morning, thank you for calling us back. How may I help you today?"

"My name is Khara Bennet. Yesterday I had been called, and told a possible relative wants to contact me."

"Please give me a minute Miss Bennet. Can I place you on hold while I search for your file?"

"Yes, I'll wait thanks."

After a short time, the lady comes back on the line.

"Miss Bennet we were contacted by a woman who said she's been looking for you for decades. We are told she did a DNA search, and you are a perfect match to her. There is no denying DNA, you are this woman's long lost sister, and she would like to be in touch with you. We do need your permission to inform her so she can be in contact with you."

"Yes, she can call me. Although I am sure no sister exists, I'll talk to her anyway to find out what kind of a scam she is trying to pull. Tell her she can call me in ten minutes or so, I'll be going to the city, but I'll be able to speak to her on my car phone's speaker. Thank you."

Done with the phone call she hangs up and finishes getting dressed. In her mind, she doesn't think this is a real DNA match but is willing to listen to her talk.

Finally ready to go out, and armed, she walks to the front door to leave her apartment.

With more than enough time to drive into Manhattan to Police Plaza, the valet is bringing her M3 to the building for her to drive her car instead of taking the subway into the city. Plus it is much quieter than if she took the train. This way if the woman does call she is able to turn off the music, and speak to her in private. After going downstairs she waits by the entry awning for her M3 to arrive.

Ready to drive to Manhattan she throws the manual transmission into first and takes off for the Belt Parkway. The morning commuter traffic is heavy but flowing. The phone rings and the Wi-Fi in the car bring her incoming call through the car's speakers. The caller Id on the radio shows a number she does not recognize as she pushes the answer button on the steering wheel.

"Hello, can I help you?"

"Is this Khara Bennet?"

"Yes, and you are?"

"My name is Dixie Pearl Jefferson, and I searched for you for decades."

"Well, Dixie you found me."

"My friends and family call me Dixie Pearl, they use both names, but you can call me Dixie if you like."

"Dixie Pearl, please explain to me how we are sisters. To my knowledge, there are no living relatives as I am an only child, let alone a sister I never knew even existed."

The M3 is passing the Bay 8th Street exit on the Belt Parkway, in a second will start rounding the curve in front of Fort Hamilton, and soon be going under the Verrazano Bridge.

"Believe me I understand what you are saying Khara, it is a long story, but I know we are sisters. The DNA match confirms it."

"What DNA match? How and when did I do a DNA test? For some reason, I don't ever remember doing any cheek swabs."

"Last year you were in a terrible shooting incident in Times Square, and you were shot several times. The shooting was on the television news reports from New York, and I read about you in the newspapers too. It was big news on all the national stations, even the local ones here in Virginia. You are a true American hero."

"Yer, but I never did a DNA test."

"The hospital took a blood sample for a transfusion. The FBI also tests all blood samples at the scene of a terrorist shooting trying to trace who those terrorists are. Guess your blood was found at the crime scene, and it ended up in their data bank with a DNA search included."

"Maybe, but how did you get access to the FBI data bank?"

"My husband is older than me, and he is a semiretired deputy sheriff here in Virginia. The sheriff is an old friend of his. They grew up together, and he helps him with his search requests. Once a year he asks for a DNA search for me. For many years I searched for you, and praise the lord I finally found you."

The M3 is curving around Bay Ridge and heading for the Battery Tunnel as traffic grinds to a halt. Downshifting the transmission to second gear to slow the car to a crawl she continues talking.

"Dixie Pearl...my mother never told me about any sister. Mother committed suicide when I was young, and while she was alive she never mentioned to me anything about her having other children."

Dixie Pearl continues describing to her how they are related.

"What a tragedy Khara, I am so sorry to hear about our mother's death, I was never informed about it. Many years ago I was told your mom was in a terrible car accident with her parents, and they were killed. My grandparents took her in and raised her with their daughter, who is my adopted mother, as sisters. My adopted mom and your mother were childhood friends and literally grew up together in the same house. My grandfather is a preacher in South Carolina, and my grandmother is the choir leader. They took care of your mother as if she were their own daughter, and as my mom's sister. They both were raised in the church."

"As a teenager, your mother became pregnant while dating a white boy, and she gave birth to me. Her childhood friend, my adopted mother, once told me the boy would not marry her because she is black. His parents sent him away to a private boarding school in Georgia. My maiden name on the birth certificate is Thurmond. Mom told me your mother was embarrassed, ashamed, and could not afford to raise me while being a single parent. Before going away she asked my mother, her adopted sister if you will, to adopt me, and she left South Carolina and headed north. The formal adoption papers were signed, and my grandparents and their daughter took me in, and raised me as their own blood."

"Khara, my adopted mother always told me she would get a call every so often from your mother, I mean our mother, to see how I am doing, but the calls stopped. My mom had no idea where or what happened to your mother. It must have been difficult for your mother, I imagine, as I was born on December 25th, Christmas day. She had to be a hurting every year due her giving birth on that day...I'm sure of it."

"Dixie Pearl I can understand it happening. When I was a young girl my mother was always depressed. The winter holidays were not a happy time for us. Looking back I remember every Christmas she would start crying, and I never understood why. About the time I was eight she committed suicide by hanging herself in our kitchen during my Christmas week vacation from school. The city sent me to foster homes after her death until I was eighteen. I left the foster care system when I married my husband."

"What about your father Khara, didn't he care for you after that?"

"My drunken abusive father was killed in a terrible knife fight a few weeks before my mom died. My dad was an abusive drunk and would beat us when he started to drink. Guess he picked one too many fights in a bar."

The car is now below ground level on the highway leading to the Brooklyn Bridge, approaching Park Slope, and soon her exit will be coming along.

"I am so sorry to hear about what happened in your life Khara. My mom knew you were born but was not told our mother died. The calls faded and eventually stopped. Almost forever I always wanted to meet you, to see how you look, if there is a family resemblance, and to hug you."

About to turn on the Brooklyn Bridge entry ramp Khara is heading into Manhattan. One Police Plaza is not far from the exit in Manhattan.

"Listen Dixie Pearl I must go now. I'm almost at my destination. The number you used is on my cell phone, and I'll try to call you back either later or tomorrow."

"Please do call me, I would love to speak to you some more. I appreciate your calling me back and talking to me today. Thank you sister, and have a blessed day."

"Thanks... you too... bye."

In the moment of silence after hanging up Khara thinks to herself "Shit, I'm related to a holy roller."

The turn off the bridge is coming up fast, and exiting onto the congested Manhattan streets she makes her way to Park Row. Trying to find a garage to leave her car, and meet with the deputy commissioner is not an easy task. With so many automobiles coming in the city it is difficult finding a parking spot near headquarters so she decides to park near City Hall, walk up Park Row to the Civic Center, and Police Plaza.

The first outer perimeter security office is a small building in front of One Police Plaza, and Khara informs them she has an appointment on the fourteenth floor. Her identification is checked, and a call is made upstairs to confirm the appointment.

Last year a police escort brought her to headquarters to speak to the intelligence unit about the Ecru Cartel. Since having eliminated most of the drug cartel by herself she does not need to look over her shoulders often. Now she will see what Don arranged for her with the top brass. Unlike the average person, her nerves are usually made of steel, and she is not apprehensive about the meeting.

After leaving the elevator she enters the deputy commissioner's office and walks up to a civilian receptionist at the front desk.

Showing her badge she stated, "I am Detective Khara Bennet, and I have a noon appointment with the deputy commissioner."

"Yes your meeting is scheduled for now Detective Bennet, please take a seat, and I'll tell her you are here."

Against the wall is a blue armchair she chose to sit in, noticing it is much nicer than those in the precincts she worked in the past. "Not bad to be a political hack," she thought to herself.

"Detective, please follow me. The Deputy Commissioner will see you."

Standing she walks behind her through two doors to an inner office overlooking Park Row. Upon entering she is looking at a thin older woman wearing a green plaid men's suit. To many people she appears professional, her blond hair is cut short with bright blue eyes, and her facial features are chiseled with a high cheekbone. The lipstick is a soothing shade of red against her tanned skin. Noticing her nails are also done, but slightly chipped, Khara said nothing.

The deputy commissioner stood and walked around her desk to shake Khara's hand.

"Thank you for coming in today on your day off detective. I'm sure you know FBI Special Agent Don Weber spoke to me about your being transferred to the terrorism bureau."

"Yes, I am interested in transferring, and I discussed it with him at length. I do have some experience dealing with terrorists as I am sure you are aware" Khara said.

"Please sit and let's talk about a little."

Plunking herself in a sturdy solid oak armchair in front of the deputy commissioner's massive walnut stained desk she waited to respond to a question. The deputy sat behind her desk in a burnt umber colored and tufted leather executive office chair. No questions are asked for a minute or so as they each tried to size up the other in their mind.

"Detective I am going, to be honest with you. Your file has been checked with Internal Affairs, Intelligence, and Terrorism people here at headquarters about your background. A lot of positive affirmations for you are on file with them. Of course, I am not concerned about those, but there are some open questions which are not fully explainable. Our intelligence people tell me you showed up in Nuevo Laredo Mexico where dozens of Ecru Cartel gunmen were killed in a warehouse shooting according to our sources. Our Terrorism Bureau has been tracking you ever since the Times Square incident. Can you explain it to me please?"

"In all honesty, I can say it is a coincidence regarding my being in Mexico at the same time, I can't say anything else."

The deputy commissioner stares at Khara for a moment, a slight smile appears on her lips, and she doesn't say a word. Probably her suspicions on the Mexican episode are plenty, but she continues speaking to her anyway.

"I don't think I want to hear any answers you might tell me. Miss Bennet, you are the type of officer I am looking to put into a special team I am assembling. The people on it must be fearless, direct and experienced in handling dangerous situations. The police department, under my directive, is forming a quick response group of officers based in local precincts but will be placed at my individual command. There will be no acknowledgment of this project by anyone except myself, your precinct captain, and your teammates once they are selected. Tomorrow you will be promoted to detective first grade, be given a higher salary, and sent into potentially dangerous situations where you will be expected to act accordingly, and on your own initiative. The team will be reporting directly to me and only to me on those assignments. Do not worry I will have your back. Do you understand what I am saying?"

"Yes, and I am ready."

"Good, I will send out your orders this afternoon to your precinct. Report back on Monday as normal until the formal paperwork goes through. If everything goes according to regulations it should take a week or so. Meantime please continue to work as usual in Staten Island. The precinct captain will release you from regular duties when I inform him I need you for an assignment"

"Thank you, I am anxious to be working with you," Khara said.

"No, thank you, Detective Bennet, please enjoy your two days off."

Khara stands, shakes her hand, and turns to leave but she is called back by the Deputy Commissioner.

"I'm sorry to call you back here Detective, but a thought crossed my mind. Later today I must go to a meeting with the mayor. One of the presidential candidates is arriving in New York today from Texas to hold a private sit-down at city hall. Would like you to join me at the Mayor's office?"

"Sure why not? My plans for this afternoon are not set. The last time I met the mayor I was in bed.

What I intended to say is I was shot in Times Square by the Ecru Cartel, and in a hospital bed when he came to visit me."

"That is a funny detective; I understood what you meant to say. Are you hungry I didn't eat yet, and the meeting is not till a little later? Come with me to lunch."

***

Together they walk out of the office and go down to the lobby in a crowded elevator, leaving the building. An unmarked police car is waiting for the women with two detectives in the front seat. The detective in the passenger seat hopped out, and opened the rear door for the deputy commissioner who entered, and sat in the car. Walking around to the other side of the car Khara slid in next to her new boss. The car drove off to a restaurant on Reade Street not far from City Hall.

The Hashery is a rustic looking place, and on the dark intimate side. There are banquets running around the perimeter of the room with small tables in front of it, and a chair or two on the other side. The Deputy Commissioner asked for her regular table in the corner. She sat on one side of the ninety-degree table, and Khara on the other side of the corner next to her, shoulder to shoulder.

"Do you mind if I call you Khara when we are alone?"

"No, not at all."

"Please call me Johanna when we are not in public."

"Not a problem, what's good here?"

"The eggs or French toast are good, and their dry rubbed burger with bacon and caramelized onions are fantastic. Believe me, I can honestly say everything here is not only good, it's excellent"

"Sounds delicious, I'll try the burger and a light beer, whatever brand they serve here, I'm not working today."

"Good choice Khara, I think I'll order the same as you, but with a soda as I'm on the clock."

The waiter comes over to the table, and they place their order. After he walks away Johanna turns to Khara and starts to speak in a whisper so no one else hears her.

"If you do not mind I would like more personal information about you Khara. From the reports, I read you are a take no prisoners kind of person. A quality like that in a woman I admire because there are too many weak ones who lack solid self-confidence in themselves."

"What you said is a good summary of me."

"So how long have you been seeing Don Weber, anything serious?"

"No, not really. We are good friends when we need each other."

Johanna smiles when Khara said they are friends, and she slides her left hand under the table and places it deftly on top of Khara's right thigh.

"Do you think it is possible I could also be good friends with you too Khara? How does it sound?"

Unexpectedly the presidential candidate from Texas walks into the restaurant with his entourage. They sit at tables on the other side of the room before Khara can answer her. Seated, Khara and Johanna look up at them. His Texas for Texans security team sits with him while the Secret Service detail stands by the front entrance on Reade Street.

Behind the candidate is a large young woman who sits to his right. Khara recognizes her as the daughter of the leader of the Texas for Texans hate group she put in a coma near Laredo when she visited there.

The New York City campaign manager spots Johanna sitting in the corner, and whispers in the candidate's ear. The politician rises, and as he walks over to Johanna's table with his New York manager to introduce himself to the women he combs forward his bleached blond hair.

"Howdy, I'm Congressman Ted Ferry, and I am running for president. If the commissioner here would vote for me it would be helpful."

"A pleasure to meet you Congressman Ferry, but I need to correct you. I am a deputy police commissioner, and sitting with me is Detective Khara Bennet."

The candidate and Khara stare at each other in silence for an awkward moment. There is recognition by each of the other, but nothing is said aloud.

Ted Ferry had been told Khara's name before, but he never met her in person or saw what she looked like. Now he is two feet away from her, and staring her in the face.

"I've heard about you detective, you are quite a hero I am told," Congressman Ferry said. The tone of his voice was dry with a slight edge.

Wedged in the corner of the banquet Khara glances up at him never having seen him in person, but knowing of him.

The picture of him from Laredo with an underage naked Mexican girl in the back seat of his Cadillac was shown to her when she returned from

Laredo. It was emailed it to her by Al, and she saved it on her cell phone.

Congressman Ferry extends his right hand and shakes Johanna's. Khara is sitting to the left of Johanna, and she lifts her left hand across the table to shake hands with him. The candidate extends his left arm across the table in an awkward movement to shake Khara's hand as his sleeve rides up a little. There on the underside of his left wrist is a small red cross with four droplets of blood tattooed on it. Khara notices it, realizes he is the real head of the Ecru Cartel, and what Alejandro had told Olga is true.

While he is talking to Johanna telling her how magnificent the city is the large young woman who is at the Texan's table looks over and gawks at the two women speaking to her father's boss.

The girl is massive and tall. Getting up she plods side to side as she walks over to where Johanna is sitting. Now standing next to the candidate she is in front of the table intently staring at Khara. Silently Khara places her right hand in her jacket pocket and grips the handle of her snub nose .38mm revolver. It will only take a second for her to take it out, and use it if she is attacked.

"This is my first time to New York, but I have a feeling I met you somewhere before, did we ever meet?" the girl said.

"Sorry Miss, but I do not recognize you."

"Your face is so familiar yet I can't place it. It'll come to me, and I'll get back to you when I remember where we met before" she said.

The candidate and young woman turn to walk back to their table. Johanna watches her sit by her father.

"Khara...those Texans are a bunch of racists, and up to no good."

"Nothing new there Johanna, I know all about them."

"Are you aware the young girl who stood here was found last year in a coma in a bathroom in a city near Laredo after a fight?"

"Yes, I heard about it."

"Did you have anything to do with it Khara? The reports state you stayed in Laredo last year about the same time it happened to her."

"This is a delicious burger Johanna, a good recommendation, thanks."

Johanna did not become a deputy commissioner because she is a stupid person. She decides not to ask any more questions, or pursue an answer to the one she asked.

"Let's finish up here Khara, and we'll go to city hall. I'll introduce you to the mayor and the new police commissioner. They would sure like to meet you now you are back on duty."

***

The deputy commissioner's security detail drives the two women to city hall and pulls in the front parking lot by City Hall Park. Both of the women leave the car and walk up the steep entry steps as Johanna, in a hushed voice, tells Khara she "heard the candidate is starting a militia indoctrination facility in upstate New York. The congressman proclaims he wants to protect the second amendment and family values. Our sources tell us he is buying land near Utica for a training camp for his recruits. The department thinks you should go up there once he makes the purchase so we are informed as to what he is doing in New York."

"Not a problem Johanna. Tell me when and where, and I am ready."

The women are now standing on the front portico of City Hall as they look out over City Hall Park, and see the candidate with his entourage drive into the parking lot. There are no media reporters around as this is supposedly an unscheduled and non-published stop. The local political campaign manager wants to try to get the mayor's endorsement, or at least get an unofficial picture of them together. The presidential campaign will spin it later as a warm meeting, and discussion, as a news leak.

The meeting Khara has with the mayor is uneventful although he does remember her regarding the Times Square incident. Afterwards, she leaves Johanna at City Hall, walks a few blocks to get her car from the garage, and drives to Staten Island.

Now she decides it is time to tell Al what is going on with the conspiracy to kill him and Olga. With the shooting at the club and Matt getting shot she did not have enough time to speak to him about what she knew. Now she has more confirmed information after seeing Ted Ferry's left wrist, and it is time to start the ball rolling.

The Staten Island ferry stopped allowing cars on it since 911 happened. Leaving downtown Manhattan Khara realized it is late in the afternoon. Traffic on Canal Street, driving to the Holland Tunnel, is heavy as she heads for Bayonne. Anxious to speak to Al about her transfer she is heading for Staten Island. This is what he wanted her to do, and she knew it is more for his best interests than it is hers. Khara felt it could be an interesting job going forward. In her bones, she thought there would be a lot of excitement in the future.

Once on Staten Island she heads for the back 440 highway, driving as usual like a maniac, and arrives at the club about dinner time to speak to Al. The regular valets are back today as the M3 screeches to a halt. Exiting the car she flips her key fob to the young valet. The M3 is parked, as usual, in front near Al's red Cadillac with the other high-end cars.

Stepping out of her car she stares at the ground and scans the pavement, and it is clean with no blood residue. Gazing up at the door Big Boy is still not standing outside yet, and there is a new security man at the front door. Khara does not recognize him, but he is aware of who she is as she walks up the stairs to the entrance as he opens the door for her.

"Hi Khara, how are you doing today?" the doorman said.

"I'm sorry do I know you?"

"Yes, we both were in Newark last year when I drove the tractor-trailer filled with the drugs we stole. When you went inside with Big Boy I took the truck, and left the city."

'Oh... it went so fast. You must have been in the second car behind me" Khara responded.

"Yes, good to see you again, Al is in the rear restaurant."

It is a strange feeling for her not to see Big Boy at the entry door. The new front door bouncer does not personally know Khara, but recognizes her, and is aware who she is dating. The new security guard lets her pass without any questioning.

Entering the front lobby a familiar waitress greets her as she knows Khara is now dating the boss and informs her he is in the restaurant at the back of the club. Once inside she walks by the hostess stand and Al waves for her to sit with him.

"Hey Khara, want something to eat? The cafe put Philly cheese steaks on the menu yesterday. It's the real deal, try it."

"No thanks I'll order a black coffee, and a buttered roll."

"You come here at lunchtime, and you're not eating? If someone sees this they'll think you're not Italian."

"No kidding Al, all they need to do is notice the color of my skin."

"Yer I know but it's soft, and I like it. Come here, I need a kiss."

Al leant over the table and kisses her on the lips, and it is reciprocated.

"Can we talk here Al, or do you want to go outside by the dumpster because I have some information for you?"

"No there are no bugs in here now. A new security firm came in, and they swept the whole club for wireless devices."

"How well do you know the company? Are you sure it is not an FBI front?" Khara asked.

"Yer my cousin owns it, and I grew up with him in Red Hook. A few months ago I set him up in business so I can do private talks in here without freezing my ass off in winter. The weather was freezing last year when we went to the dumpster outside. What's happening with the transfer Khara?"

With Don sleeping over last night, and Dixie Pearl on the phone, she forgot to find out how Big Boy is doing. The question about the transfer is ignored for the moment.

"How is Biggie coming along after his surgery yesterday?" she asked.

"He'll survive. The surgeon worked on him for a while, but he'll be fine. The anesthesia will knock him out for a few days until it leaves his system. He'll need to go for some minor rehab."

'No kidding, I know all about it. The same thing happened to me last year when the Ecru Cartel shot me in the Times Square ambush. Listen I must talk to you about my new assignment."

"You're being transferred to the Terrorism squad?"

"No, it's even better because I am being placed on a new strike force which is not being publicized. It is a secret team directly under the supervision of the deputy director. The mayor may not even know about it yet."

"And that is good because...?"

"I will obtain knowledge of things happening as they happen. For an example today I met the presidential candidate while I ate lunch with the deputy commissioner. Shaking my hand his sleeve rode up a little, and I saw a tattooed small cross with four red teardrops on it. The Congressman is the big boss of the cartel, he knew me by name only, and froze for a second when we were formally introduced by Johanna."

"No surprise here, you know he is the top guy of the Ecru Cartel already. Alejandro told you this before you killed him."

"Yes but this confirms it. Also, did you know he is in a conspiracy with the Mexican Secret Police to kill you? That is why gunmen were in here yesterday. With you out of the picture, they can get half of the profits, instead of the third split with you and Olga. With no question in my mind, I'm sure she will be the next in line they'll try to kill."

"This means they are going after Olga also. Does she know this yet?" Al asked.

"No, I figured it out today when I saw his wrist tattoo."

"When you go home you must tell her what is going on. As long as she is in an all brick fortress of an apartment house she is safe."

"Yes, I agree. After I finish my coffee I'll drive home, and tell her. By the way, do you feel like some company late tonight? Let's say about two in the morning?"

"Not sure, I have some things to do now because this situation came up. I'll call you."

Chapter Six

Staten Island commuter traffic is terrible. A turtle with three legs moves faster. After placing her magnetic flashing light on top of her BMW Khara turns on the siren and takes off heading home via the Verrazano Bridge at seventy-five miles per hour.

The M3 passes several cars while she is driving in the left lane when she glances in her rearview mirror and catches a glimpse of something strange in a car behind her. The driver and passenger are wearing a cowboy hat. Nobody normal, according to Khara's way of thinking, wears those kinds of hats in New York.

In her mind, she thinks they are following her, and her Adrenalin is pumping with thoughts of how to evade them flash in her mind. Now she is on the highest point of the bridge going about fifty miles an hour, and only two feet from the car in front of her. The cars to her right are packed in tight so she cannot do an evasive maneuver. In bumper to bumper traffic, she will not be able to lose them here. Her gut instinct takes over and tells her what to do.

With her right foot stomping hard on the brakes the M3 screeches to a halt. The car behind her nosedives to a stop almost rear-ending her new BMW. The door opens and she jumps out of her car scurrying to the car in the back while ignoring the traffic swirling around her. In a flash, she pulls out her badge on a chain from her blouse and draws her Sig Sauer .45. The young driver raises his hands shouting "don't shoot, don't shoot."

"Police... get out of the car and put your hands where I can see them, or I'll kill you where you sit. Get out now, and lay face down."

Two young men leave their car and do as they are told. Now lying face down on the dirty cold asphalt of the Verrazano Bridge car horns are blaring, drivers are opening their windows yelling profanities at them while whizzing by the two stopped cars. The strong breeze from the bay blows their cowboy hats off, and they float over the gray steel railings into the choppy harbor water below.

The Sig Sauer is shoved against the neck of the young man who exited the front driver's door as she demands an answer to a question.

"Who are you, and why are you following me?"

"We're not following you. We are going to a Friday night square dance at my girlfriends church in Brooklyn. Really we aren't lady, honest."

With her left hand, she pats them down and realizes they are unarmed.

"This is your lucky day boys. Stay down on the ground until I drive away, understand?"

"Yes, ma'am."

Seated back in her car she breathes a sigh of relief and continues to Brighton Beach leaving two bewildered young men lying on black asphalt on top of the bridge.

As she drives up to the parking area by her apartment she spots Olga walking out of the building with her usual security team, and with a short blast on the horn loud enough to grab her attention.

"Hi Khara what's doing?"

The key fob is given to the valet as she walks up to Olga, and begins to clue her in on what is happening.

"Alejandro is right. The presidential candidate from Texas is the head of the Ecru Cartel. Today I met him, and I saw four teardrops of blood tattooed on a small red cross on his left wrist. And I found out from the FBI he and the Mexican Secret Police want to eliminate their new partners, you and Al, and split the profits two ways with Ted Ferry instead of three."

"Thanks for telling me. I'll speak to Al later, and we'll deal with this. It is easier to knock off one person, the candidate than it is to kill two people."

"Right, I guess he will clue me in on what's going to happen. Now I'm going upstairs to chill out a bit."

***

About two in the morning Kara's phone rings. Still awake she is waiting up to contact Al for a sleepover at his place tonight.

"Hello Khara this is Johanna. Sorry to call so late but an assignment came in tonight for you."

"No, not a problem, I am watching my VCR for shows I missed. What do you need?"

"Tomorrow morning I need you to go to the Torino-Ashley Hotel in Manhattan to work security. The Texas crew is staying there for a week while Ted Ferry does a lot of fundraising in the city. Try to find out as much as you can about the upstate New York training camp they are planning on building."

"Tomorrow I'll be reporting to the hotel early at seven to catch the 8 am shift change."

"Good I want you to report to the lieutenant on duty by the front desk in the lobby. He will tell you where to go, any questions?"

"Not at this time, I'll be where I am supposed to be, don't worry."

"Thanks, sorry if I woke you."

"Nope, everything is cool Johanna. Good night."

After she hung up with her new boss she called Al on his private number with her burner cell phone.

"Al Khara, are you home? The deputy commissioner contacted me a few minutes ago to tell me I'll be guarding the Texas assholes in their Manhattan hotel tomorrow, and might also be there for the rest of the week.

"Good Khara, call me when you find out more because I need a plan to take care of the competition."

"Okay, speak to you soon, good night."

Before she sits back on her sofa and falls asleep her alarm is set for five in the morning. The three-hour nap is all she can do at the moment and will need to suffice.

The clock goes off a set, she wakes up, showers, gets dressed, and arms herself as usual as per her daily routine. Her gold detective's badge is pinned to her pants by the waist, and she slings her shoulder holster over her blouse on the left side. The always present leather jacket is put on as she secures her .38 snub-nose in the right pocket, and closes the small Velcro sewn on the underside of the jacket flap to keep the gun secure.

The top drawer of her dresser is opened as she withdraws her small over the shoulder bag, and places a hand grenade with a short fuse in her pocketbook. In her left pocket she puts in six .38 mm bullets in case she needs them, and inside her jacket goes two loaded .45 mm clips. The throwing knife and sheath slide with ease into the top of her right boot. Now she is ready to report to work.

On her way out of her apartment, she fills a small glass with water and pops two caffeine loaded tablets to wake her up. In midtown Manhattan are plenty of coffee shops all over the place, and she'll grab a cup of black Colombian brew with a buttered roll when she arrives.

After locking her door she takes the elevator down to the first floor. The pills start to juice her up as the meditative music is playing over her head. For a few moments, her nerves are on edge. The energy rush brings a wave of nausea, but the feeling is only momentary.

Khara meanders into the lobby and the concierge, standing behind the tall marble desk, calls for the valet to bring the M3 around to the front of the building for her. This way she doesn't need to stand outside waiting for her car. The young man drives her car up to the awning, blows the horn as she saunters out to the curb, and hops in the driver's seat. At this time of the morning, the Belt Parkway is busy with commuters trying to go to Manhattan. Traffic is stop and go all the way into the city.

The parking for guests is valet driven, and she pulls into their underground garage when she arrives for work. By eight in the morning, most commercial garages will be full. The Torino-Ashley Hotel built theirs under the building for lodgers, and she is able to pull in and park. The attendant gives her the claim ticket to retrieve her M3 later, and she hands him five dollars. "Please be careful when you drive this car. Your name is on your shirt, and I won't forget it."

The skyscraper, at street level, is filled with commercial stores and restaurants. The second to sixth floors are market-rate rental apartments, and the seventh to tenth are residential condominiums. Khara walks to the elevator in the garage and takes it to the hotel registration desk on the eleventh floor. As she enters the main lobby a police lieutenant spots her and approaches to give her instructions. In an instant, he recognizes her from her past fame in the department.

"Welcome Detective Bennet, I heard you will be assigned to this detail. The Texas group, and the candidate is on the fifteenth floor on the west side of the building. On the floor with them is the Secret Service who is only guarding the congressman."

"Going up now, and I'll be on their floor watching them like a hawk" Khara said.

"Yes, the Deputy Commissioner wants to learn about everything they are doing, or discussing, if possible. Think you can find anything out?"

"Yes, I will try. I'll go upstairs to check in with the detail on the floor."

"Good, I'll speak to you later."

Khara turns around and steps to the side. The hotel elevators are to the right of the one from the basement as she presses the button in the lobby to go up. The door opens and she enters on an empty elevator. But she hears someone calling out to hold the door as they are running, and want to go upstairs. The door button on the inside wall is pressed, and the sliding chrome doors remain open.

Through the open doors, a handful of Texas for Texans security men come rushing in.

Now she decides is a better time than later to try to meet them.

"Hey guys, welcome to New York"

One of the men responds in his western drawl.

"Howdy ma'am, how are you today?"

"Fine, thank you. The people of The United States appreciate what your group is doing keeping out of Texas, and America, all those Mexicans and South American rapists and killers from coming into our safe country."

"Although what you said is true you don't sound like a Texan."

"If a person believes in what you are doing, and is a natural born American, we are all Texans, right? This is why I'm going to vote for your candidate Congressman Ted Ferry."

"You are right on Miss. Did you ever come to our big and beautiful State of Texas?"

"Yes, last year I visited someone I knew in Cotulla, north of Laredo. Did you ever hear of the place?"

"Matter of fact our boss lives with his wife and two daughters in Cotulla. The oldest daughter came along on this trip with her dad and us. We will introduce you to him if we ever meet again."

"I would like it if you can make the introduction for me. The police department assigned me here to assist you with anything you might need help with. Ask me, and I'll see what I can do."

"We appreciate the offer, thank you."

One of the Texans glances at Khara's body and takes her up on the statement.

"Later if you could stop by my room tonight we can talk about Texas all evening long. By the way, we are in room 1508" he said.

"Don't be surprised if I take you up on the offer, thanks."

The elevator doors open, and the men walk out past the N.Y.P.D. security detail. While they go down the hall to their rooms laughing and joking with each other Khara stays back, observes them go to their room, and introduces herself to the two uniformed officers standing in the lobby.

"I'm Detective Bennet, and I'll be in charge of this position when I'm here. About what time do they leave their rooms?"

"In the morning they go for breakfast and don't return till much later. The campaign manager reserved a whole wing in the north hallway. The Secret Service is stationed by the rear stairs, and one man is outside the candidate's room. The Secret Service also placed one agent here with us, but he goes to the men's room while we are here or usually stays by the back staircase. At dinner time if the Texans don't go out they order room service from the kitchen upstairs. When the candidate exits the building the Secret Service follows him."

"Officers I do appreciate you filling me in."

After her first half of the shift is over Khara enters the elevator to the thirty-fifth floor for a meal break. The hotel runs an enclosed bar on the roof overlooking Manhattan. Relaxed, and looking out the all-glass restaurant and bar at the city below she sits at a small brown marble slab on a pedestal near the rear of the room with her back to the wall. Since lunchtime starts about now not too many people are sitting in the room yet and having alcohol or food. The minutes fly by as more people show up, and they sit at the bar or a table.

A waiter approaches, and Khara takes a quick gander at the menu. For now, she only orders a bacon cheeseburger with cheddar cheese and caramelized onions on a toasted brioche roll. For a drink, she asks for her favorite, Amstel Light Lager on tap. The beer comes in a frosted glass and is ice cold.

Positive no one is seated near her within earshot she calls Al on her burner phone.

"Hi Al it's me, and you must send someone to register for a room, but not on the fifteenth floor of the Torino-Ashley Hotel in the city tonight. Book the room for a week, and make sure Olga gives your person the package I asked her to save for me. This evening we are going to deliver a message to the candidate."

"Guess I'll go to Olga's office myself this morning to meet with her before I go to the club, and hope she understands what you are talking about."

"She will don't worry, I don't want to speak on the phone. Later when we meet in person I'll tell you more."

"Thanks, Khara, I'll tell Olga what you said."

The chrome doors open as she hangs up and gazes inside as three men wearing cowboy hats stroll out of the elevator with their leader's huge daughter trailing behind them. The small herd of Texans is seated at a table on the other side of the room, and they order a few drinks with some food. The large girl does a once-over around the room and spots Khara sitting in the back by herself. The heavyset girl plods over to talk to her having seen her the other day.

An immense shadow is cast over Khara's table while the tall obese young lady stands motionless and stares at her face.

"Damn I am sure I met you somewhere before, but I can't place where. There is like a fog in my memory, yet you are so familiar to me, did you ever stay in Texas?"

The question is ignored as Khara answers with an inquiry which changes the subject to throw her off.

"Is this the first time you are visiting New York City?"

"Yes, we arrived here the other day for some private meetings with the mayor, and a few rich political donors."

"That must be it because we met yesterday in the restaurant downtown on Reade Street. Also, I attended the meeting at City Hall doing security for the deputy commissioner."

"Yes I remember yesterday, but somehow I think we encountered each other before, and I can't recall where."

"I doubt it, but you never know."

Without saying another word the girl smirks and waddles back to her table to eat her lunch. The next time they meet Khara realizes she must finish her off for good, and not leave her in a coma as she did before in Cotulla.

While the food is being prepared Khara is able to peer out on the cityscape below. The burger is served and she is enjoying every bite and leaves a large tip when finished. It is time to go back on duty. Walking to the elevator she notices the Texans following her with their eyes. Not looking back, wanting to show her self-confidence she enters an empty elevator and gets off on the kitchen floor of the hotel.

In Spanish, Khara identifies herself to the hotel security guard standing in the utility lobby as she walks past them to the rear area where the stoves are situated.

In the midst of a bustling kitchen, she is searching for someone in charge when she sees a bunch of busboys milling about.

"Which one of you does room service to the fifteenth floor at night?" Khara asks in English and Spanish.

The four boys point to the smallest of them standing in the group.

In Spanish, she asks him where he is from. The young man responds he is from Puerto Rico and came here for work. Khara pulls him aside, and they walk to a quiet corner of the kitchen.

"Do you carry a phone with you?"

"Yes, I keep it in my pocket."

"Good, how would you like to make five thousand dollars in cash this week?"

"Tell me what I need to do."

"Give me your phone. I am entering a number in the memory with an X for a name. Tomorrow if there is a room service request to the fifteenth floor I want you to call me, and follow my instructions. You will be given cash and a plane ticket back to Puerto Rico. Do not tell anybody about this, do you understand me? If you don't do as I instruct you there will not be any money."

The leather jacket is pulled back a little so her shoulder holster shows, and the message is driven home.

Finished in the kitchen she goes back to the fifteenth floor to be at her post.

At the end of her shift, Khara calls Don from the main lobby.

"Hi Don, I'm in the city tonight do you feel like getting together?"

"Sure why not? At the moment I am in midtown on the east side, where are you?"

"I'm off Times Square, and I can meet you in front of Radio City in twenty minutes or so."

"Good, I need about thirty-five minutes to walk there. At this moment I am busy, but I'll see you soon Khara, bye."

Later in the day a middle-aged couple signs in at the Torino-Ashley hotel. The couple parks their vehicle in the underground garage, and wheels their large oversized luggage from their car to the elevator themselves ignoring a bellhop who offers to take the bags for them. Upon reaching the eleventh-floor main lobby they approach the check-in counter, and tell the desk clerk they reserved a room on the sixteenth floor.

The room they chose happens to be one above the Texan's floor. To the check in clerks, everything appears normal, and the pair seems like typical tourists speaking English with a foreign accent. The tourist's cameras are hanging from their necks, Mexican passports are shown, and the couple uses a Mexican credit card for a deposit. The husband registers as Mr. and Mrs. Alejandro Gonzales.

***

On Sixth Avenue she is standing in front of Radio City watching people walk by ignoring their surroundings. One thing she always does is notice the people around her. Given the choice, she will place her back against a wall. Even now waiting for him she is propped with her back to the building. The burner cell phone rings on silent, she feels the vibrations, and a text message comes through. The text only shows a number on the screen and the letter O, sixteen forty-one, and Khara realizes it is the room the Mexican tourists checked into at the hotel.

Traffic is heavy in midtown Manhattan, and the taxi cabs are trying to cut each other off to grab a fare. The chaos on the avenue is cheap entertainment to her as she watches them. To her, the people are like a Broadway show which costs her nothing. Turning to her right she recognizes Don walking up the block to where she is standing.

"Hey Khara, I am happy to be with you again."

The couple kisses on the lips while giving and enjoying a big hug.

"How about dinner, are you hungry? Nearby is a fine dining steakhouse and we can get in without waiting because I am friends with the manager" Don said.

She is inquisitive about how he met the manager of an expensive steak establishment in the city as they are walking.

"How do you know him, Don?"

"A few years ago the FBI stationed me in New Orleans, and he owned a small restaurant where I ate almost every night. No one can beat homemade Cajun food from New Orleans. Over time we became friends, and use to go fishing in the bayou together. Sometimes it is hard if he talks too fast but with patience, you can understand his deep Louisiana accent and I enjoyed some good times with him."

"So tell me how did he end up here in New York City?"

"When Hurricane Katrina hit Louisiana his restaurant washed away. Too bad because I miss the wonderful food he uses to cook. After the flood, a lot of Federal employees transferred out since no office space was left for them in the city. The bureau sent me to New York, but I kept in touch with him.

"One day I am on a case, and the Bureau needed me to investigate someone who continued to eat at this restaurant we are going to now. The FBI is setting up a sting, and I am talking to the owner when he mentioned he needed a manager so I recommended my friend. The rest is history."

"I didn't realize you are such a foodie Don."

"No I am not, but I do like a good steak every so often. Plus the owner, who is also a chef, appreciated my recommendation, and when I go to his restaurant he always comps me with a free meal. Because I don't want to take advantage of his courtesy I don't go too often."

"You are such a goody two shoes it's disgusting sometimes."

Don laughs to himself when she called him a goody two shoes because he heard it before from his family.

"Come on in, we're here. Let me open the door for you."

Don grabs the door handle and holds it open for her as she goes in first. The hostess greets them and asks if they would like a table for two. Asking for the manager Don explains to the woman he is a personal friend of his. The young woman calls over an older man, and the two men hug as they greet each other.

"Hey Don I'm happy to see you again, I missed being with you."

"Yes, it is a long time. The Bureau sends me out on a lot of domestic trips on terrorism cases, and I don't take off vacation time for myself like I used to anymore. Thought I would drop in to see you for dinner, and this is my good friend Detective Khara Bennet."

"Hi Khara, I met Don a long time. Don't want to say how long, but we go back to New Orleans before Hurricane Katrina."

"Yes, he told me on the way here. It is a pleasure to meet you."

"Come follow me, and I'll seat you at a quiet corner table."

The manager brings them to their table and leaves when he is called to the kitchen for a moment while they sit and read the menu.

"This is going to be a delicious meal tonight Don, and I love what they offer on the menu."

"Order whatever you like."

"Would you like to share an appetizer with me? The cheesesteak egg rolls sound tasty."

"Sounds good to me, what else would you like?"

"I could go for their hand rubbed and aged certified prime sirloin steak with a side of pan braized mushrooms and potatoes; how about you?"

"My stomach is growling Khara, I'm hungry, and your dinner sounds good to me so I'll order the same."

After the meal, they glance at the dessert menu. They both decide on the hot chocolate cake with freshly made vanilla ice cream topped with a unique homemade raspberry sauce. Desert is almost finished and Khara's cell phone rings on silent. Without looking she excuses herself to go to the ladies room. Once inside she enters a stall with a solid wooden door and locks the door shut.

With her phone in her hand, she views her caller ID and the number shows it is the busboy from the hotel. In Spanish, she answers the phone. The young Spanish boy tells her an order came in for the fifteenth floor, and he will deliver the food. The plan is set in play, and Don will be her alibi for where she is this evening.

Her fingers move like lightening texting him the room sixteen forty-one then she puts on a pair of latex gloves, takes out an alcohol wipe from a pouch, and wipes the burner phone clean of her fingerprints. Finished with her texts she goes back to the table and asks Don if he "would like some company tonight at his place."

Khara asked if he would like her to come home with him as she never visited him at his apartment, or even stayed over one night. They are always together at her place. A night with Khara is always an adventure, he smiles at her and calls over the waiter to ask for the check.

"The manager said the meal is on the house, thank you for coming, and I hope you enjoyed the food," the waiter said.

"Yes the steak is tasty and cooked right too, thank you."

Don reaches into his pocket and leaves a hundred dollar tip on the table. On the way out of the restaurant he thanks his friend, and hugs him goodbye.

Together they walk to Madison Avenue where Khara spots a homeless person begging for money. The man is sitting on the sidewalk with a cardboard sign saying he is a disabled veteran in need of help. One of his legs is missing, and a pair of crutches is lying next to him on the sidewalk. Don continues to go ahead as she stops and yells out this will only take a second. A twenty dollar bill is taken out of her pocket, and she wraps the money around the burner phone without touching the phone with her fingers. She stoops over and places the money, with the burner phone sandwiched inside the cash right into the man's large tin coffee container. Khara straightens up and runs to catch up to Don.

The homeless man takes out the money and is surprised to find the cell phone placed in the can. Two young men walk by, and he offers them the phone for a few dollars. Without even a discussion among themselves, they buy the cell phone. The phone is an unlocked one which anyone can use. One of the boys slips the cell phone into his pocket so nobody should view him with it. They continue on their way not realizing they are now capable of being tracked for a soon to be murder.

Don hails a cab, and they go to the Upper West Side of Manhattan to his apartment house. The cab arrives at his home, he pays the cabby with a credit card, and both of them walk to the front door.

The brick apartment houses stand at attention like soldiers row after row as far as the eye can see. Most of them are built without a parking garage underneath. A number of years ago the city constructed a multistory parking facility a block away, and the monthly fees are high.

"Somehow I never asked you Don, but do you own a car?"

"No, I do not need one. If I need to go somewhere I drive the agency's car, or I rent one for my personal use."

The keys to the building are in his hand as he unlocks the front door, and enters the building's lobby. Khara raises her eyes upward and discovers small video cameras perched on each wall of the entry.

"Do you know if the videos are time stamped Don?"

"Yes, they are because I inquired about the cameras when I moved into the apartment house as a safety precaution."

To her thinking, this is an opportunity because it reinforces her alibi in case an investigation comes along, and she needs to prove where she is tonight.

Although the building is an older one it is well maintained and clean. The apartment is furnished in middle-aged bachelor contemporary. Nothing too wild, yet not sedate either she thought the furniture is comfortable and relaxed.

In the center of his living room she is standing, turns places her arms around his neck, and starts to kiss him.

"Come on Don, join me in the shower, afterward we'll go to bed for the night."

***

The next morning Don wakes, walks into the kitchen to make coffee while turning on the television with the remote control, and the morning news shows are on. The weather is being given when a bulletin flashes across the screen. The local broadcast switches from the studio to the national lead where a reporter is in front of the Torino-Ashley Hotel reporting a double murder happened in the hotel last night while candidate Ted Ferry is out for dinner. Two members of the Texas for Texans security team the presidential candidate travels with are found shot to death in their room. The police and the Secret Service are investigating. The congressman left early today canceling the rest of his scheduled week in New York and is on his way to Virginia for a campaign rally.

"Khara wake up. Listen to this. A murder happened last night at the hotel where you are working."

"No kidding?"

"Yes, it came over the news this morning."

"Don you do acknowledge there is no way I can be involved. Last night I spent the whole evening with you in bed, and you are now smiling ear to ear to prove it."

"Funny Khara, I'll find out more when I go into the office today."

"Well I need to dress also, and I must report into Johanna this morning. I don't know where she'll want me to go. First I will shower before I leave. Do you have any body wash here?"

"Nope, I only use soap."

"Remind me to buy some coconut body wash for the next time I'm going to be here with you."

Chapter Seven

The front door to the apartment building opens as they leave, and Don hails a taxi to take her back to the hotel in Times Square. On the way, the yellow cab will stop to drop him off at his office. When she arrives at the Torino-Ashley Hotel she gives the taxi driver the fifty dollars he gave her to pay with. Ambulances and police cars are double parked all along the side street making driving difficult for traffic to navigate around them.

The hotel's small street entry lobby door automatically opens for Khara as she walks in, and takes the elevator up to the main entrance level. As she exits out of the elevator she spots Johanna standing near the registration desk talking with the Mayor, and the

Chief of Police. The Deputy Commissioner point's one finger up into the air signing for her to wait a moment, and continues with her conversation while Khara understands what she is signaling.

For a few minutes, she is milling around, and waiting as she meanders over to the floor to ceiling windows to stare out at the bustling street eleven flights below. Mesmerized by all the activity going on she is oblivious to Johanna walking over to the window, and now standing on her left side. Khara takes a quick look around to make sure they are out of earshot of other people as a question is asked.

"Guess you heard what happened here yesterday Khara?"

"Yes, the shooting is on all this morning's news shows."

"This couldn't happen to a nicer bunch of racists, but we need to find out who did this. Although I am your superior officer I might not want to be told the answer to my next question, but where were you yesterday evening?"

"Not a problem Johanna. Last night I ate dinner with Don Weber at a great steak place right near Rockefeller Center. After we finished eating we went back to his apartment on the upper west side, and I stayed the whole night with him. If needed he can obtain the cab receipts and the building video to prove I spent the night with him if you want them."

"No, obtaining them for me won't be necessary Khara, and to be honest I wouldn't be upset if you are in involved in this killing. Somehow I would find a way to protect you." With a light touch, she rubs Khara's upper arm and stands for a moment looking out the high windows with her.

"Thanks, Johanna, I appreciate the thought."

"Don't forget I'm here for you. Also, our sources tell us the leader of the group instructed his lawyer to close on some property in northern New York State yesterday. The Foundation bought some acreage near Boonville deep in the woods. In a week or so I need you to go up to Utica to find out what is going on. In the meantime go back to your precinct in Staten Island, and I will be in touch with you very soon."

"Today I'll report back to my precinct."

"Come on Khara and I'll go down with you."

The women turn to the elevators as Johanna pushes the button, and they walk on when it arrives at their floor. Alone on a slow ride down to the ground level, in a stealth move, Johanna takes Khara's hand in hers. "Is this thing with Don Weber serious?"

The doors open on the street level lobby before she can answer. People are walking onto the elevator as the two women exit and leave the building.

On the crowded city sidewalk, standing with pedestrians hustling around and past them, Khara answers her question.

"The truth is I enjoy Don's company. Believe me, nothing serious is going on. This is only a physical attraction between us. My psychiatrist tells me all the time my high sex drive is part of my clinical diagnosis."

Silence, as no follow-up from Johanna comes regarding the unknown condition mentioned. Khara thinks she is ignoring her answer because she does not care what the problem is as long as she can be intimate with her. Being bisexual Khara picks up the vibes from the lipstick lesbian deputy commissioner.

With the explanation about Don being told to her, the deputy commissioner extends her hand to shake goodbye when Khara places her left hand over

Johanna's and smiles at her. The signal is sent and received.

"The FBI scheduled a meeting at their New York office, and I must go now. Later I will try to call you when I leave the conference" Johanna said. She walks out to the curb and sits in the back of a waiting unmarked police car.

Finished here Khara goes back into the lobby to wait for the elevator to go down to the basement to retrieve her M3, and head back to her office. With a five dollar bill, she tips the valet, drives up and out into traffic heading for the Thirty-Fourth Street entrance to the Lincoln Tunnel. From midtown, she heads south on the New Jersey Turnpike to the Goethals Bridge, and into Staten Island.

Her car is parked head on by her precinct. Exiting the car she saunters into the building, past the desk sergeant, and takes the stairs to her desk on the second floor. Matt spots her come in and walks over to Khara's desk while leaning on the wall of the cubicle. A question which crossed his mind when he watched the early morning news reports is asked of her.

"So Khara, are you involved in the Texan's shooting last night?"

"Believe it or not Detective McMann, Don and I spent the whole night together, and nowhere near the hotel."

"Wow, what a change for once."

"Come on Matt we'll go meet the anger management doctor, I'll drive."

With the doctor's business card in hand, they head to the Eltingville section for a visit. The trip only takes a few minutes or so, and they pull into a residential neighborhood where the office is located.

"Matt, don't you think it is strange a doctor operates out of a home in this quiet neighborhood? Are you aware of any sign outside? How in the world do people find out about her?"

"Beats me, let's stop and go in to find out some information about her practice."

The unmarked squad car is blocking the driveway as they leave the vehicle, walk to the front door, and ring the bell. Three times they press the doorbell before someone comes to the door.

A young lady opens the door, stands still holding the door ajar, and is looking at them.

"Can I help you?"

"Yes, we are detectives investigating some deaths related to anger management issues. Is the doctor in? I am Detective Bennet, and my partner is Detective McMann."

"Please come in, I am the person you are looking for. What can I assist you with today?"

"Is this your office, in your home?" Khara said.

"Yes, follow me and we can sit inside if you don't mind, we can talk downstairs."

Inside the home, they walk behind her down to an inner room in the basement strolling by a wall filled with the woman's diplomas hung side by side.

"So you didn't go to any American universities from what I can tell. All the diplomas are from unknown schools, and are also hanging on some cheap wood paneling."

"Yes, of course, I did Detective Bennet. The advanced degree on my left side here I received at the Universal Foundation of Hypnotherapy in Iowa and the paneling is not cheap."

"So you are not a real doctor?"

"Do not even imply I am not a doctor, I earned a doctorate in hypnotherapy from the Foundation."

"Bull shit and you know it too."

"Detective Bennet I resent your implication I am not qualified to treat my patients. Also, I sense some anger in your voice."

Only standing a few feet from her Khara steps closer to the woman, and is about two inches from her face, nose to nose.

"Not sure what you are pulling here and I don't believe anything you say you are doing. If another patient of yours kills someone, or themselves, I will be back to you before their body hits the ground. Do I make myself understood?"

"Yes, I understand the threat Detective. Would you like me to treat you as a patient for anger management? With luck, I may be able to squeeze you in my busy schedule."

"Bet you would love to try and treat me."

Finished speaking to her the detectives leave the home, and head back to the precinct. In the car, they engage in a short conversation about the doctor.

"Matt I think she is full of shit. What is your impression of her? Maybe only a week or two, or sooner, will pass before we revisit her again. Or, I am thinking out loud, I might go to her by myself to attempt to find things out, this will be kind of undercover work. What do you think?"

"Khara try not to kill her, please. Too much paperwork involved."

***

On the way back a call comes in from dispatch a ten-year-old girl near an elementary school reported a man approached her. A white van with a pink cow on

110

the side is said to be the vehicle from which the man enticed the girl with candy.

Matt responds to dispatch they will pick up the call. The police car is close to the school and Khara is able to drive there in a matter of minutes so they can interview the young student. The assistant administrator is watching her while sitting in the nurse's office waiting for the police, and her mother to arrive. Both of the detectives question the ten-year-old girl, but the nurse and girl tell them nothing new which will help in their investigation. Only a standing pink cow on the van is what they can go on. Finished they leave the elementary school and return to their office. A call is put out on the evening news to look for the described vehicle. With any luck, the van will turn up again somewhere on Staten Island, and soon.

The time is late so they clock out, Matt heads home to Far Rockaway Queens, and Khara goes to the club to meet with Al.

The back 440 highway is almost empty of vehicles. Rush hour traffic is going in the opposite direction. A firm grip on the gear shifter enables her to throw the transmission into second gear, pop the clutch while stomping the gas pedal to the floor and the car springs to life. With the speed of a professional, she is in third and redlining the tachometer when she slows down because the exit is coming up fast.

The M3 coasts to the front awning stops, and she gives the valet her key fob. Big Boy is not back at work yet and the new bouncers are aware who she is, and let her in without searching her for weapons.

Upon entering the lobby a pert young cocktail waitress approaches, and after Khara inquiries about where Al is in the building, she tells her he is in his office, but not where the location is. Khara is aware the girl's answer is a security measure so she leaves the bubbly young girl, and walks down a hidden flight of stairs waving at the video cameras on the wall of the stairway aware Al is watching her descend to the basement.

A few knocks on the steel door is only protocol as she waits for a response.

"Come in Khara everything last night went as planned at the Torino-Ashley."

"Tonight I am going to ask Olga about the hotel when I am home, but I figured you would be told the details by now."

"This morning I spoke to her and she is home. They left early today for Brooklyn. Too bad no camera is present because I would love to see the Texan's faces when they find out Alejandro checked in yesterday."

"What happened? I'm anxious to find out."

"Sit down for a moment and I will tell you. Yer, this is how the operation went down. Olga and one of her team registered at the hotel as Mexican tourists. A room is reserved for them on the sixteenth floor above the candidate's floor. The room service waiter delivered the cart to their room as you instructed him. The young boy is handcuffed, gagged, and placed in the bathroom for the time being, and she began working on the platter."

"The small main serving dish is removed. In Olga's larger suitcase she brought a larger serving dish and a chrome cover to fit over the plate. Your package is taken out of the dry ice and placed on the dinner plate, and the dome replaced. A black waiter's uniform with a white shirt Olga took with her is put on because she is going to switch with the real waiter. The room service order will be her ticket onto the secure floor as she prepared to leave her room. Right before she pushed the button to go down one flight Olga takes out a tiny butane flame starter people use to light a barbecue. The fire starter is enough to heat the chrome dome so the top is hot to the touch."

"When she walks off on the fifteenth floor two city cops asked her where she is going. No secret service agents are present. My guess is the congressman went out for the evening. The policemen stationed on the floor wanted to lift the cover and inspect the food. She told them if they would touch the cover they could sense the heat so the contents would remain warm, and be alright."

"The police are told if the candidate receives a cold meal they would be responsible, not her. The officers allowed her to pass through, and she went to the room number which ordered the dinner way down the hall."

"After she knocked on the door they let her in, and two men in different stages of undress are sitting on the beds. The men see Olga in a short waitress outfit and they started to proposition her. In her Russian accented English, she said servicing them is not a problem. First, she wants to go to the bathroom to change out of her clothes, and they need to be naked when she comes out. The men point to a small door at the rear of the room, and she went into undress. Once inside she lifted her jacket, took out her .45 from her holster tucked behind her back, and screwed a silencer on the barrel. With her jacket now pulled back down she opened the door. The men are undressed, and waiting for her. With a few pops from her pistol, they are all dead. In no rush, she searched the room for any information they might be in possession of, placed the pistol back in her holster, and went out the door to the elevator, and back upstairs to her room."

Continuing the story he said "soon as she walked in her room Olga changed into her dress and blouse, then she left the hotel to go home taking the large suitcase with her. By the way, the young Spanish waiter is stuffed in the luggage. I can only assume when the candidate, and the leader of the hate group, came back they discovered the dead men. My only wish is if I could be in the room when Ted Ferry lifted the chrome dome on the cart and recognized Alejandro's head on a platter. The head of his right-hand man must have been a real shock to him".

"I am sure they all got the message, Al."

"Now we need to track down the son of a bitch when he comes back into the area. At the moment the situation is too dangerous to send you back to Mexico until we eliminate our domestic competition."

"How's Biggie doing?"

"He'll be back soon. Big Boy still must rest a while, but he's coming around."

"Good I will be going home now. Talk to you later."

Khara goes upstairs, and out the front entrance to wait for her car to be brought around. Under the awning waiting, her phone rings, and the caller ID tells her Johanna is calling.

"Hi, Johanna what's doing?

"I need you to go to Brooklyn. A large house explosion took place in a residential neighborhood, and the fire marshals think explosives are the cause. Check out the situation for me."

"Text me the address, and I will be on my way."

***

The location comes in, and Khara drives by the docks in Bay Ridge Brooklyn. The home is on West Fifty-First Street between First and Third Avenues.

Now on Staten Island, she is not too far from the next destination. Back in her own car she turns on a siren to take the express lanes, takes out her magnetic flashing light, and sticks the unit on the top of her M3. This helps a little, but the traffic is dense and slow moving.

At last, she gets to the destination, and the street is blocked off with fire trucks and police cars. Colored emergency lights are twirling and glaring all over the place and the area is organized mayhem trying to fight an inferno in a building which is crumbling before their eyes. The explosion structurally damaged the over one-hundred-year-old row house and its neighboring homes too.

The M3 is parked in a way blocking the beginning of the street with all the flashing lights on the car remaining on. With her right hand, she takes out her badge on a chain and slips it out of her blouse and around her neck as she tries to find the police commander in charge. Only a moment or two later she spots him about fifty feet away. Amidst the chaos of the scene, she approaches and identifies herself as being on assignment from the deputy commissioner.

The commander starts to tell Khara what is happening. "An undercover unit received a call from one of our confidential sources a drug operation is making a bomb here. The remnants of a cartel wanted to murder a big drug boss on Staten Island. The department tried but they could never find out who the person is. A SWAT team came here to take out the bomb makers. The educated guess is they looked out the window and saw us arriving. I asked the fire chief and he said the fire marshals thought they tried to move the explosives, and the homemade bomb went off. Most of them make their own TATP [triacetone triperoxide] which is established to be an unstable explosive. TATP is the stuff suicide bombers in the Middle East use to blow themselves up. The slightest friction and boom they are gone."

"Are any witnesses around? Did anyone manage to walk out alive?" Khara asked.

"Doubt someone escaped but we don't know Detective Bennet, and if anybody did escape from this mess they'll be covered with soot, torn clothes, and pretty beat up from the pressure of the explosion."

"Did the officers check the bus stops and subway stations yet?"

"The local cops are canvassing the neighborhood now. Can you also check those out, and help us?"

"Give me a few minutes, and I will be back."

For a moment she sits in her car thinking the problem through, and realizes if someone did survive the blast they would not be standing on the corner waiting for a bus. The smart thing she thought is they would run to the subway station only two blocks away. So she jumps in her car, turns the flashing light on, and drives to Fifty-Third Street to check out the subway station. When approaching the station she is able to find an open parking spot and scurried down the steps to the train tracks.

With her badge hanging around her neck on a chain she hops the turnstile and is on the train platform. The adrenaline is rushing through her body as she scans the station for anything out of the ordinary. She spots someone sitting on the concrete floor at the far end of the platform with their back leaning on the wall. A flick of her finger unlocks her service gun from the shoulder holster while she approaches the person with caution aiming her pistol down facing the floor.

A train pulls in and a lot of people are getting off the crowded subway due to rush hour. The commuters are going home from work. The mass of people flee as fast as they can when they sight Khara walking with her gun drawn, and her gold detective's badge swinging over the front of her blouse. But this person is motionless.

As Khara gets closer she spots a gaunt skeletal young girl in her early twenties or so. The woman is still, her head is bent forward into her chest, and her legs are straight out and split apart. The girl's chest is not moving. The clothes are shredded, filthy and burn marks are on her arms. With the first two fingers of her hand, she presses against the slumping girl's neck trying to find a pulse, but none can be felt.

"Are you alright Miss?" She asked.

Silence, the girl does not reply. Now on one knee and bending over to look at the girls face white foam is coming out of her thin petite lips. With one step back she realizes the girl is either dead or dying. Either way, nothing can be done at the moment which will help the girl's situation.

Not getting a pulse, or an answer, she calls on her phone for an ambulance, and also for backup.

With ease, she lays her down on the floor and searches through her clothes for identification. Nothing is found on her, and the girl's pockets are empty except for a ten dollar bill with a phone number on the front. The money Khara places in her leather jacket pocket and waits for the backup she requested to arrive. Later she will try to find out who belongs to the unknown number.

The girl's body is lying on the cold concrete platform, and Khara detects the girl's hands are clinched closed. Curious as to why they are in a fist Khara pries them open and finds small glassine capsules wrapped in a thin rubber band. The pills are recognized due to her drug training, as cyanide capsules. The girl committed suicide.

At last, the ambulance arrives with uniformed officers, and she is able to leave the subway station walking upstairs to the street level to go home. First, she has to go back to report to the officer in charge and explain she found one of the people from the explosion. Now in her car again she heads for Brighton Beach. It's been a long day, and she can't wait to shower, and refresh herself by putting on her favorite coconut body wash again.

Once home she presses star 67 and calls the number on the ten dollar bill. The telephone rings once, twice, and on the third ring, a voice message answers the call. The message is in Spanish and says to call back at midnight if you need assistance. The area code looks familiar as she realizes 204 is a Dallas Texas number. In a flash, she assumes they must be making or trying to make, a bomb to attack either Olga or Al. Now she needs to drink cups of coffee to stay awake till midnight. The shower will be taken later. To pass the time she takes out her guns, including the MP7 submachine gun, and starts to oil and clean them.

The hours tick by, and now it is midnight in Dallas. The number is dialed, and she speaks in Spanish when a man answers.

"Hello, you want help in New York?"

"Yes, I am in trouble, and need assistance."

"We thought you died in the explosion, everyone is dead, all the national news reports said so."

"No I escaped through the basement moments before, and I am carrying one device with me in a backpack" Khara answers.

"Meet us at Owls Head Park in Brooklyn tomorrow morning at seven. A black car will pick you up so make sure to bring the bomb with you."

The man hangs up on her.

The time is a little after midnight, and Khara is aware Al will still be at the club. The quick dial function on her phone calls him. She needs to make sure he is working, and not on a date with some pretty young waitress. In a few seconds, he answers the call.

"Al I need to speak to you. Give me thirty minutes, and I will be in Staten Island because what I must tell you is important."

"No rush, I'll be here waiting."

Tired but determined she grabs her weapons, puts on her leather jacket, and goes downstairs to retrieve her M3 from the valet. After midnight the roads are still filled with traffic, but not as much as in daytime. Khara speeds to the Verrazano Bridge, and soon is pulling into the parking lot at Al's club.

He is waiting outside for her he strolls over to the car when she drives up and sits in the passenger seat next to her.

"What's up Khara?"

"At seven this morning I am meeting someone in a park in Brooklyn. Due to my speaking with them on the phone I believe they are the Mexican Secret Police, and they hired some people to make homemade explosive devices to blow up the club, or Olga's building, or both. Place extra men outside the building for the next few weeks, because I couldn't chance to tell you this on the telephone."

"Thanks for the warning. Do you need help with your meeting? Tonight I can send some of my men to help out if you need them."

"No I can handle them myself thanks, but I do miss being with you."

The smile on her face is meant to reassure him of his masculinity. Although in truth she did not miss him at all. What she did miss is the attention, sex, and gifts he gave her, and she thought what she said at the moment would be appropriate. Being a psychopath she does not possess true emotional feelings for anyone.

"And I miss you too Khara. How about after you finish with them this morning you call me? I should still be home."

"Depending on if I am not stuck somewhere, I will."

Al leant over to her, kisses her goodbye on her lips, opens the door, and hops out. Khara drives off to survey the location around the park and to prepare her plan of attack.

The sun is not out when as she pulls up to the park. The first thing she does is drive around the perimeter casing the area. Looking and thinking how she is going to do this she decides on a course of action.

The park is small and situated on Sixty-Eighth Street and Colonial Road in Bay Ridge off the Belt Parkway. From Staten Island, this is an easy trip, and Khara parks walks about one hundred feet from the curb to some wood and concrete benches situated near a brick public restroom building.

Looking around she can make out a dog walk path and a small hill in the center of the park. Still early she goes back to her car to wait, and try to relax a little. The M3 is parked on Colonial Road facing the way to the entrance to Route 287 from Sixty Eight Street.

***

Now almost seven in the morning Khara reaches inside her jacket to take the safety off her Sig Sauer, makes sure her knife is loose enough in her boot and swings her pocket book's strap over her neck. The small pocket book holding the grenade is hanging behind and at her left hip.

Opening her door she marches on the grass to a set of wooden benches by the brick building housing the bathrooms, and waits. The building is to her back, the concrete path is in front of her, and leads to the street. The backpack with the MP7 is hanging by its strap on the bench's concrete post at her side. The bag with its zipper halfway down looks full as if a small device is in it, but her MP7 is inside instead, and ready to fire.

At seven sharp a black limousine pulls up and stops by the curb. A dark tinted window rolls down, and a man yells out in Spanish "is it with you?"

"Yes, the bomb is in here" as she points to the canvas bag on the post next to her.

The grounds are illuminated with soft lighting from a few fancy lamp posts spread too far apart to give off any bright glaring light. An eerie feeling is cast over the park with only enough dull illumination on the pathways to make it difficult to see someone walking.

A voice calls out in Spanish from the car "aqui por favor" [bring it here please].

"No," Khara said.

Two men exit out of the car and start to walk towards Khara. Unzipping the bag a little more, she reaches into hold the MP7 and keeps her hand inside the bag with her finger on the trigger. The safety is off, the gun is at the ready, and she is waiting for their next move.

The men come closer when she can view bulges through their jackets by their hips. Khara assumes they are armed, and figures they are from the Mexican

Secret Police. One man halts half way between her and the limousine. The other continues walking towards where she is sitting.

Nothing is said to her and no introduction of any kind take place. The man stops on the path about twelve feet opposite the bench she is sitting on.

"Is the bomb in the backpack?"

"What is in here is for you. Who are you?"

"The Colonel sent us to pick up the device, and dispose of any witnesses."

The man reaches into his jacket to a holster on his waist and begins to raise his arm holding a gun in an attempt to shoot at Khara.

With her hand on the MP7's trigger, she fires a short burst at close range spinning the man around, and he falls to the ground. The second man further down the path also starts to reach into his jacket after the short machine gun burst, and he too starts to withdraw a gun. Seeing this Khara raises the backpack a little higher, and he is also shot with a quick burst of semiautomatic gunfire. Twisting around from the impact of the bullets he falls backward on the hard brown dirt of the dog run, and off the concrete path.

A third man, upon witnessing this, jumps out of the front passenger side of the limousine, and charges at her shooting as he is running. Bullets begin to speed toward Khara who is about fifty feet away. With the MP7 in both hands, she stands facing him and sprays bullets in a left to right swaying motion aiming at his legs and shooting him in the knees. The bullets which miss him spray into the limousine's doors and fenders. The man falls to the ground crippled and crying out in anguish. Racing to him she kicks the pistol away from his writhing and collapsed body. A car motor starts and Khara glances up as the parked limousine inches backward to move away. With her arms pumping, she breaks into a sprint running as fast as she can towards the vehicle.

The limo backs up and starts to pull out of the parking spot when Khara jumps through the open back door landing in the rear seat. She reaches up and points the backpack to the front seat squeezing the trigger. The burst of bullets hit the driver. Wounded in the lower back he steps on the gas in a reflexive move causing the limo to lurch forward as he yells out in agony, and over the curb into the park itself. A tall robust tree stops the limo from going any further as smoke rises from the hood of the engine.

The driver is moaning due to a smattering of bullets in his back near his spinal cord. She reaches down and pulls her knife out of her boot, in Spanish she demands to be told if any more men are here in New York. Against his neck, she places the point of the blade and there is no patience on her part for a stalling answer.

"Leave me alone I don't know anything, I'm hurt, call an ambulance."

The man is speaking in a low tone of voice as Khara is leaning over the back of his seat trying to listen, and watching him. In a move not quite quick enough he reaches into his jacket, and she catches sight of the handle to a pistol. Not waiting for him to take the gun out she jabs the knife into his throat, twisting the blade trying to sever an artery. The driver is bleeding out all over the seat as she gets out of the limo and goes back to the third man she shot in the knees.

The man appears to be in severe pain holding both of his knees, while in a fetal position, as she runs to where he is lying. Again in Spanish, she questions him.

"Are others here with you?"

"No, only the Texans are left. We are to go to a military training camp they are setting up in New York somewhere. Call a doctor, I need help, I am in pain."

"Tell me the truth; your orders are to kill me, correct?"

"No, no only to scare you."

"You are lying to me, too bad."

With one pull of the trigger, his brain matter fertilizes the park's almost green grass.

Time is of the essence causing her to run out of the park at breakneck speed. In the distance, she can hear sirens approaching. Someone from the neighborhood must have heard the gunfire and called the police. With sweat dripping down her forehead she is running over a small mound as she heads away from the bodies. In a sprint, she races to her car which is parked on Colonial Road a half block away.

With her thumb pressing her key fob she pops the trunk, throws the backpack in, and opens her driver's door to sit behind the wheel. Pushing the button she starts the car, pulls out, and makes a U-turn to go in the opposite direction away from where the gunfire took place. The escape plan changed due to the sirens.

The time is ten after seven in the morning, and she already killed four armed men in a ten-minute span.

With her Adrenalin pumping, she calls Al on her cell phone. Still too early to go to work, and she is too excited to go home to sleep. Al's condo is only a few blocks away so she calls him and asks if he would like some early morning company. Of course, he welcomes her to stop in to be with him.

Chapter Eight

"Come on its time to wake up, I need to go to work, and so do you."

"What time is it Al?"

"Almost two in the afternoon and your phone's been ringing, but you never woke up to answer the call. You were in a deep sleep."

"Yer I know, I was exhausted, and I spent almost twenty-four hours awake. Hand me my cell phone so I can find out who called."

The caller ID said Johanna rang her a few times, but before she calls her back Khara first needs to shower and afterward she will call her. In the bathroom stall is her coconut body wash because Al wants to make sure some is always available for her. The medicine cabinet is also now stocked with the Chanel No.5 she loves to spray all over her body.

All dry and dressed she returns the call on her personal cell phone.

"Hi, Johanna this is Khara, what's up?"

"A report came in four armed Mexican policemen were shot dead in a park in Brooklyn this morning. A neighbor spotted a black woman driving away in a small black car. Where were you about seven today?"

The answer to the question is a question. "How did you find out they were Mexican police?"

"The bodies all had identification on them when our lab people searched each corpse. Did you have anything to do with this?"

"What if I hypothetically told you they were connected to the bomb explosion you sent me to investigate yesterday?"

"Tell me the cases are tied together, and I would say to you well done, I'll talk to you soon, bye."

With a sigh of relief, Khara is satisfied Johanna meant what she said when she was with her earlier. She told her she would have her back. Johanna listened and read between the lines.

"Who was on the phone?" Al asked.

"The Deputy Commissioner for Terrorism wanted to find out if I was responsible for four dead Mexican Secret Policemen being killed this morning in Bay Ridge."

"Know what, you don't need to tell me the answer, I can guess."

Now ready to leave his condo she walks with him down to the basement garage. The BMW is parked next to his red Cadillac in one of the three contiguous parking spaces he owns. The black M3 pulls out of the garage and heads for the Verrazano Bridge, and her precinct.

Once on the Staten Island side of the bridge by the toll booths, she spots a white van with a pink cow on its side two lanes over on her right. In a flash, she remembers the school girl who was almost abducted the other day and decides to tail the van. Traffic is heavy as she tries to get closer so she can be able to read the license plate. On her voice-activated car phone she calls Matt, reads the plate number, explains what she is doing, and asks him to send her the registered address. In second gear the M3 is going to move away from the tolls at speed, and follow him.

The suspected van is followed at a comfortable distance behind as she trails him to a residential neighborhood where he drives into the back of an overgrown hedged driveway.

The car phone rings and Matt is calling her back. The address is the same home she is in front of at the moment.

"Call the officer in charge Matt and tell him where I am. Mention I'll be parked in my personal car waiting for backup."

Now she stops and parks a few houses down on the tree-lined street. Home after home the neighborhood is packed with over seventy-year-old residences. Not a rundown area, but one which is established, and showing its age on a lot of the homes. Many are in need of paint, residing, patchy lawns, and rusted iron gates from years of neglect. From a distance, these things are not too noticeable except when you are closer to the homes, and it becomes apparent this is a lower middle income working class neighborhood.

The need to be closer to the house where the driver parked to investigate comes to mind as she leaves her BMW, and saunters down the block at a casual pace not wanting to bring attention to herself. The shades are drawn all the way down on every window in the house. Stopped at the beginning of the driveway she peers down the side of the home. She becomes aware the small basement windows are painted a frosted white to prevent anyone from looking in, yet allows light to flow through the glass.

On her way back to her car her phone rings again. The caller ID reads the recent number and Khara discovers her newfound relative Dixie Pearl is calling. There may not be enough time now to speak to her as her backup should be there in a minute or so, Her new found sister will need wait a little while longer before she can call her back. The phone is placed back in her pocket, and having her cell phone ringer is slid to silent.

This time she doesn't want to experience another club incident where her cell rings at the wrong time.

In the distance, sirens are wailing as they are approaching closer to the area.

From both sides of the one-way street marked squad cars with their lights flashing rush to the address, and pull in front of the home she is watching. The commander in charge is approached as Khara explains what she saw and why. A court order is obtained and the police are ready, in force, to break through the front door.

The doorbell is rung three times, and no one is coming to the door.

"This is ridiculous I am sure he is in the house because I saw him enter and park his van in the driveway" Khara informs the officer in charge.

The main entry door is smashed open and with a handful of officers Khara dashes inside. A few go upstairs, some search the first floor, while she and Matt decide to investigate downstairs. A squeak is heard while opening the small basement door as they go to flip on the light switch. To their surprise, the lights are on downstairs. Someone must be down there. With their guns at the ready, the safety is flicked off, and they descend the narrow stairway to the concrete floor below.

The basement is empty except for a washing machine, a dryer, a small refrigerator, and a wall of bookcases filled with groceries. To everyone's surprise, no one is in the semi-finished cellar.

"What is the awful thing I smell Matt?"

"Don't know, and I can't place what the odor is. The stink is terrible in here. What do you think it is?"

"Not sure, but the disgusting aroma is coming from down here somewhere."

The detectives start to open the washing machine, the dryer, and even the refrigerator to try to find where the smell is emanating from. Both glance down at the floor noticing curved grooves on the top of the concrete starting from the left corner of the refrigerator, and swings out to the center of the room.

"Matt help me turn this refrigerator in the direction of the scratches."

Both pull together as they move the unit away from the wall with ease. The unit is on castors, and the odor hits them again with renewed strength. A small square opening in the sheetrock is now exposed to them. In her hand is a high impact LED flashlight enabling both of them to spot another room behind the wall. In the center of the small room's floor, they both see a hole with a ladder coming out of the ground.

"Matt I'm going down. Call the captain upstairs to tell him what we found."

One leg is placed through the square hole and then the other as she crawls through the opening. Khara enters a tiny room on the other side of the wall. There is not a lot of room to stand due to the short ceiling height. With the small high-intensity flashlight in her hand, she shines the light into the hole, and another narrow wood door one level below where she is standing is spotted and open a little. One foot at a time climbing down the ladder she is now facing the wooden door, and there is a faint glow shining out. With her other hand, she grabs the unfinished door and opens it. Once inside she spots the man who drove the van to this house, and two naked young girls, in their late teens or early twenties, tied to a post in a room with a dirt floor. The girls are filthy and appear to also be malnourished.

The stench is unbearable.

The girls yell at her for help while the man is stunned to find someone else in the room with him.

Forced to holster her gun to fit in the hole, and climb down she is not armed when confronted. Only her gold detective's badge on a chain around her neck is shining in the subdued light. The rest of the room is darkish and gloomy.

Not seeing a weapon in her hand the man lets out a blood-curdling yell and rushes at Khara.

In the somewhat darkened room, he throws a punch at her face which she dodges, grabs his extended forearm, and twists it behind his back. With a firm grip on the wrist, she shoves his arm in an upward motion toward his neck when a bone in his arm snaps and breaks, and there is no longer any resistance. With her other free hand, she takes hold his hair in an iron grasp and yanks him to the ground pounding his face many times onto the filth-strewn floor. The room is too dark so the blood, due to the inflicted smashing of his face goes unnoticed. There is so much unknown fluid spread around on the loose dirt floor Khara is starting to slip and lose her footing. The lighting is almost non-existent except for her flashlight. The man is lying face down yelling at her with animalistic guttural sounds which are unintelligible because of immense pain.

With no hesitation on his part, Matt follows her down and cuts the two hostages free. The young girls, crying at being freed, follow him scurrying up the ladder to waiting EMT's with blankets and an ambulance.

In the basement, the man calmed down and is now able to talk to Khara. The pervert, talking in mumbles due to broken teeth, is trying to make a deal with her to let him escape.

"Let me go, and I'll pay you over five thousand dollars in cash. The money is hidden upstairs in the wall over the transom of my clothes closet in my bedroom. You can keep it if you let me leave."

"You are beginning to piss me off, don't fall getting up"

Again she grabs a handful of his hair, lifts his head upwards, and slams his face into the wooden ladder four or five times shattering his nose, cracking bones in his face, more of his teeth, and again cutting his lips. Blood is starting to flow down his chin onto his neck and shirt.

"Do not try to escape from me again. Do you understand? Now stand, and start climbing to the top of the ladder through the ceiling."

Forced to reach down to help lift the man as his right arm is dangling at his side, Matt sees he is having trouble using the ladder.

By now plenty of officers are in the basement of the house waiting for them to bring the man out of the hole. The perp is handcuffed, and two policemen take him out of the house to a police van, but he now needs an ambulance.

Not wanting to waste any time Khara runs upstairs to the man's bedroom and searches his clothes closet for the money he said he hid. With care, she starts to rub her right hand over the transom until she feels a hole in the wall. On her tiptoes she reaches in and takes out thousands of dollars wrapped in rubber bands. With his cash in her two hands, she walks downstairs, and the two young girls are now sitting in an ambulance, wrapped in blankets, about to be taken to the hospital for observation.

With the currency in both hands, she splits the cash into two bundles and gives each girl one. "Girls you forgot your money from the house, here it is."

The two of them stare at her puzzled and decide to take and hide the money in the folds of their blankets as Khara goes back into the house to wash some dried blood off her hands. The ambulance pulls away with the girls inside bringing them to a hospital.

Matt approaches her in the kitchen as she is rinsing off the perp's blood.

"What you did is a kind thing Khara."

"No, I didn't do anything. I figured they earned the money, screw him. Hope they sue him for the house, and everything else the bastard owns."

The officer in charge comes into the kitchen and goes up to Khara. "You did a fantastic job finding those girls Detective Bennet. There is going to be a commendation for this one to add to your personnel file."

"Thank you, sir, it is appreciated."

"Please tell me something detective. Judging by his face as he was placed in the ambulance is he another perp who resisted arrest?"

"The man attacked me and had to be subdued. I'm doing my job, nothing more."

'Somebody upstairs must like you because all I can say is anyone else would be thrown off the force many years ago."

The faucet is turned off, her hands dry on some paper towels left on the counter, and she decides not to give him any kind of an answer.

The commander shrugs his shoulders and walks out of the room.

Matt and Khara leave the garbage-strewn home and drive back to the office to file their reports.

***

In no rush driving to the precinct, she elects to return Dixie Pearl's earlier phone call to her from the morning.

"Hello" Dixie Pearl answers.

"Hi Dixie Pearl, its Khara returning your call."

"Bless Jesus it is good to hear from you sister. This morning I was talking to my husband, and we would like you to visit with us and sleep in our home. Can you come down here because I would like to know you a little better? We have a lot of catching up to do."

Now remembering the Texas presidential candidate will be campaigning in Virginia this month she has an idea. Should she mention it to Johanna, and hope she'll send her down to investigate, where she can try to kill two birds with one stone.

"Let me find out what I can do about my trip. This will be on official business so I must speak to my supervisor about going to Virginia, I'll be back to you in a little while."

"A vacation stop here with me would be wonderful Khara, I hope you can come and stay with us."

"Never know, I'll try but I must go now. Talk to you soon, bye."

Both hang up, and when she arrives at the precinct parks and climbs up the back stairwell to the second floor. Matt is waiting as he hands her a piece of paper.

"Hey, I did the incident report for you Khara. All you need to do is sign it, and I'll hand it in for the two of us."

"Thanks, Matt."

After signing the form she picks up the phone and goes to call the deputy commissioner in Manhattan when her office telephone rings in her hand, it is Johanna calling her.

"Detective Bennet, can I help you?"

"Khara this is Johanna, I am speaking to the New York State Police a lot about the foundation, and they are interested in why the Texas for Texans bought land in Booneville. The State Troopers took some aerial shots of dirt being moved around showing what is going on, and they wanted to find out if we knew anything."

"Do you think I should drive up to Utica, and snoop around a little."

"Not a bad idea Khara, but it is too early yet. The Texans are still moving earth around up there, and they need to file plans for any construction they want to do."

"In the meantime, Johanna would you like me to go to Virginia? The candidate is campaigning down there, and I might find something out before I go up to Booneville."

"Today I'll do the paperwork so you can leave tomorrow, and I'll be able to give you one week to discover any information you can."

"Appreciate it, Johanna, I'll take off early in the morning."

"Good, talk to you soon."

Finished on the phone she looks up at Matt who is standing at the entrance to her cubicle.

"So now you're going to Virginia, I never see you anymore," Matt said.

"After I return I'm going to ask Johanna to assign you to the special team she put me on. What do you think?"

"Yes, I would be happy if you did. Things are boring here when you are not around, thanks."

"Listen I'm going to the bank to take out a few bucks from the ATM. After I am finished I'll be going next door to the bank for something to eat for dinner. Some of the fellers said the new coffee shop makes delicious sandwiches, and are well priced. Give me about thirty minutes or so and I'll be back."

In a hurry, she skips down the back stairwell and rushes outside to her parked car. The key fob clicks the lock open on her M3, and she is off to the cash machine. At her destination, she parks in front of the branch gets out and takes her ATM card from her wallet. The gold detective's badge is tucked back in the top of her blouse and is not visible.

This is a new branch office with glass windows all around it on three sides, a spacious lobby, and the gleaming steel vault door is left open so people can be secure in the knowledge in how thick the door is. The walk-in safe is in the background and can be seen from in front of the teller's counter. The lighting inside the place is almost glaring it is so bright, yet it appears inviting for depositors to enter. With a pull the glass entry door opens, she walks in, and a handful of people are standing on line with only two tellers behind the low-level partition.

The trip will require some cash, and she wants to withdraw money for her Virginia journey. The sign on the ATM digital screen declares a limit on how much can be withdrawn from it. Not realizing it she needs more money than the machine allows. The only way to do this is to go to a teller and make the withdrawal using her debit card. The time is late in the afternoon, and the bank does business till eight at night for walk-up inside service as Khara strolls to the back of the line and waits for her turn.

Three men enter brandishing guns and wearing masks. One of them announces "this is a robbery, everyone on the ground and don't move if you want to live."

The robbers had to be casing the branch for a while because only thirty minutes before an armored truck made a drop of a lot of money. The next day, Friday is payroll cashing for many businesses in the area. All the cash bags are lying in the vault unopened, unsecured, and the huge polished steel door is left open.

The head robber screams out "I want everyone to go behind the counter, and sit on the floor."

All the customers online hurried to do as they were ordered. A trained investigator Khara now realizes by sitting behind the teller's desk the building seems empty. A passerby would not realize what was going on and think it was closed.

One of the men stands in the middle of the entrance, only feet from the exterior front door as the other two men run into the vault to grab full money bags of cash. The safe is set behind the teller's cage, off to the side. Everyone is on the floor watching the men in masks enter through the open vault door. No robber is now guarding the sitting customers. With a quick move her gold detective's badge is pulled out of her blouse, shows it to the others, and now it is hanging down on her chest. The Sig Sauer is taken out of its shoulder holster from under her jacket; the safety released and is held with a tight grip in her hand.

On her knees she maneuvers as close to the massive door as she can without the armed robber who is standing in the lobby, by the entry door, seeing her.

The other customers inch away from her. In a moment Khara will almost be in the path of the robbers when they come out of the safe. Everyone is silent as she overhears them talking about loading the money on a cart which is in the vault. The employees use it to transfer the bags from the armored truck to inside the building. Things are going quickly in the bank.

Sirens can be heard in the distance. One of the tellers, or customer service people at a desk, had to set off a silent alarm. Khara realizes the robbery is soon going to become a hostage situation.

The sun is starting to go down, it's now dusk, and getting dark. Squad cars pull up facing into the tall glass windows with their headlights on high beams and sighting the robber in the bank's lobby area.

The two men in the vault start to run out, and when they see Khara with her gold badge around her neck, sitting with her pistol pointing at them they freeze for a second. One of the men turns to face her with his gun, and before he even thinks about a chance to shoot she blows him away. Two quick shots hit him in the chest knocking him back where he lands on the small cart loaded with bags of cash. The full tan canvas money bag he is holding drops to the floor. The second bank robber realizing what the situation is running back in the vault to hide, and take cover.

The police now start to speak to the lone gunman standing in the glare of the head lights, via a loudspeaker.

"The building is surrounded. Place your weapon on the ground. Put your hands with fingers interlocked behind your head. Our sharpshooters are aiming at you."

From experience, Khara is well aware the department's marksmen will have their laser scopes pointed at his chest, and he has to see it on his body. By doing this showing the lasers on his chest the snipers force him to acknowledge he is a target and a dead man.

The phone in the bank starts to ring. An officer using a bullhorn, from the squad cars facing into the branch, asks the bank robber inside the safe to answer the call. Aware this is the beginning of a hostage negotiation Khara sits still, the others mumble in hushed voices to each other due to nerves. The telephone in the vault rings and the surviving vault robber answers it.

The conversation is in a hushed tone, and she cannot overhear what is said. After a few minutes the man in the safe yells to his buddy "put your weapon down, and place your hands behind your head, or we're both dead men. Don't shoot I'm coming out."

"Place your gun on the ground, and come out with your arms extended so I can see your hands" Khara commands.

The man walks out hands first doing as ordered. The man in the lobby also gives up, and the police come rushing into the building to secure both of the men.

The commanding officer on the scene comes over to Khara when he finds her.

"Detective Bennet twice in one day I've seen you. Good thing those men listened to me, and I imagine they don't realize how lucky they are to be alive."

"Why did they give up so fast Commander?"

"The one in the safe started to make demands, and he mentioned one of his men had been shot by a female cop with a gold badge hanging around her neck. So I asked him if the female officer who was wearing a gold shield also had an afro haircut. After he said yes I told him I am not going to negotiate with him. Surrender now or the detective inside is going to kill you, she is deadly. The lead robber told me you shot and killed one of his men. Guess shooting one of them convinced him to give up."

"Thank you for the vote of confidence commander, but I still need to make a withdrawal. Tomorrow I'll drive back here to get my money."

***

Finished at the bank she is driving back to her precinct, and now must begin to fill out another report due to her using her weapon. With her hands-free phone, she calls Johanna on her private line.

"Hello, Johanna speaking."

'Hi it's Khara, today I was involved in stopping a bank robbery, and need to file an event report. I'm going to be late leaving tomorrow for Virginia. A lot of time was wasted there, and I wasn't able to withdraw enough money which I will need for the trip."

"Why don't you stop by my place tonight, and I'll give you a department charge card for undercover work. My condo is in Jersey City by the waterfront at Caven Point. Hop over the Bayonne Bridge to the back 440 highway and you'll be here in no time."

"Yes, thanks, I know where it is. Fast question, I thought to be appointed by the mayor you must live in the city proper?"

"In Manhattan, I sublease a room as my official residence, but I own this condominium. The water ferry goes from here to the battery, and I'm at work pretty quick every day I need to be in the city. Give me a minute and I'll text you my home address. I look forward to seeing you soon, bye."

After she finishes the report she drives to Jersey City to meet with her. The condo is situated facing lower Manhattan, and she parks underneath the building in a public garage.

In a hurry, she took the elevator up to the third floor where she finds the apartment number she is looking for and rings the bell. Johanna opens the door and is wearing a bathrobe with pink furry slippers.

"Come on in Khara, glad you came because I opened a bottle of my favorite wine two minutes ago, and I don't like to drink alone. Care to join me?"

"Sounds inviting, and I would but tonight I must pack because I'm leaving early tomorrow morning, and I'm running late as it is."

Johanna sighed. "Well do come in for a minute because I am going to take out the official police department credit card for you."

"Time is short and I would love to stay longer and hang with you Johanna, but I will only be gone a week to work in Virginia."

"Do you think if I make it two weeks you might want to linger here tonight?"

Not saying anything, and standing in the doorway she stares as Johanna pulls the bathrobe wide open in a teasing manner exposing herself to be undressed.

"What kind of body wash do you use in your shower?" Khara asked.

***

The next morning Johanna makes some eggs and bacon with toast for breakfast for both of them. The fresh coffee is brewed and waiting on the marble counter. The stools in the kitchen are comfortable as they sit and begin to talk about their backgrounds, and get to know each other better.

"Were you ever married Khara?"

"Yes, but it didn't last too long. At eighteen I was married, and he paid for my education, but he was a real pussy, I couldn't stand him, and he sucked in bed too. What about you Johanna, ever been hitched?"

"Yes I was married to an Army colonel, and he was stationed at Fort Bragg in North Carolina. My husband was a graduate of Duke, Harvard, and Oxford. My ex-husband had twenty-five years in the military. One day he took up with a married female reserve captain who had a Master's degree and a Ph.D. in psychology. The woman had four children of which only the last one was her second husband's son. My husband was a nasty bastard. The only reason he was never in trouble is his father is a three-star general stationed at the Pentagon in Washington and covered his ass too many times. For many years I was his wife, and I know it is almost impossible to get to him. The Captain's husband was smarter than my asshole. He was an ordinary Joe of a guy who worked hard, and had a decent job."

"What did he do Johanna. I'm kind of curious and would like to know?"

"The husband went to meet his wife, and my husband at a local restaurant to talk about the situation with them. Her husband was wearing a concealed wire to record the conversation and told them he needed to discuss the terms of a divorce with them because of the children involved. My stupid husband blabbed he was in love with the guy's wife, mentioned her by name, and wanted to marry her as soon as she could divorce him. My husband said he was sorry, but they were lovers, and couldn't live without being in each other's lives going forward. What the two cheaters didn't realize was her husband had trailed both of them to motels on numerous occasions, had videos of them entering the motel together, and kissing. Meticulous records were kept by him by tracking the dates and locations of the different hotels they registered in and had their trysts in."

"Wow...so what did he do with the information once he had it?"

"Well according to Article 134 of the Uniform Code of Military Justice adultery becomes a criminal act if three certain elements are present. The captain's husband had all the corroboration he needed to fulfill the requirements for a felony prosecution. Evidence was presented to the Judge Advocate General's office, and they had him dead to rights. His father couldn't bail him out of this situation. My husband pled guilty, was demoted in rank which is the death knell for a career in the military. My asshole was forced to retire from the Army, and he lost over $780,000 in pension benefits as a result of his adultery with a fellow officer. So I divorced the bastard and came here."

"Johanna he is much luckier than my husband because I sent him to the hospital so many times he is still paying for my psychiatrist to this day. The divorce lawyer he used insisted on it for his safety."

***

Early morning and the traffic is heavy as she drives back to Brooklyn, and begins to pack for her trip. After placing her essentials in the suitcase she puts in extra .45mm clips, and a full fast reload for her snub nose .38. The grenade with the five-second fuse is kept in the small pocket book she wears on a long strap and hangs down around her neck. Two more grenades are placed in the luggage as extras. Now she is satisfied everything needed is packed and ready to go.

It is about nine in the morning, and she needs to find a place to base herself out of in Virginia. All set to call her sister she picks up her phone and dials Dixie Pearl to say she is leaving this morning to come visit her. The expectation is she can stay near her as a cover while following the candidate around the Virginia Washington area.

"Hello Dixie Pearl, this is Khara."

"Well, what a pleasant morning call. It is so good to hear from you today Khara."

"Yes, I wanted to tell you I am leaving this morning for Virginia, and I thought I might visit with you later today?"

"My husband and I would love for you to come. Our home has an extra bedroom, and you are more than welcome to stay with us instead of a hotel. We moved from Leesburg to Ashburn a year ago to a smaller place. There is still plenty of space for guests. I'll send you a text with our address in it."

"Thanks for the offer. I figure it will take me about four hours to get to your home. See you soon."

"This is a heaven-sent day for me Khara. I am looking forward to seeing you. Please have a blessed day, and a safe trip."

Now her plans are complete.

Upon reaching the ground level she is wheeling a small suitcase to the front door so she can get her car from the valet. In the main vestibule, she recognizes Viktor, Olga's lover, from pictures in her apartment. He is talking to two security men by the sofa in the rear of the lobby when he spots her, and wave's hello.

In all the months she lived in the building she never met him, but figures he must have been told about her. There are no other African American people living in the same apartment house. Viktor calls out to wait for a second as he stops his conversation with the two men, and walks over to her.

"Hi Khara, I am Viktor, and I wanted to say hello to you. Olga has told me many good things about your abilities. Listen if you ever get tired of police work I can use a woman like yourself in my organization. Of course, you helping me out can only happen if Al approves as I don't want to step on his toes."

"Thank you, I appreciate the offer, and I'll keep it in mind. A person never knows what the future holds."

Viktor said something in Russian, and one of the men picked up Khara's luggage. The man walked outside holding it for her while her M3 was brought around to the valet station. The young man pops the trunk, and the security guard placed her suitcase in it and closes the lid.

The valet hustles around and opens her driver's side door for Khara to enter. After sitting she turns on the GPS to put in Dixie Pearl's home address. The time shown on the lower right side of the screen indicates it will take a little under four hours. Traffic is a bitch around the D.C. loop, and she doesn't want to go through Washington so she inputs Gettysburg. This allows her to take the Pennsylvanian Turnpike to Harrisburg which has less congestion but is a little longer. From there she will head south to Leesburg, and on to Fenwick Drive in Ashburn. The town is only a fifteen minute or so ride away to where Dixie Pearl now lives.

The highway will permit Khara to let the M3 roar on the Pennsylvania Turnpike's straight and empty traffic roads. Once she is past the Philadelphia exits and hits the areas where there is only farmland on both sides of the highway, and little population, she will open up the throttle to let it roar.

The M3 is approaching the Verrazano Bridge and she calls Al on his phone and asks him to meet her downstairs at his building. The detour is only a quick loop to his Bay Ridge condo, and back to the highway.

The BMW approaches the garage when she finds he is standing outside the building's lobby. Double parked in front of the condo he spots her, and scrambles around the car and gets in the passenger side door.

"What's so important you need to see me this morning?" Al said.

"Tomorrow I'm heading to Virginia, and I wanted to tell you I might need your help. The goal, if at all possible, is I am going to go after the presidential candidate. His Texas for Texans security group is as ruthless a bunch as the Ecru Cartel. Be careful you must be aware of this danger because they are after you and Olga."

"Not an issue with me, I understand, and you know if you need me here is what I want you to say. Only you and I will know the meaning."

Al leant over to her and whispers two phrases in her ear. One is for help for her, and the other is a warning of danger for him."

With the words whispered to her, he puts his hand on the back of her head, and pulls her close to him for a kiss."

Finished talking he gets out of the car and walks back to his building's lobby as Khara drives away.

Chapter Nine

The trip is uneventful until she hit a rest stop on the Pennsylvania Turnpike a little before the Route 15 interchange by Harrisburg. The M3 slows down from ninety miles per hour and glides into the parking lot. The car must refuel, and she wants to grab a small bite to eat.

Not wanting her door to be dinged by another vehicle she parks the BMW in the back by the grass where no other cars are parked. The M3 is locked, the alarm is set, and she turns to walk to the food court inside the building.

An old pickup truck pulls up next to her ignoring half an empty lot, and is filled with four country boys laughing and happy. In the cab are two of the young men, and two are in the rear truck bed. The pickup's door is opened and they hop out when her nose picks up a strong pungent odor coming from the truck's interior.

The scent is ignored knowing what it is they are smoking, but Khara stops to watch they don't slam their door into her car. The men are lucky they are careful not to hit her BMW, and appear to be in a mellow mood.

Once inside she grabs a black coffee, small cherry Danish, and sits down to relax. Nobody comes to sit near her except this unshaven man, wearing a bandana on his head, with his hamburger and soda at the next table. The stranger tries to start a conversation with her, but she ignores him.

"Are you driving far?" He said.

Khara continues to drink her coffee and does not answer him.

"Excuse me miss, I am talking to you. Are you deaf or something?"

Annoyed she sits back in her chair and turns to face him while sliding her jacket open a little, and exposing her holstered Sig Sauer.

With no emotion in her face, she stares at him for a moment.

The strong message is sent. The man turns away and continues eating. Finished he stands and in a casual way strolls to the restroom.

In silence, she visually follows his walk to the men's room. Now she turns back to finish her black coffee, goes to buy a muffin for the road, and marches back to her car not realizing the man wearing a bandana is trailing after her at a distance.

The sun is at her back, and as she approaches her car a shadow on the ground appears behind her. She places her right hand inside her waist-length leather jacket while going behind the pickup truck, and the Sig Sauer is withdrawn from her shoulder holster. The man following does not spot the gun is out, and ready to use until it is too late.

The man tailing her turns by the front of the truck and is surprised to be confronted by her Sig Sauer .45 pointed at his face. Startled he is frozen in his tracks. With her left hand, Khara grabs him by his shirt and swings him around to the side of the vehicle so no one can spot them. In a stern tone of voice, she demands an answer.

"You have three seconds to tell me why you are following me, or I'll blow your brains all over the parking lot."

"I'm a private detective from Dallas, and a political campaign hired me to trail after you, and report back to them."

"Which organization, I want to know now."

"The Presidential Election Committee of Congressman Ted Ferry from Texas employed me, and I didn't understand why until early today. The information shook me up a lot when I found out the real reason why they hired me. The campaign director who I dealt with said the candidate did not forget what you did in Mexico. He saw you in a restaurant in New York with a police commissioner, and he wants to get even and needed me to map your movements to decide on the right time for him to strike. Right before I left the director informed me you are deadly, and to be careful."

"How much is the organization paying you to follow me?"

"The pay is three hundred dollars a day plus expenses, and I need the money. The job of trailing you is a twenty-four hour a day job."

"What else do you know?"

"The man who hired me is an Anglo, and I didn't know the real employer who is hiring me until this morning. My mother is an illegal alien from Mexico and is living here for forty years, and if Congressman Ferry gets elected president he said he will deport my mother back to Guadalajara. This is the reason why I am telling you this. I caught up with you at the rest stop when you parked because you drive like a crazy person."

"Did you tell the campaign manager I am here?"

"No, I told him you are driving and will contact him tonight when I am sure where you are. One of the provisions of the employment is I must call him every night."

"Here is what I need you to do. Speak to him tonight, and tell him I am in Long Island New York staying in the Hamptons. Do this, and I'll make sure you are paid double for the time you spent following me. Do you understand?"

'Yes, I'll phone him later as you asked me to do."

"Good, give me some information so I can reach you."

With one hand he reaches into a pocket on his jeans, pulls out a business card, and hands it to her.

"Tonight I'll call and make sure a friend of mine pays you in cash. The information on your card is all I require so he will know how to contact you, and you'll be compensated by him; he's on Staten Island."

"At the dance club off of the back 440 highway, you go to all the time?"

Thrown off guard for a moment when he mentioned the club she now understands she is being followed, and for a long time too. Not showing any emotion she remains collected.

"Yes, ask for Al, and he'll arrange for you to be paid in cash."

The man backs away and turns to walk to his car.

The nondescript vehicle pulls away while Khara waits to be certain he leaves the rest stop as a security measure for herself. The M3 is started, pulls over to the gas pumps, and she starts to fill up the tank for the rest of the drive.

The gas tank is filled, the clutch released, and the gas pedal pushed down to continue her drive on the turnpike. In a few minutes, she reaches Harrisburg and heads south to Virginia on State Route 15 past Gettysburg. In Maryland, a little before crossing the state line to Leesburg she stops at a roadside stand selling fresh apple-cranberry pies. The thought is this the pie will be a tasty gift to bring to Dixie Pearl when she arrives in an hour or so. In the rural market, she also buys a diet orange soda and a small bag of 6 baked apple cider donuts to munch on while she is driving.

The remainder of the trip is uneventful, and now she is on Route 7 to Ashburn and Fenwick Drive.

***

Ashburn Village is a planned community. The different neighborhoods are in a kind of pod with each one having its own unique cluster of stores, offices, and restaurants surrounded by single family homes, attached senior developments, and small three-story apartment buildings spread out to appear to give an airy feel to the region.

The BMW turns right into the Ashburn Village neighborhood, and in a few minutes will be at her sister's home. The car cruises up the block at a slow speed while she is looking at the house numbers until she spots the one she is searching for and stops by the driveway. The slope of the land causes the driveway to be on a steep incline. The thought of the front of the M3 bottoming out if she drives up the slope and scrapes the bottom in her mind causes her to park in front of the home on the street.

About to unlock her car door the front entrance to the home opens, and this tall caramel skinned woman comes out. With her hair straight, her makeup not overdone and natural looking she is dressed in a modest outfit but in style. The sight of Khara makes her smile, and she walks towards her with arms outstretched to deliver a heartfelt embrace.

"For too many years, bless the Lord, I wanted to be with you in person. I am so excited to hug my little sister."

Tears of joy and happiness are streaming down Dixie Pearl's face as she embraces her for a long time, kissing her cheeks, and hugging her till it seems this will go on forever.

"My heart is bursting holding you in my arms Khara. The Lord answered my prayers, praise Jesus" Dixie Pearl said. "Come inside with me, and greet some of your relatives. Your great aunt is here also. Sweet

Jesus sent you to us, our prayers are fulfilled, and the family is reunited."

Dixie Pearl walks with her to the front steps of her home clutching Khara's hand in hers. The husband holds the door open for them and kisses Khara politely on the cheek, and welcomes her into the house.

"My husband will carry your bags in Khara. Give him the car keys and he'll pop the trunk and bring them in the house. Upstairs is a bedroom all set up for you to stay here with us while you are in Virginia."

"Thank you, you are too kind Dixie Pearl, but I am not planning on staying in your home. There are plenty of hotels nearby at Dulles Airport where I thought I could check in for the night."

"Don't be silly, I will not hear of it. I want to know you better during your time here with me, and I insist you stay with us, please."

"To sleep here tonight is fine with me, but you need to understand I am here on an assignment and will be gone a few days at a time."

"Not a problem Khara. Come with me I want to introduce you to your aunt who is sitting inside on the sofa. She is your maternal grandmother's sister. Also a handful of cousins I hope to introduce you to also."

Not wanting to offend anyone Khara is trying to seem interested in meeting her relatives, although she is not able to express any real emotional ties to them. Khara puts a small smile on her face. In reality, her thoughts are on finding the presidential candidate, and killing him, not family reunions.

Together they all enter the living room and find a place to sit. Dixie Pearl introduces her to her aunt.

"Please tell us about your life Khara. The family is so curious about getting to learn all about you. Last year we read about the shooting in Times Square. The terrorist attack was on all the news channels. Are you alright now after being shot?"

"The doctors made me undergo a lot of physical rehabilitation, but everything is fine now. Almost daily I work out at the gym and still do my Krav Maga martial arts training. The department asked me to teach it at the police academy."

"You'll need to tell us more about it, sounds so exciting. How about we let you freshen up before we all go out for dinner and celebrate" Dixie Pearl said.

A short while later Dixie Pearl invites everyone to pile into her large six-passenger van and they all go to eat at a steak restaurant in the Dulles Town Center mall.

The time is late afternoon, and they are seated right away. Dixie Pearl is sitting on one side of Khara, and her husband on the other when she asks a question. "Can you tell us what police business you are doing down here in Virginia?"

"The New York City Deputy Commissioner on Terrorism assigned me to follow Congressman Ted Ferry, and his Texas for Texans security group."

The husband turned to Khara, and mentioned to her he read in today's newspaper the presidential candidate will be at a convention in the area tomorrow. "The congressman is going to run a dinner fundraiser and a voter rally afterward. The turnout they expect is almost fifteen thousand people to attend the gathering."

"Are you sure? Fifteen thousand is a lot of people."

"Yup, the sheriff also asked me to come back part time to pitch in for this event. The affair is supposed to start about one in the afternoon. The campaign is also doing a five hundred dollars a plate dinner for a ton of people afterward."

"Do you think I can tag along with you tomorrow? I never met the candidate, and I would like to see what he looks like in person."

The last statement is a lie because she needs to be up and personal if at all possible. Dixie Pearl's husband said she can go with him in the morning if she would like. After excusing herself she strolls to the ladies lounge in the restaurant. Once in the restroom she enters a stall and calls Al on a new burner phone.

"Hello Al, I plan to be staying at a hotel near the Big Top Convention Center by Dulles airport tomorrow." The secret phrase is said to him.

"Big Boy will meet you at the convention center, be careful"

The code is mentioned again in case someone is listening in on their phone call. Their meeting is arranged for him to engage with her at the rally the next day. Big Boy is now able to walk and feeling better although not yet able to run. Not that he ever could run, but he is still deadly. The white Cadillac leaves at night with three armed members of his crew and will join her in the morning at the Dulles Center. All Big Boy's guys grew up on the streets of Brooklyn, and are all men who in the past killed someone as ordered.

Finished with her call she returns, and again sits next to Dixie Pearl. To continue the conversation Khara turns to her sister to speak to her a bit longer.

"To me, it seems like your husband is a kind man. How did you meet him?"

"One night my church sponsored a young person's social, and we met at a dance. So I guess I'm a lot like my mother because I fell for a white guy, and he is the sweetest man I ever met. For over twenty-five years we are married and have a son and daughter. The kids are twins and are away at college. Tell me did you ever marry"

"Yes but it was not a good marriage, I was eighteen, and am about to be discharged from the foster home program when we hitched up together. Too young, and I could not go back to foster care to live while I worked security for his company, and he asked me to marry him. After we married he took care of all my college costs, and when I graduated and became a cop we divorced. There are no children, and I am alone in New York."

"Well, now you know a lot of family is here for you. Remember you can always come down here to retire, settle in here, and be with me."

"The offer is appreciated, but my life is up north at the moment. Maybe in years to come, I'll move down south, but not at this time."

"So sorry for you, but I understand. Let's finish up and return home, I think you must be tired from your long drive here."

***

The next morning Khara woke up at five, put on her running shoes, slipped on workout clothes, and went outside to do a run. Behind the house is a footpath Dixie Pearl told her about, and it goes between the developments. The new sneakers she bought helped her run on the path for almost thirty minutes and returned to the house to shower and start to dress.

Afterwards, she came downstairs to the kitchen with her suitcase and saw her sister cooking breakfast.

"You're leaving so soon Khara? I thought you would be staying with us for a while."

"Yes, I need to go because I'm on assignment. Do you mind if I tag along with your husband today because I must follow the candidate on the campaign trail? I'll try to come back to spend some time with you on my way home if I can."

During the night she awoke early and packed her bag placing it in her car without waking everybody up in the house.

"I would like to spend more time with you in the future Khara. Come sit down, I made eggs for you with buttered toast and hand squeezed orange juice. How do you like your coffee?"

"Black please, and thanks for breakfast, you didn't need to do it."

"Not a big deal for me, I am so happy you are here. It's a pleasure for me to stare at you."

Dixie Pearl sits at the table next to her, and with a soft touch rubs Khara's arm with love.

After eating Khara gets up, her sister hugs her, and she leaves for the Dulles Center in her BMW following Dixie Pearl's husband.

Once she arrives at the convention center, and parks near his car they walk to the security entrance together. The husband says hello to his buddies, and tells the deputies he works with she is here with him. With a flip of her wrist, she shows her gold detectives badge from under her shirt, and they let her pass without a body search for weapons.

The Secret Service agents are walking the hall inspecting it. The arena is a massive hundred thousand square feet, and she is amazed at how large it is. About halfway back it is walled off with portable gray walls. The wait staff is setting up the tables on the other side of a row of endless temporary walls while she meanders around the room.

In front of the stage are roped off areas to maintain crowd control. While strolling through the place she sees no video cameras are placed in the adjacent hallways behind the theatre platform, only at the main entry point where people will be entering. The restrooms located in the back of the facility are not being videoed either, only the large garage entrance behind the building is equipped with cameras, and Khara also viewed them.

Dixie Pearl's husband must leave now to report to his station by a side door near the front of the building.

Although retired he still does do per diem work when needed if asked by the county sheriff's department.

The musicians arrive and begin to set up next to the central stage. The stagehands help unpack their instruments, set up their music stands, start to tune their instruments and practice. The public announcement staff is testing the system for clarity and volume, and the noise is deafening in the busy passageways.

In a coincidence of timing, Khara is walking by the big platform at the same time the Texas group enters the staging area through the extra-large garage door. The candidates luxury touring bus home away from home is parked only fifty feet or so from the building in the back lot. Secret Service agents are guarding the vehicle along with the Texan's security team.

The phone in her pants starts to vibrate indicating a call is coming in. The vibration is the only way she can know since the racket in the cavernous room is so loud, even behind the platform. The cell phone is opened and it is Big Boy calling her. About ten feet ahead Khara spots a ladies room, she walks in, and enters a stall to talk to him in private.

"Khara where is the candidate's bus parked?"

"The tour bus is parked in parking lot letter H way back from the street. I'll go in the kitchen on the southern side of the building to let you in the food service entrance as most kitchens lack security in there."

"Give us a few minutes, I'm here with my crew from Brooklyn, and we'll meet you there."

The call ends, she places the phone in her back pocket again and opens the stall door to leave.

Only one step out from the stall, and she is face to face with the huge young girl who is the daughter of the head of the Texans as she enters the restroom. The woman is well over six feet tall and three hundred plus pounds. The girl spots her and stops, as does Khara when the women stare at each other in surprise and are motionless for a moment. In a slow move, each faces the other in deadly silence with neither one going forward.

A sudden flashback of memory strikes the girl, and now she remembers the last violent time they met. The previous altercation was back in Texas when Khara beat her into a coma in a pizza joint restroom. The sudden sight of her tormentor again in a restroom brings to life the lost memories of this humongous girl.

"You son of a bitch you did this to me."

Her forefinger points to her flattened nose, two scars on the top of her head where doctors sewed almost a hundred stitches as she makes a fist with each of her hands. The daughter gives out a primal scream from the depths of her large being which echoes in the small non-acoustic tiled bathroom. Without hesitation, she bolts towards Khara who is standing about ten feet away, grabs her with both hands by her leather jacket lapels, and lifts her high into the air. The heavy girl continues running and puts all her weight behind her effort of slamming Khara's body against the rear cinderblock wall. The wind is knocked out of her, and Khara's body goes limp trying to breathe.

Still holding her arch nemesis in her clenched fists, and in a rage, she turns and throws Khara clear across the restroom. A hard landing when she hits the marble tile floor hurts and her body continues to roll over to where the sinks are. In pain and moaning, Khara now realizes this is a deathmatch, and only one of them is going to walk out of the bathroom alive.

Almost flat and lying on the floor trying to catch her breath Khara is motionless as the girl jostles her body as fast as her swollen legs allow coming over to inflict more physical harm. The thick roll of fat at her waist prevents her from reaching down in a quick motion to grab at her again. This gives Khara only seconds to raise her left leg, and kick her in the knee. The blow stuns her for a second because she is bending, and does little damage other than inflicting some minor distress. Now still on the tile floor the kick gave her some additional time to inhale and fill her lungs.

A reflex move brings Khara's leg back up, and ready to kick again while enabling her to withdraw her throwing knife from her boot. This is done in a speedy and fluid motion while the three hundred pound girl dives on Khara's body as in a wrestling match, intent on choking her, and falls on the sharp point. The blade tears into her right arm cutting deep into her bicep causing her to yell out in pain. This plunge onto her smaller foe lands the massive girl on Khara's rib cage and tears cartilage on her chest inflicting painful damage.

After being stabbed in the arm the monster of a woman rolls off Khara and is stretched out on the filthy restroom floor next to her. Still holding her wounded arm in agony, the girl is attempting to stop the bleeding and ignores her mortal enemy for a brief fatal moment.

In a quick movement Khara, in pain from her chest injury, takes her left hand which still holds the knife and swings it around trying to stab her in the neck. With difficulty, she strains her muscles and is able to puncture the girl's neck with it, but not a major artery or airway. The girl's eyes widen, and she now realizes she is in real serious medical trouble if she stays in the ladies room.

A strenuous effort helps move her immense body as she now tries to roll over on her side so she can reach the sink's countertop, and try to pull herself up. With difficulty, she is getting into a sitting position by the sink while Khara is able to stand on her knees behind the girl with sweat flowing down her face. To lean forward is a struggle, and with all her strength Khara plunges the knife into the girl's back hitting her spine, and withdraws it in a twisting motion. The always sharp cutting point shreds through a cotton shirt and between folds of blubber as it lands between vertebra causing the girl to yell out in anguish, and fall backward on Khara again.

The daughter is again on top of her, this time facing the ceiling, and she raises her left arm as high as she can and crashing her elbow downwards into Khara's rib cage inducing her to cry out in pangs of severe pain.

Determined to finish her off, and still holding the knife Khara is having difficulty breathing. With all the energy left in her body, she strains to push the heavy girl off her, withdraw the blade, and plunge it back into her thick fatty neck again. This time the sleek stainless steel is twisting as it cuts into the carotid artery. The girl rolls off her, and blood is now pouring out of the girl's mouth. The knife is again withdrawn as she wipes it on the girl's blouse in an attempt to clean it in haste, and slips it back in her boot sheath.

Strange gurgling sounds come from the giant of a girl as she is thrashing around, almost in slow motion, on the floor. Now able to stand holding onto the sink's counter Khara is motionless while trying to get her bearings back.

The female racist is slowing down, and lying almost still. In a swift fling of her small pocketbook around to her side, she opens it and takes out the hand grenade. In a determined move she pulls out the pin, wedges the grenade between the floor and the large girl's immense stomach, and dashes out of the ladies room as fast as she can. The girl is still moaning as she is attempting to turn her dying body over.

Now hobbling to the food preparation room Khara is in constant distress from her rib injuries but needs to open the southern kitchen door for Big Boy and his men. While she rumbles past the waiters carrying plates and glassware to the dining floor there is an explosion which rocks the convention center. Fire alarms go off, and people are in a panic. There is mayhem in the place with people flying all over trying to escape the building. Big Boy, limping, walks in the side door Khara opened while the staff runs out. The crew from Brooklyn is running in to be with her as they leave the kitchen to enter the hall looking for the Texans.

Big Boy looked at her and made a comment. "No kidding Khara you look like shit, you okay?" There is no time to answer as she waves for them to follow her.

The guys from Brooklyn and Khara approach the main stage from the back hallway as the head of the Texas for Texans spots Khara. The presidential candidate told him about Detective Bennet and showed him a newspaper picture of her from the Times Square incident. The leader catches a glimpse of her in the hallway, and yells for his men to "kill the black bitch."

Visibility is terrible due to smoke filling the hallways from the explosion and the resulting fire. The video cameras are useless because of the dense smoky fog in the halls. Sirens are going off outside and inside as firetrucks and police converge on the building.

In the hallways, it is helter-skelter as the Texas cowboys and Big Boy's urban men engage in a raw street fight inside the building's hallway. Guns are taken out by both sides and shots are fired into sightless clouds of gray smoke.

One of Big Boy's crew grabs a large brass fire nozzle attached to the wall and uses it as a bat hitting cowboys with it while trailing the hose behind him.

Total chaos breaks out and two of the Texans run to attack Big Boy. With each hand, he grips a Texan by the throat and lifts him off the floor with their legs twirling in the air. In an instant, Khara takes out her .38mm snub nose from her jacket and begins shooting hollow point bullets at anyone wearing a cowboy hat she can view through the smoke in the hall. The sound of gunshots reverberates throughout the hallway. Three men fall to the pavement due to her deadly aim. The remaining men withdraw. Big Boy drops the two men to the floor as they gasp for air. With his massive legs, he pounds down on their each of their throats with the heel of his shoe using all his body weight to kill them.

"Hey, Biggie let's get out of here. I will call you later."

All Big Boy's men fly out of the building through the kitchen exit. Once outside, Khara goes around to the front parking lot to get her car. Every step she takes is painful due to her ribs. The same time this is happening Big Boy gets in his white Cadillac, and pulls to the back of the building where the tour bus is situated. The Texans guarding it ran inside the building to help their pals leaving only two Secret Service agents standing by the entry door of the bus. The Caddy swings around the other side of the bus from where the Federal Agents are standing. One of Big Boy's men shimmies up into the open sunroof spraying submachine gun fire into the bus. The guy in the seat behind Big Boy, who is driving, fires a pump action shotgun at the darkened bus windows hoping to kill the drug dealing presidential candidate. The Cadillac speeds off melding in with the local traffic, and the crew waits to hear from Khara.

Once seated inside the M3, and in agony, she looks up a walk-in medical facility on her cellphone. With her ribs throbbing she drives to the clinic for treatment. Every time she goes to shift gears, and move her arm a sharp pulsating pain shoots through her ribcage.

In the examination room, she tells the doctor she fell, and he tapes up her upper torso after taking a few x-rays. Now it is about noon, and she must find a place to lay low for a while.

In distress and needing a safe haven to rest she goes to a four-star hotel by Dulles Airport, and checks in under an assumed name. The deposit is paid with a pay on demand credit card which is loaded with five thousand dollars in it. A bellhop is asked to carry her bags for her, and she goes to her room to lie down.

After tipping the boy she double locks the door, places her guns on the night table next to the bed, takes one of the pain pills the clinic gave her for discomfort and exhausted falls asleep on the bed while still dressed.

Chapter Ten

The pain pill enables her to sleep through the rest of the day, and the entire night, but leaves her groggy the next morning when she awakes.

Still sitting in bed she picks up the phone, and orders two black coffees with a buttered roll from room service. About thirty minutes later there is a knock on her door. Without thinking she reaches for her snub nose .38, and peers out the peephole to make sure a uniformed waiter is on the other side. She lets him in tipping him five dollars.

The server places a tray on a round dining table in the room and leaves. Khara grabs a chair and pulls in the seat to the table so she can eat her breakfast. Relaxed and sitting at the table she starts to drink her coffee while looking out the window at the passing cars below and hoping the caffeine will kick in to wake her up. In her left hand, she takes the remote control for the television and turns on the morning news station.

The local reporter out of Washington D.C. is standing in front of the convention center with fire trucks and police cars with their emergency lights flashing in the background. The woman is reporting an explosion happened at the rally, and at least four people are dead. The news now switches to the presidential candidate saying his head of security lost his daughter in the explosion. The congressman will continue with his campaign relying only on the Secret Service for the next week or so until the funeral of the girl is completed.

Khara's burner phone rings, and in a lot of discomforts she gets up to answer the call.

"Good morning Khara, I spoke to Big Boy last night, how are you feeling?"

"Like shit Al. My ribs hurt, they are bruised not broken, and I'm wrapped up like an Egyptian mummy."

"Yes, Big Boy told me you are in rough shape. The media is carrying the story of the convention turmoil and deaths because Congressman Ted Ferry happened to be in the building when the fire started. Otherwise, this would be a local news item."

"I agree the report on this morning's news went national. The fat bitch daughter is dead and gone. I'm going to rest up a few days in the hotel because I am too sore to do much else at the moment."

"After what you told me I can understand. By the way, I also sent Big Boy with something you might need. Would you be able to meet him tonight somewhere?"

"The pain pills I am on make me light headed, and I don't want to drive. The hotel I registered in is near 50 and 28. I'll text Big Boy my address, and he can meet me at my car."

"Okay Khara take care of yourself."

"Thanks, Al."

Not dressed yet she hangs up and places her burner phone on the table and returns to finish her usual light breakfast.

As she starts to sip her coffee again her personal phone rings this time. The caller ID shows the number calling is Johanna's, and her name is popping up on the screen.

"Hello, Johanna what's doing?"

"Good morning Khara how are you? Last night I caught the news about an explosion in the convention center where Congressman Ted Ferry is."

"Yes I caught the news also"

"My intelligence division tells me at least four Texas security men died in the hallway of the center. Did you by chance have anything to do with the deaths?"

"Honest Johanna I never used my service gun, it never left my holster."

"And what about the explosion in the convention center, Khara? The Secret Service reports to us they believe a grenade is responsible for starting the fire. The ATF crime lab found shrapnel in the walls, and in body parts in the ladies bathroom. The Federal lab overnight reported the shrapnel markers match those recovered in Far Rockaway from last year."

Khara did not answer her.

There is no hard push from her to find out if Khara is responsible because knowing more than she should would not be a smart move. Johanna stopped asking about the explosion.

"The local news reported the leader of the Texas for Texans daughter is missing," Khara said. The fact is she knew the news reported her death, but Khara is testing Johanna to find out what she is aware of.

"No, she's not missing. The police found her body parts all over a woman's restroom where the explosion happened. What someone would be doing with a grenade in a convention center I can't imagine, do you?"

"This couldn't happen to a nicer person Johanna. Some people might call it karma."

"In any event, I want to fill you in on the shooting at the Torino-Ashley Hotel you missed the night you spent with Don Weber."

"What information do the police know about this?"

"To start with they found Alejandro Gonzales' head on a platter in the room with the two dead Texas security men. Congressman Ferry viewed the head and our sources in the campaign reported to us his face turned ashen white, and he checked out of the hotel within the hour."

"Did the department obtain any leads on who shot the men yet?"

"Sort of a lead, one of the Latino waiters is missing. The department believes he is the one sent to the room where they found the bodies. The police traced the waiter's cell signal. The cell tower lines led to another cell phone. Detectives caught up with two young men in the Bronx with the cell phone in their possession. The District Attorney believes they might be gang members, and now they are denying anything to do with the murder. But they admit to getting the phone in Times Square the night of the shooting."

"You never know what young gang bangers are capable of doing Johanna."

"So did you find out anything about the Texans foundation yet Khara?"

"No, I couldn't because the fire and smoke forced everyone to evacuate the building. Do you know where the candidate is heading next?"

"Yes he is going to Charleston West Virginia today, and later is swinging south to Richmond. Our intelligence bureau told me tomorrow he is going to be flying back to Texas and will be in the southwest states for the rest of the week. You might as well come back."

"Do you think I can stay here for another day or so? This week I met my long lost sister, and want to spend some time with her. Would my staying here a little longer be a problem for you Johanna?"

Khara did not plan to go back to Ashburn to visit Dixie Pearl again, but she needs another day or so to recuperate.

"Oh, I don't remember you telling me a sister lives in Virginia. Take the rest of the week off, and I look forward to seeing you when you come back."

"Me too, I didn't know my sister existed until a few weeks ago. Next Monday I'll be back with you, bye."

In the room by herself, she started to wonder what Al gave Big Boy to bring down for her. The anticipation is killing her so she sent a text to Big Boy to meet her for lunch because she can't wait for dinner. A message came back he will pick her up in front of her hotel, they will grab a bite to eat, and he will put the meal on Al's American Express credit card.

After sending him the information she undressed and started the shower. Her bag is still unpacked so she opens the suitcase, takes out fresh clothes, and her coconut body wash. With care, the elastic bands are unwrapped from her rib cage. Unstrapped she steps into a hot stall, and is much fresher when she finishes.

After drying off, and getting dressed it is almost lunchtime. In a careful way, she rearms herself and takes the elevator down to the lobby. By taking small careful steps due to some rib pain she manages to walk outside and sits on a wooden bench situated near the entrance.

Big Boy drives up in a large white Cadillac, and two of his men are with him. In a slow downward move gritting her teeth in pain, she slips into the front passenger seat, and they drive to the Dulles Town Center for lunch.

"So what do you feel like eating for lunch Biggie?"

"Today I am in the mood for a steak like a sirloin or two. Can you deal with a tasty steak?"

"Good for me, let's go."

Big Boy drives to a steak restaurant on the perimeter of the mall.

As they walk in the two men with Big Boy go to sit at the bar. The crew leaves Big Boy and Khara alone to eat at a table, and speak in private. Seated, she surveys the menu.

Both of them decide to order the fried pickles for an appetizer. For lunch, she orders the spicy brisket sandwich with cheese, chili sauce and fried onions on top. Big Boy is more mundane and orders two cheeseburgers as an additional appetizer while they order fries well done on the side. Big Boy wants a twelve-ounce sirloin steak cooked medium well. An Amstel Light is ordered for her, and Big Boy orders a twenty-ounce glass of Heineken on tap.

"Are you heading back home soon Khara?"

"Not sure Biggie could be in a day or two. My ribs are still killing me from the fat bitch jumping on me. It hurts when I shift gears using my arm. The pain stings in my ribs and is hard for me sometimes. Think I'll buy a book and read something while I take it easy here in Virginia. The hotel clerk at the registration desk told me a steam room is next to the indoor pool. Later I'll go try and relax in it. But after lunch, I need to stop in the mall and buy a bathing suit because their pool looks inviting."

"Not a problem Khara. On the sign outside the mall, it said four big department stores are in here, I'm sure you'll find something."

"Thanks, Biggie."

"Listen when we go back to the Cadillac Al sent something for you. Let me open my trunk because I placed the package in there. Later when we go back to your hotel I'll pull around to your car, and put the bag in the M3 for you."

"Sounds good, let's eat here comes our food."

After the meal, they go shopping for a bathing suit for her, and drive back to the hotel with her purchase, as Big Boy pulls around to her M3 parked in the rear lot. The Cadillac stops next to her car, and he pops the trunk.

"Come on Khara I want to show you what's in the package"

Together they walk to the back of the car and look in.

"Al sent you a Remington Defense CSR [Concealable Sniper Rifle] which is a lightweight and compact Winchester bolt-action breakdown single bolt action sniper rifle with a Fast-Attach Silencer/Suppressor. Olga and Viktor obtained the weapon for you from their European NATO sources.

This is a long distance weapon which I am told is accurate, and I placed the gun in this backpack. If you like I'll carry the bag to your room for you. There is some extra ammunition in the bag too."

"Thanks, Biggie I appreciate your help. Follow me to the lobby elevator where I will be able to take the bag from you."

Once on the elevator, Khara is able to bring the bag to her room, lock her door, open the backpack, and start to assemble the rifle. This does not take her long, and she likes the weight of the gun. Her arm braces the weapon on the table top as she peers through the scope, and takes aim through her fourth story hotel window following someone who is walking a long distance away. Now she tries on the silencer and screws the piece on without a hitch. She'll add this weapon to her personal arsenal along with the MP7 submachine gun she obtained on her Mexican adventure.

After a while, she takes the rifle apart and returns the parts to the backpack the gun came in. Reaching for the channel changer she puts the television on and lies on the bed to take a short late afternoon nap.

About an hour later her phone rings, and Johanna is calling again.

"Hey, Khara good afternoon it's Johanna."

"Hi, what's doing?"

"The intelligence division this morning informed us the presidential candidate changed his travel plans. From Richmond tomorrow he is traveling to Washington to speak to the chairman of his right-wing political party. Ferry is upset about a rules change for dedicated convention delegates. This is a top secret meeting and is not acknowledged to anybody except his inner circle of consultants. One is the head of the Texas for Texans, and the other is his campaign manager."

"What is the Richmond address?"

"Give me a minute and I'll text it to you. After his meeting at party headquarters, he scheduled a quick flash rally at Union Station in D.C. The campaign did not want to announce the rally yet, and the press will be told about the stop only minutes before he appears. The press manager for the congressman wants the media to report the crowd as a spontaneous demonstration. The department's intelligence unit found out he scheduled the stop through our Secret Service liaison. Tomorrow I'll see what else I can find out."

The call is finished and Khara decides to go to the hotel pool and try their steam room. A pair of workout clothes is put on, and she wraps her small snub nose .38 in a large bath towel to take with her as she heads to the elevator to go downstairs to the pool.

The lifeguard gives her a key for a locker, and a beach towel to wrap around her. A sign states the steam room is not gender specific, but sharing a steam room does not bother her. A few minutes after she sits in the room, with her snub nose still wrapped in a towel from the room sitting next to her, a young man enters wearing a towel and sits on a wooden bench opposite Khara. A short conversation ensues.

"Where are you from Miss?"

"New York, I came down to Ashburn to visit a relative. Where are you from?"

"Texas and I am working for the campaign to elect Congressman Ted Perry president. Part of my job is I handle some of their event stops, and do advance work when he schedules a rally somewhere. Sometimes I fly all over the country setting up meetings, and making hotel and security arrangements for him."

"Your position with the congressman sounds like an interesting job. Do you think I can meet him since I admire the congressman?"

Khara thought to herself this guy might be useful to her.

"With luck, I might be able to obtain a press pass for you to his rally tomorrow in Richmond. Later when he is done at the rally he is flying back to Texas for a week or so because I handle his travel plans also. Would you like to meet me for dinner tonight?"

"How about the lobby at seven thirty, is the time good with you?" Khara said.

"Great, I could use a date with a pretty woman. In a little while, I'm going to go for a dip in the pool, care to join me?"

"Sounds like fun, I'll be wearing a new bikini I bought today at lunch. After the steam room, I must go to the locker room to change. Let's jump in the cold water when we leave the sauna. But I do need one question answered."

"What would you like to know?"

"If you do all his travel plans, are you sure he is going to Texas tomorrow? Yes, I know the plan is what the campaign announced on television, but I heard something different from a friend of mine about his plans for tomorrow."

With no warning, he springs across the small steam room and attacks Khara hitting her on the side of her head with a glancing blow as she tries to duck from the punch. The pain in her ribs prevented her from moving too quickly. Knocked to the floor her Krav Maga training causes her to use a sweeping motion with her leg and hits him in the back of his right knee. His leg buckles and he falls to the floor in front of Khara.

Their towels fly off in the tussle. Trying to come up with a good grip on him to give her an advantage in the fight is difficult. The two squirm around on top of each other due to the sweat on their bodies preventing a good dry power hold. In desperation, he manages to wiggle away from her grasp and reaches out to grab Khara's hair. With all his strength he yanks her head against the bottom of the wooden bench. With her right leg, Khara in an instinctive response swings it in a defensive motion towards his head and hits him in his temple. His eyes flash open, he lets go of her hair and falls back on the floor holding his head. To her, he appears dazed.

Scurrying on her bottom Khara gets back to where she is sitting on the bench, grasps the towel hiding her snub nose, bends over his prone body, and shoves the barrel in his mouth smashing and chipping his two front teeth.

The young man now realizes he is going to die unless he stops fighting her.

"Who are you, and how did you find me?" Khara demands.

With blood sputtering out of his mouth he answers her.

"I witnessed you shoot the three men because I stood in the rear hall against the wall at the convention center. What I saw I reported to Ted Ferry, and I am a witness to everything you did in the hallway fight."

"So you don't possess a press pass to give me so I can enter into the Union Station flash rally?"

"Yes, I do, the pass is in my room upstairs. If I couldn't kill you they wanted me to give you one for Richmond, not Washington. The Texans are going to finish you off in Richmond where they will set up an ambush at a rally they are planning. The director offered me a lot of money to terminate you if I could."

Now she is standing, and he is sitting on the floor, the gun is out of his mouth, and pointing to his head with his back to her. To stem the bleeding he is holding a towel to his lips by his missing front teeth.

"Lie on your stomach, and don't look up at me" Khara commands.

He stretches out on the floor and spreads his arms out as far as they can go.

Without saying another word she presses her knee into his back, grasps his head in a firm grip, and twists as hard as she can. Khara is wincing with pain from her ribs but she is successful. Without making a loud noise she is able to finish off another would be assassin.

Now starting to feel a throbbing pain in her side since her adrenalin subsided from the fight she grabs onto the bench to stand. Gingerly grabbing her towel to hide her gun she prepares to go back upstairs. With a tremendous effort, she bends her knees and lifts him off the floor by holding him from under his arms. In a corner, she props him up on the wood steam room bench so he appears to be asleep, and she departs the room believing nobody will bother him for a while thinking he is resting.

To remove the gym key off his wrist before leaving she sits next to him, and slips it off and then opens his gym locker taking out his hotel room key.

Changing into her workout clothes she heads upstairs to his room to retrieve the press pass. As Khara slides the room key in the lock she opens the door, the towel is hanging over her snub nose .38 and hiding the gun.

To her amazement, a man is sitting on one of the two beds watching television. Surprised he sees her walk in the hotel room and his eyes pop open. On the round dining table by the window are two Glock pistols, and a box of bullets.

Khara kicks the door closed with the back of her foot and slides the towel off her gun so he can view the pistol.

While attempting to reach under the pillow next to where he is sitting, and pull out a gun he takes his eyes off her, as she is removing the towel from her gun. With one shot Khara shoots him in the chest. The bullet penetrates the heart as he is thrust back into the headboard, falls to the side of the bed, and tumbles off to the carpeted floor.

On top of the dresser is an open attaché case, and she stops and rifles through a bunch of papers. On top are press passes, and under them are reams of typed notes. Not wanting to stay in the room any longer than needed she closes the cover, and using the towel she opens the door handle and takes the case to her room.

Back in her hotel room she takes out a few alcohol wipes, starts to swab the bathroom and other surfaces clean making sure no fingerprints are left in the room to trace her presence.

In a hurry, she packs her bag and calls downstairs asking for a bellhop to come up with a cart so she can wheel her stuff out. With a hand towel, she turns the handle leaving the door a little ajar. The bellhop will grab the door for her when they leave so she does not need to touch anything else once the room is sanitized of her presence. A few minutes later a knock on the opened door tells her the bellhop and a cart is here. The young man places her bags on the wheeled cart, and they both leave for the main lobby.

Wearing the backpack she is also holding the attaché case she took from the dead man's room.

As they walk off the elevator Khara asks the bellhop if he would like to make a quick hundred dollars. The young man answers in the affirmative, and she asks where the utility room is.

"Go down the side hallway to the right of the check-in desk to the back entrance, and at the end is an ice machine in a small alcove. In the alcove is a door to the utility room."

"Thanks please help me place my bags in the car, and I'll give you another hundred to go for lunch for an hour, and disappear."

175

After loading up the trunk she goes back in and checks out of the hotel under the fake name she used to register. The reloadable burner credit card she used more than covers the hotel bill. Al made sure five thousand dollars is always in the account for her to use. At the lobby desk, she finishes paying and takes the side hallway to the ice machine alcove.

As Khara turns into the alcove the door is on her left. The handle is a normal household type with a simple key lock. No deadbolt, steel security plate or a number dial lock on the door. The utility room door is only three feet from the vending machines. On one foot, and steadying her back against the ice machine, bracing each hand against a wall and a soda machine, she rears up, and with both of her legs jolts the door open after two hard thrusts.

Her ribs are hurting after her exercise in breaking and entering.

Now in the utility room, the video recorder is on a small shelf. The unit is not a tape recorder type but attached to the internet. There is a keyboard next to the unit with a page of instructions and password codes. A chain hotel, because of high turnover of employees, leaves the typed codes for new management in the room. The password codes are input and she is able to delete the past five days of recordings. Before Khara leaves she disconnects the wires to the system and heads out of the hotel as if she never stayed.

Sharp pangs shoot through her side as she rushes to her car, and drives a few miles away. In the distance, she spots a busy gas station, pulls in and parks on the side of the building. The latch on the case is flipped up and she opens the top cover. With care, Khara starts to go through the papers. In the attaché case, she finds the candidate's schedule of campaign stops. On the bottom is a reservation for a whole wing of a hotel near Utica New York for the end of the month.

On her GPS she punches in the Richmond address and heads south on I-95 to Richmond to confront the Texans. The train of thought is they don't expect her so soon, and the excitement of combat sends an adrenalin rush through her body.

Ted Ferry is staying at an elegant five-star hotel, and as is the case his campaign is paying for the room and food at over four hundred dollars a day per room. Tonight he is having a private fundraiser/dinner in a small ballroom at the hotel for ten thousand dollars a plate.

The BMW M3 is speeding along over eighty-nine miles an hour when she decides to call ahead on her car phone to reserve a room at the same hotel.

Upon arriving in Richmond she drives to the front of the hotel where the parking signs are, and she gives the key fob to the young valet. Khara opens the trunk and lifts out the backpack with her new sniper rifle herself. The bellhop grabs her suitcase on wheels and takes the luggage inside. While she is wearing the backpack with the rifle they enter a magnificent lobby.

Not used to classic Southern elegance Khara stops in her tracks when she walks through the ornate brass and glass entrance doors and enters the hotel.

The main entrance lobby is stunning and reminds her of a fairytale castle with thick golden marble columns rising up to a three-story ceiling. The balcony with thick white marble balusters running around the perimeter of the room on a mezzanine level fascinates her. The furniture in the lobby is massive with carved wood frames with gold-leaf on the wood, and red velvet upholstery. To Khara, the lobby seems like time stood still since the civil war.

The main lobby is bustling with people. The bellhop turns to Khara and explains the reason the hotel is so busy at this late hour. "A presidential candidate is staying in the hotel, and he is greeting potential donors in private meeting rooms upstairs on the mezzanine level by the balcony. Did you ever hear of Congressman Ted Ferry?"

Not answering him a crowd on the mezzanine catches her attention. The Texas security men with their cowboy hats are walking around on the balcony, and standing by two meeting rooms while Secret Service agents are blocking the stairway going upstairs.

"Guess I am out of luck meeting the candidate?"

"Yup, unless you can give a hundred thousand dollars to his presidential campaign," the bellhop said. "Ten thousand will only enable you to look at him at the front of the dining room upstairs."

Khara checks in at the front desk and is assigned a room on an upper floor. The bellhop walks with her to the elevator and presses the button to go upstairs. When the elevator doors open they enter along with other new guests, and a second bellhop carrying their three suitcases. Someone presses the button for the floor they want to go to, and the doors close. The elevator is full with no spare space as it rises but stops on the mezzanine level on its way because someone pressed the elevator button waiting on the mezzanine level.

The elevator doors open, and waiting for an elevator is a group of Texas security men with Ted Ferry ensconced amongst them. With so many people and luggage crammed in no space is left for anyone to enter the elevator. The group waiting remains on the mezzanine smiling at the elevator occupants as the doors start to close. In the center of the men is the candidate himself. In a flash of recognition Khara's eyes meet Ted Ferry's, and his face freezes. Due to the sighting, Khara understands her advantage of surprise is lost. It will only be minutes before his goons find out what room she is in. Holed up in a hotel room with only one entrance and no second way to exit is not the best place she wants to be in a gunfight if possible.

The elevator stops on her floor, and she walks out of the elevator with the bellhop.

"Your room is down the hall on the right. Follow me please, and I'll lead you there."

"Is a service elevator here?"

"Yes on the other side of the hall on the left as you leave the elevator," the bellhop said.

Some hotels use special keys for their service elevator so the guest doesn't take it by mistake. Khara asks him to take the service elevator down with her.

"Bring me to it now, and I'll give you one hundred dollars."

"Follow me please ma'am" as he leads her down the other hallway.

The service elevator is smaller though empty as the doors open, and both of them walk on.

"Take me to the basement I need to leave the hotel unnoticed." On the way down she explains she is "a police detective and criminals are in the hotel. The element of surprise is the reason you are helping me."

The bellhop pushes the basement button with beads of sweat now appearing on his forehead.

When the doors open he leads her to the rear service entrance past the laundry room. As both walk out the back door two Texas security men guarding the hotel see her leaving the building. "There's the black cop from New York" they yell out as they take out their guns.

With a leap back in the doorway she pulls out her Sig Sauer and returns fire. With her valet stub in her hand, she presses it into the bellhop's palm telling him to go out the front lobby, and get her car for her. "I'll be there in a few minutes, now go get it for me."

The bellhop begins to shake, but listens, and then runs back inside. He goes up some stairs to the lobby.

Aware the two men shooting at her called for backup she opens her pocketbook and pulls out the short fuse grenade. Opening the rear door she pulls the pin and drops it on the floor expecting the men to rush inside after her. Not waiting for the blast she hustles up the stairs two at a time, and through the main lobby to retrieve her car.

The grenade goes off and the old building shakes. A rush of security men run to the rear exit in the lobby hallway and down the stairs through the billowing rising smoke.

With her ticket in hand the bellhop handed it to the first valet he spots so her car can be brought around to the front of the hotel.

The M3 is driven to the front entrance, and her bags are put back in the trunk by the bellhop.

Before she gets in Khara hands the bellhop two one hundred dollar bills and a warning.

"The Texas security men are going to find out you took me to my room. Tell them yes, I entered the room by myself and tipped you a hundred dollars. If you tell them you helped me leave the hotel they will kill you. Do you understand?"

The bellhop now seems more worried after she tells him this, and what he witnessed by the rear entrance. He shakes his head yes, and runs back inside the hotel.

Khara drove off heading north on I-95 to Washington.

When she approached Fredericksburg Virginia she pulled off the highway and saw a national motel chain with a vacancy sign. The M3 parks in the front as she checks in for the night. Although tired, and sore, she asks if a shipping and printing store is nearby. The desk clerk told her three are located in the city, and she is directed to the nearest one. The shop is still open for business when she arrives, but will be closing soon.

The door to the M3 opens and she heads for the store to fax the papers to Al. She is positive he will keep them safe for her. Khara felt it is too dangerous to send the schedules to Johanna via email due to possible hacking. A fax, to Khara, is much more secure. When she gets back she will hand deliver them to Johanna in her apartment condo after retrieving them from Al's office.

The papers in the attaché case contain the candidate's schedule and information about the military training camp they are setting up near Booneville New York, near Utica.

The young male clerk thanks her for using the store's services, and asks her if there is anything else he can do for her.

'Yes, as matter of fact. Are you a citizen of Virginia?"

"Yes, ma'am. Born and raised right here in Fredericksburg."

"Interested in making a quick two hundred dollars? I'll pay you two hundred to buy a gun for me."

"Sure c'mon, and follow me after I close the place. Down the road, a piece is a large gun shop only a few minutes away from here."

The papers must be faxed first so she leaves and returns in a short time span as he is being relieved by the arriving night desk clerk.

Khara follows him in her car and they pull into a well-lit parking lot. The gun shop is open, and in a total surprise to her, a lot of people are in the store too.

A man behind the counter asks if he can help her with something.

"Yes sir, I would like to buy a .38 snub nose with a two-inch barrel."

The clerk walks a few feet down the counter and takes out three guns for her to inspect. Khara places each one in her hand and decides on the snub nose with the medium chestnut finish on the handle. The pistol is a Rock Island Armory Spurless M206, and the gun holds six rounds, not five as some others pistols hold. Small and concealable the Spurless is the perfect gun for her. In the past, Khara only needed a snub nose for close range shooting, and this new one fits the bill.

"Can I also buy a box of Federal 158 grain bullets, hollow point if you stock them?"

Khara wants a bullet with force, and the projectile must be deadly. When she shoots her gun the intent is not to wound someone, but to kill a person. Not too often will she be able to take a second shot.

The counterman takes the gun back from her and reaches down to retrieve the box the .38 came with from the factory. The clerk turns around as he reaches up on a shelf to take down a box of the specified bullets she requested.

"Can I copy your driver's license please miss?"

"This is for him, I'm paying for the gun, is cash alright?"

"As long as he is a resident in Virginia we are fine with everything else."

Khara pays for the gun, the shipping clerk signs the papers, and Khara gives him his money.

"Would you like to try out your new gun? Our store maintains an indoor range in the building you can use. The entrance is on the left, headsets will be loaned to you upon payment of the range fee."

"Yes I would like to do some shooting, thank you."

Both Khara and the store clerk walk to the end of the counter where she pays the range fee, takes a headset to muffle the gunshots, and is allowed in the indoor range behind the retail gun display wall. The young shipping clerk trails along behind her.

After shooting off six rounds she refills the gun. The young clerk is impressed with her accuracy. Round after round she uses up the whole box she purchased a short while ago. Satisfied with her target practice she stops on the way out and buys two more boxes of ammunition.

Together they leave the gun shop. Before the shipping clerk gets in his car Khara stops him and gives him an extra hundred for using his identification to buy the gun.

Almost a year passed since she dabbled with a total stranger. The shipping clerk, although about twenty, and much younger than Khara, is invited back to the motel room to shower with her. He is tall, muscular, and a good-looking young man. Well after midnight he leaves her room and goes home to sleep.

Chapter Eleven

The next morning Khara disassembles her old snub nose in as many parts as she can. Too many people were whacked with the .38, and she wants to dispose of the pieces so they can't be traced back to her if the gun is found in her possession.

Since it is early, and still dark out she walks behind the motel where some woods are located. The lighting is dim as she goes down the back stairway, and strolls to the edge of the tree line. The striking hammer from her old snub-nose is in her hand as she throws the piece as far as she can into the trees. Tomorrow on her way to Washington she will stop a few times, and throw away the remaining parts so the snub nose gun can never be put back together with the original traceable metal.

Finished with the task at hand she packs the car and is ready to roll onto Washington.

The BMW continues on the highway until she arrives at exit 152B. Turning off the road she heads to a rest area to refuel the car and goes inside to grab a bite to eat for lunch. On her way back to her car she places two more gun pieces in a paper bag from the food store and throws the parts in a dumpster sitting in the back of the building. With her right hand, she reaches up and closes the garbage receptacle, gets in the M3, and continues driving on I-95.

Back on the interstate again she is heading for D.C. when Don calls her on the car phone.

"Hi Khara, Don here, I need you to come back to New York as soon as you can."

"Why, what's going on?"

"Our FBI intelligence sources tell us the remnants of the Ecru Cartel are being ordered by their old Numero Uno to eliminate the new American kingpin who is running the drug trade from Mexico to the States. There is no data on who the old boss is or the new one either. But if they are on the hunt they might be gunning for you also, so I would rather you be back here under our protection."

"I understand what you are saying Don but I'm almost in Washington, and I must make a quick stop after I finish there I'll continue home. Talk to you later, bye."

Her foot slams on the gas pedal, and the M3 is roaring along the interstate to reach Union Station before the candidate. The schedule in the attaché case stated he will go to the site sometime in the afternoon. First, he will be in a political meeting trying to mend fences, and then he'll go to the fake impromptu rally at the entrance of the train station.

The M3 arrives in Washington and the GPS enables her to drive around the area casing the plaza. When she parks, on E. St. NE across from where the congressman will step out of his limo, she is very close to the train station. Two buildings are in the sight line of the main station doorway. If she can enter one of the buildings, and be on the rooftop, she'll be able to take a clear shot at Ted Ferry.

After parking, she puts on her backpack with the sniper rifle tucked inside and walks to the front of the building. Armed private security guards are gathered by the entrance, and a metal detector is present also. The fact she cannot enter through the main lobby doors causes her to continue to walk around to the back by the service area. A young good looking guard is standing by himself. The guy, she figures, must be a newbie since he is unarmed so she unbuttons the top two buttons on her blouse, and saunters up to him asking if she can go into use the ladies restroom inside.

"I'm sightseeing here from New York, and I ate something for breakfast which doesn't agree with me. Can I go in and use the ladies room, please?"

With a smile on her face, and stroking his arm with a feather touch the guard agrees to let her in. He slides his pass in the reader, and the rear door opens allowing her to enter.

The young man yells out to her as she walks in the building "the ladies room is on the left a little past the stairs going up."

The door closes, and she starts to climb the steps to the roof. The building is not very tall with only six floors, and upon reaching the top landing she wants to make sure the door stays open. With her right hand, she retrieves from her jacket pocket a cartridge, bends on her knees to wedge a .38 bullet in the door jam at the bottom. This prevents the door from closing behind her, trapping her outside, and not being able to escape.

The sky is cloudless and bright as she strides to the edge of the roof and peers out at Union Station. She needs to make sure there is a clear sight line to the main entrance. All she will be capable to do today is one attempt at him. The important part of being on this particular building is the sun will be at her back, and no one can stare upward to catch a possible reflection of the glass from her scope, or even look at her.

A little tired she takes the backpack off and sits, opens the main flap, and removes the sniper rifle. With her back to the outer perimeter wall of the roof, Khara starts to assemble the weapon, loads a round in the chamber, and begins to screw on the silencer. Now standing she uses the scope and tries to estimate the wind velocity and distance to the entrance. Never having used the gun before she needs a practice shot to find out how off the sight is when she aims at a pigeon on top of the train station. The bird is landing, and she fires off a round aiming for the body as it flutters its wings, and a few feathers fly in the air. The bullet is off a little to the left. Khara checks her watch when she realizes the candidate will be here any moment, and the time is getting too close to take another trial shot.

The breeze high up is gentle as she sits on top of the office building and waits with the reloaded rifle on her lap.

The Omega Speedmaster Professional watch on her wrist reads almost two o'clock. The left earpiece to her headphones she now places in her ear, and tunes in a local television channel on an app she downloaded. With patience, she is waiting to hear a news item about a political rally at the train station. After a few boring items the reporter announces Congressman Ted Ferry will be at Union Station in five minutes for an impromptu meet and greet.

For some reason Khara senses something watching her, and glances skyward. Maybe she heard a faint motor whirring, but whatever it is unnerved her. The sound is coming from above and approaching Union Station with the sun at its back. A small drone with a video camera is about to go over the building where she is situated. With no hesitation, she pulls her hoodie over her head, bends over to conceal the sniper rifle while leaning into the tall parapet, and watches the drone fly over and away.

With the sun still at her back, she sits down for steadiness and aims for the center of the drone between the propellers.

One, two, three seconds go by, and when she is sure of her target squeezes the trigger. The drone shatters above the street, and pieces plummet to the ground three blocks away landing on top of a tour bus filled with passengers.

Now confident of mastering the scope on the rifle, with caution, she peers over the wall and waits for a convoy of limos to drive around the front of the statue.

Out of nowhere hundreds of people start to gather in the vestibule of the station and on the exterior esplanade awaiting the candidate to arrive.

Police are on the scene trying to control the crowds. On the left side of the entrance standing behind yellow and black stripped wood barricades are pickets denouncing Ted Ferry. To the right side are another group of people shouting and supporting Congressman Ferry. From the corner of the roof, she can observe in the distance more emergency vehicles arriving along with two buses filled with police reinforcements.

Curious she is thinking how those two groups appeared out of nowhere when no advance notice is given. She assumes the rally is really a staged event for the media. "You can't trust any politician," she says to herself.

Six large black SUV's drive into the semicircle in front of Union Station. A lot of cowboy hats step out of the first two SUVs, so Khara figures the third one must be carrying the candidate.

His supporters are cheering him, and the protestors are booing him. Chaos breaks out as the crowds on both sides of the barricades breakthrough, and merge in the middle trying to fight each other. The SUV's speed off to protect the congressman who she thinks is probably still inside the third vehicle and leaving the Texas security men in the free-for-all with the fighting crowd.

The problem is distinguishing who are the cowboys as their hats are knocked off by the mobs attempting to have a major brawl with each other. Frustrated by the loss of a clean kill she aims for the left side of the back seat in the third black SUV. Khara guesses he would be sitting by the side window so he can hop out at the station. With her finger on the trigger, she exhales as the rifle fires once into the top of the vehicle, and she takes a blind shot hoping for the best.

After a faint popping sound she ducks sits back on the hot tar paper and disassembles her rifle. For sure next time she will get a better opportunity at him. Right now she is putting the disassembled weapon into her backpack, and heads for the door to go back downstairs.

On the way to the stairs, she retrieves the doorway bullet as she hustles down to the back door where the security guard who let her in is standing.

"Thanks for letting me use the restroom, I appreciate your kindness."

In a calm and casual walk back to the front of the building she crosses the street and gets in her car to continue the trip back home

.

***

Leaving Washington behind she is in Maryland in a short time, and heading for the New Jersey Turnpike when Big Boy calls her on the phone.

"Hey, Khara can't you go any faster?"

"Where the hell are you Biggie? I'm going seventy-five and keeping up with traffic."

"Right behind you, what kept you? We stopped for a long lunch, and now we are behind you in the white Cadillac. You're driving like an old lady. Are you getting old or something?"

A big grin crosses her face as she downshifts from sixth to third gear while pressing the gas pedal to the floor. Pushed back into her seat she is enjoying the emotional rush of the speeding car as her body starts to pulsate from adrenalin spewing through her veins.

The Cadillac doesn't appear again until they reach the first rest stop on the New Jersey Turnpike when she pulls in for a cup of coffee ahead of him.

In the dining area, she is sitting and sipping her Java when Big Boy comes in with his three men. His hand goes in his right side pants pocket, and he slips a hundred dollar bill to one of his men to buy food when he spots Khara and sits at her table.

"Glad you caught up with me Biggie. Now, who drives like an old lady?"

"Funny, the amazing thing is you didn't kill anyone with your crazy driving. Did you listen to the news on the radio?"

"No the Stones are playing on my personal mix. Why what is going on?"

"The news stations are reporting a shooting at the Union Station rally for Congressman Ferry. A massive brawl broke out between his supporters and protestors. Ted Ferry is sitting in his black SUV and the media reported someone shot him through the vehicle."

"No shit? How could it be?" Khara said.

Big Boy looks at her and smiles.

"Don't bullshit me Khara. You don't need to say anything, but I know what I know, and I know you."

A slight smile appears on her face.

"Couldn't happen to a nicer racist, Biggie, he deserved it. Did they say he survived?"

"No news came out yet. The radio said the limo rushed him to a hospital for surgery, and I did not hear anything else about the shooting. All the stations are talking about his being hit, and nothing else. One station said a Mexican tried to kill him because of the racist statements he made, but they are not certain yet."

From her back pocket, she can feel her phone ringing. With her leftt hand, she takes it out and glances at the caller ID. The deputy commissioner is calling her.

"This call I must answer Biggie, give me a minute."

Khara steps to the corner of the seating area where no one else is present, and stands by the windows.

"Hi, Johanna, what's up."

"The department's intelligence unit informed me a few minutes ago someone tried to assassinate Congressman Ted Ferry today at Union Station in Washington. The Secret Service and the FBI are investigating. This is all the information I received at the moment. Where are you now?"

"I'm in Jersey on my way home."

"Did you obtain any intelligence on the Boonville training camp they are building?"

"In my car is a lot of stuff for you. Tomorrow evening I'll drop everything off at your condo, about seven?"

"Perfect, I'll arrange for dinner to be brought in, and we can talk."

"Meet you then, bye."

Finished with the phone call she goes back to Big Boy, sits with him and his crew, and drinks her coffee.

"So does Al miss me, Biggie?"

Big Boy smiles at her and doesn't answer. "You need to ask him a question like that, not me."

"Well, I'm almost done with my coffee so I'm heading back. In a little while, I'll be driving to the Outer Bridge to Staten Island, and I'll stop at the club to ask him myself if you're too chicken shit to answer me."

"Don't get me in trouble Khara, ask him yourself."

"Are you working the door tonight or taking the day off?"

"No I'm at the club, I'll see you later."

Khara stands and eases her way back to her car to continue north on the turnpike to the Outer Bridge.

***

The BMW pulls off the back 440 highway and she stops at the building's awning, flips her key fob to the valet, and starts to enter the building.

The bouncer standing by the front door is new and is not aware of who she is dating.

"Please open your pocketbook I must screen you for weapons."

Khara opens her leather jacket and flips her gold shield out of her blouse hanging on a chain around her neck. The sight of her badge and shoulder holster with a .45 in her jacket causes him to open the door for her.

"Thank you" as she is walking past him, and into the entry area

Al is at the side lounge, spots her entering the lobby as he puts his drink down on the polished wood bar, and walks over to greet her. After kissing and embracing he takes her by the arm and escorts her to the elevator to sit upstairs in his private booth.

The slow ride going up gives her time to hug him, and with a tenderness she kisses him on his neck.

With his hand holding hers they walk to his favorite seating area overlooking the dance floor below as she slides in first, and he sits next to her with their shoulders touching

"Missed you Khara, doing anything tonight?"

"Maybe, I'm not sure, I need to meet the deputy commissioner at seven at her Jersey City condo to report back on the stuff I found out concerning those crazy Texans."

"Don't worry about those papers you sent me, I put them in a large envelope, and hid them in my floor safe under the carpet beneath my desk."

"Hold them till I need them because if I disappear you need to send them to the deputy commissioner at One Police Plaza."

"Will do, but I doubt anything is going to happen to you tonight. You're too tough a son of a bitch to get yourself killed."

"Never know Al, shit happens all the time. Look at what happened to the asshole Ted Ferry today."

"Yes, I heard about what happened. The news said the bullet hit him in the top of his thigh while sitting in his SUV as he left Union Station. Wonder how the shooting went down, don't you?"

Ignoring his question she stares at him and smiles.

"Guess you like the special gift I sent you. Cool isn't it?" Al said.

"Yes, I appreciate a thoughtful and useful item. I like the rifle a lot, thank you. Hey, listen I'll try to be back here later tonight, tomorrow without fail. Problem is I can't tell how long I'll be at Johanna's this evening. She may want to go over the papers with me."

"Call me when you leave her place, I'll be here till three in the morning. We're hosting a big bachelor party, and I arranged to bring in a handful of Russian strippers for entertainment. The arrangements for them to come here are being made for me by Olga. Later I need to send Big Boy with a van to pick up the women in Brooklyn."

"If I'm free I'll call you to schedule something."

He leans in and starts to kiss her. After a few minutes, she pulls away, and says she needs to go home to change and rest a little from the almost six hours of driving she did today.

Al escorts her from the elevator in the rear of the dance floor to the front entry so the valet can bring her BMW around as she is leaving the building. The car is brought to the front awning and is waiting for her.

Big Boy and his crew now pull up in the white Cadillac behind the stationary M3 by the valet stand. Khara is about to sit in her car she turns, waves to him, and he smiles back at her.

Due to her being tired she is driving in a sane manner over the Verrazano Bridge and stops at the front of her building. The doorman nods a greeting as she approaches the entry, and he opens the art deco door for her.

One of the building's concierge's security men carries her bags up to her apartment and drops them off in her lobby. Once in her place, she puts the worn clothes from her luggage in the laundry basket, the attaché case on the floor by the front door, and is able to relax.

Now at last in her apartment, she undresses, takes a hot shower using her coconut body wash, sets the alarm to wake her, and slips into a comfortable bed to take a restful nap.

***

The alarm goes off; she reaches over to her phone on the nightstand, and calls Johanna to confirm she will be able to meet her later at her condo.

"Hey, it's Khara, checking to make sure you are going to be home by seven?"

"Hi Khara, yes I'll be in. Do you feel like dinner with me tonight when you arrive here?"

"Sounds good to me, I'll see you, bye."

Still tired she gets out of bed, dresses, and turns on the television. The early evening news is full of stories about Congressman Ted Ferry getting shot in Washington. People on the street are being interviewed about what happened to him. Many are sorry he didn't die, and a few are upset with a presidential candidate being fired upon. The national news media likens the shooting to the Kennedy assassination.

Finished dressing she goes downstairs to her car and drives to Jersey City. The short trip does not take her long as she goes to the Holland Tunnel, and hops on the Turnpike to Caven Point.

The M3 is parked in Johanna's parking spot, and she calls upstairs. Johanna tells her to wait for her to come down. In a few minutes, she appears and asks Khara to join her at an upscale restaurant overlooking Lower New York Bay.

At the restaurant, they are seated and inspect the menu and order their drinks once the waiter approaches. Johanna orders a sour apple martini and Khara an Amstel Light beer.

"So tell me how did you enjoy your visit with your sister?"

"Nice, considering I never knew she existed before this. My older sister is a good woman if you like a holy roller. I shouldn't say anything bad about her because I found her to be a giving person, a gracious lady, and I also met an elderly aunt."

"Sounds like a great family reunion. Tell me, when you left her house and trailed Fred did you find out anything about the training camp the Texans are building in New York?"

"Yes, I lucked out and obtained Ferry's travel schedule. His press aid left the information for me in his attaché case. I placed the papers in my car trunk. After dinner, I can bring it back to your condo with me."

The waiter brings their drinks and the conversation changes to food. Johanna decides to order first.

"Can I order the sirloin steak with the demi-glaze, sautéed mushrooms, a salted baked potato with butter only please, and the mixed vegetables."

"Sounds delicious Johanna, I'll order the same."

The waiter walks away to enter the food order and both enjoy the view looking out at the bay as a water ferry brings in commuters from lower Manhattan.

With intent, Johanna leans over, and in a soft tone of voice asks if Khara would be interested in staying the rest of the night with her. "We can spend some quality time together."

"To be honest Johanna I hoped you would say that."

Their food is brought to the table and they relax while having some small talk about Khara's favorite baseball team, The Mets. After eating they skip dessert and walk back to the M3 to grab the attaché case. The trunk pops up, and Khara lifts the case out and carries it to Johanna's condo as she is walking alongside with her.

They enter her dining area when Khara opens the case, and takes out all the papers placing them on the table. Johanna sits down next to her and begins to sort through the sheaves of notes with great care. Only a minute or two went by until she stops, and starts to stare at one piece of paper with intense interest.

"My guess Johanna is something on the sheet caught your attention?"

"Oh my God Khara, they are going to blow up two buildings, and the paper says they will kill the two new heads of the Ecru Drug Cartel. I don't care about them, but innocent bystanders can also be killed in the explosions. We must try to stop them somehow."

"Remember the home explosion you sent me to in Brooklyn a few weeks ago. I think the building which blew up was their local bomb factory. The problem is if they aren't now making the bomb themselves they must be obtaining the explosives elsewhere. Bet they got the supplies in Texas and drove them into New York. Does the sheet give any addresses?"

"No Khara, it states what their general plans are. I found it on the last page on the bottom of the case. This attaché did not belong to a public relations person, but a close advisor, or even a right-hand man, to Ted Ferry to be able to keep this highly classified date in his possession. How did you to manage to obtain this information?"

"He tried to kill me, so I took his stuff."

"Is that all you are going to tell me?

Silent, Khara smiles a sly smile at her but says nothing.

"Yes, I understand. At least you obtained the case with this information. Tomorrow I'll speak to the intelligence bureau about this, and hope they will contain other important things they would like to share with me. Report back to Staten Island, and I'll contact you if anything turns up."

With a quick shuffle Johanna bundles and stacks together with the papers and places them on a marble and iron side buffet. The case she puts by the door for Khara to dispose of later as she goes back to the kitchen, and takes her by the hand as they enter her bedroom.

***

About two o'clock in the morning Johanna's phone rings. The caller ID shows the call is from police headquarters.

Exhausted Khara does not hear the phone ring and continues sleeping. The police commissioner is telling Johanna a building exploded in Staten Island tonight, and she should be aware of it. The initial fire marshal's report stated the fire started in an area where no gas lines are present. Someone placed and set off a bomb.

"Shit, wake up Khara. A bomb went off a few minutes ago in Staten Island, and I need you to go find out what is going on. The department thinks it is terrorism-related."

With a soft shake, Khara wakes up bleary-eyed.

"What's going on Johanna?"

"A little while ago an explosion occurred in Staten Island at a dance club, and I'm waiting for an address to come through. Head for the Bayonne Bridge, and I'll text the street address to you when I receive it."

"Not a problem, I'll go right away."

Still sleepy she jumps out of bed and puts her clothes on as fast as she can. After dressing, and before she leaves Khara makes sure she is carrying all her weapons. In her haste, she forgets the attaché case on the kitchen table and heads downstairs to her car.

The drive to the Bayonne Bridge goes quickly on the back 440 highway on the outskirts of Bayonne.

The BMW slows down to seventy miles an hour and as she crosses the bridge her phone rings with the address texted to her. Khara doesn't bother to look at the address. In her gut, she knows where the bomb went off. Without even looking she assumed it is Al's place.

At the zenith of the Bayonne Bridge she slows down and in the distance, yellow and red flames are dancing in the night sky about a hundred feet highlighting up the dark night. The fire is streaking higher and higher trying to outdo the previous bursts of intense heat.

The M3 enters Staten Island and hops on the expressway going to the explosion. Though still early in the morning she can't distinguish if the smoke is emanating from the building, but she can't miss the flames. Once she saw the fire she is positive the Texans blew up Al's club.

In only a matter of minutes, she drives up to the location, and police and fire trucks are parked in front with their multicolored lights rotating in circles. The firemen are hosing down the melted metal building, or what is left of the club. The fire is still uncontrolled inside the heart of the structure.

In a rush to leave her car she swings her neck chain and badge out of her blouse, and runs to the edge of the burning building. The police instituted a perimeter, but they allowed Khara, a detective, to go past.

The sounds of sirens are ringing in her ears. More firetrucks and squad cars are arriving as well as a few ambulances. Khara starts to walk around the site looking for someone she recognizes, even a police commander will do. She needs to find out if anyone survived.

In the distance standing next to the fire chief is the area police commander on duty as she approaches him, and asks if there are survivors from the blast. "At this time Detective, I don't know. The ambulances took a few people to a hospital in Brooklyn to the burn unit. The rest are being transported to a local hospital emergency room. What are you doing here? Are you on duty now?" the commander asked.

"No, the deputy police commissioner for terrorism sent me here to investigate if this is a terrorist act. The information she obtained says this explosion might be drug related to the Ecru Cartel from Mexico."

"Okay detective I'll keep you in the loop if any more information comes in tonight," he said.

"Thanks, I appreciate your help commander."

Khara steps away from the fire, and goes to her car to call Olga, and warn her The Texans blew up Al's place and killed him in the process. Something must be going on at the building in Brooklyn because she tried dialing her, but she did not answer her phone. Khara thought it is unusual for someone not to pick up. Something must be going on at the building in Brooklyn.

Tired and sitting in her car watching the firemen her cell phone rings, Big Boy is calling her.

"Hey, Biggie where are you?"

"I'm in Brooklyn at Al's son's place. Tonight I picked up the Russian party girls in Brighton Beach, and am bringing them back for the night's entertainment. As I was about to turn off the highway and pull in the club's driveway the building exploded right before my eyes. With flames shooting straight up I parked on the shoulder of the road and left the girls sitting in the van while I ran up to the club to try and help. The unbearable heat prevented me from approaching anywhere near the building. With my cell phone, I called 911 to report the fire and drove away to bring the entertainment back to Brooklyn. Where are you now Khara?"

"I'm sitting in my car at the inferno. The city fire marshal's initial investigation said someone set the explosion. The Texans must be responsible. Those assholes are out to kill Al, and I warned him about this before I went to Virginia."

"Believe me I am aware they are the culprits, he told me all about them. Listen... meet me in Brooklyn at The Fattachie Family Funeral Home tonight. Ring the back delivery bell, and they'll let you in. I'll be there and introduce you to Al Junior, he owns the place."

"Biggie I'm on my way. There is nothing I can help with here."

In a hurry backing out of the parking lot, she comes close but avoid hitting another firetruck racing to the scene. The red fire truck comes screeching to a halt on the driveway entrance, leaving only enough space for Khara to squeeze her car by, and drive away.

Before heading for the Verrazano Bridge she places her magnetic flashing light on her car roof and flips on the siren she installed in her M3. Now speeding over the suspension bridge she arrives at the funeral home in record time. The place is off Bay Parkway, and a large parking lot is located on the back. The BMW is parked near the rear door under the high-intensity floodlights.

Parked in the back she walks to the door and rings the bell as instructed. A middle-aged man with a pencil thin mustache, gray hair swept back, and wearing a tight-fitting black suit opens the door for her. The slender gentleman greets her by name although she never met him before, she thinks nothing of it. Khara is not the typical person ringing their bell at night so she knew he expected someone like her.

"Please follow me to Junior's office upstairs, and to the left."

The man turns, and they both take the stairs up to the first floor. The stairway opens to the main entry lobby. In a slow walk, she follows behind him on the imported Italian marble floors. The metal taps on her boot heels make a clickity click sound on the tiles. The hall has three doors, and he stops by a plain wooden door with no signage and knocks two times.

The door opens, and Big Boy is standing expressionless.

"Come in" Junior beckons.

Big Boy steps aside and sits on a sofa by the wall as she enters the room. She is surprised to meet Al Junior. In the time she spent with his father she never knew he had a son or any kids for that matter. Only the three of them are in the office. As a trained investigator Khara looks at him and places him to be in his mid-twenties, and handsome. This is obvious to her his father set him up. No way could this kid afford to be in a big funeral business like this.

"Hello Detective Bennet, I am sorry we are meeting under these conditions. My father said many complimentary things about you."

"Thank you. To be honest I never knew you existed until a few minutes ago when Big Boy asked me to come here."

"Yes, I can understand why. Dad never mixed pleasure with family, but he did talk about you to me quite often, and the conversation always was favorable regarding you. To be truthful he told me many times he is crazy about you."

"And she is also good at what she does" Big Boy chimed in.

"Thanks for the confirmation Biggie," Khara said.

Al Junior stands from behind his polished imported Italian walnut desk, walks in front of it, and sits on the edge facing her." The reason I asked you here is to find out if we can hit those bastards back somehow. Is there information on where we can find them? My guys are going to kill every one of them, and their entire families too. Their wives, their children, their parents I want all of them killed. Where ever they are they ain't going to be able to hide."

"Junior, I faxed to your father their travel plans while I investigated them in Virginia this past week. He said he placed them under the carpet by his desk. The papers I'm sure are destroyed due to the fire. The police have a copy also" Khara said.

"Don't be so sure Detective, as you know Dad's office is in a basement, but not under the club itself. The room is built outside the perimeter walls of the structure. Why do you think the doorway to his downstairs office is well hidden, and hard to find. The building department doesn't know the office even exists because it is not on the architect's final certified plans. Dad designed the club, and he constructed his underground room like it is a bomb shelter. The contractors reinforced the concrete walls with rebar, and placed two steel doors you need to open in the hidden hallway to enter his stairwell. If he was in his private room, at the time of the explosion, he might still be alive. Plus he also installed a safe placed in the floor under the carpet by the outside right corner of his desk. The safe is set in concrete so the papers in there are in good shape. We need to break into retrieve them."

Curious Khara asked Junior "how are you going to enter into the basement office to find out?"

"We also own a construction company in Red Hook. Tomorrow we'll pull the permits from the building department so we can start to tear down the remaining parts of the club and cart the debris away. The place will be fenced off with six-foot high solid wood fences before the sun comes up. Nobody will be able to watch what is going on. The solid barrier will be installed instead of a chain link one. We will first concentrate on the side where the office would be below ground, and I'll bring in an earth mover and dump trucks. Before lunchtime we'll be underground level with jackhammers breaking into the reinforced concrete walls. Big Boy and I will be supervising the work site. Once we enter into the room we'll move the desk, and disclose the floor safe. Don't worry I memorized the combination to open the safe. In a day or two, I'll call you for another meeting, and we'll plan out our attack on those Texas assholes. We might also be surprised to find out Dad survived the explosion."

Chapter Twelve

On her way home, Khara tries to call Olga again, but there is still no answer.

She pulls off the Belt Parkway onto the city streets and begins to feel a little unnerved as the M3 approaches her apartment house. Something is peculiar about the street in front of her home. Not stopping at the yellow valet line by her building to drop off her car she keeps driving, and scans for movement of any kind which doesn't seem to belong.

On the next block, she stops, makes a U-turn from the far right lane, and parks in an open spot next to a fire hydrant between two parked cars. With difficulty, she is trying to figure out what is different, yet continues staring down the street. Her burner phone rings and the caller identification recognizes Olga's number.

"Do not stay here, leave now. The Texans are expected at any moment, and we are watching you in your car. My men are all set and waiting for them, and I'll call you when the shooting is over."

Now when Olga said she is observing her Khara starts to move her eyes upward, and she never noticed anything before but does this time. On almost every lamp post, situated on the top, is a video camera. Turning her head up and down the road, she sees them as far away as five blocks in each direction. "How the hell did Olga ever place them up on the posts, and remained on city lights with no one ever noticing them?" She wonders to herself.

The night's anticipation made time fly by, and dawn is almost here. Exhausted from the excitement at the club her heart is now starting to beat a little faster expecting a gunfight in front of where she lives.

With reckless abandon, she ignores Olga's warning as she turns off her car lights, but keeps the engine idling, in case she needs to drive away in a hurry. With her right hand, she reaches into her jacket, withdraws her Sig Sauer .45 slightly from its holster, and flips off the safety. The gun is placed on the car seat next to her and within easy reach.

In the distance, two vehicles are approaching the block where her apartment is located, and being led by a small box truck, but not yet by the building.

The hair on the back of her neck starts to rise and her instincts tell Khara the vehicle must be loaded with explosives. The Texans are going to blow up the apartment house when they bring the truck close enough to the front door. The cowboys are mimicking the suicide terrorists from the Middle East or the crazy right wing nut jobs from Oklahoma where they blew up a Federal building. A gut instinct tells her after the explosion they will leave their vehicles, and run inside the apartment house killing everyone they can find.

At a slow speed, the delivery truck gets ever closer to the beginning of the street where she lives. Khara spots multiple red lasers shoot down from the roof of the building. The mist from the ocean acts as a backdrop making the colored beams visible. The two cars driving behind the truck must also observe it as they stopped following, and stood motionless.

With a push of a button, she lowered her window and can discern a faint boom. The echo might be coming from the open waters, but she is not sure. Out of the corner of her eye, she turns her head and is cognizant of a small ship off the coast. It is too far away to make out what kind it is, but it is the only one out at sea at this moment. Without warning the box truck explodes into a fireball of flames shooting high into the night sky. Secondary explosions go off in the rear of the vehicle. The impact of the laser-sighted RPGs sets off whatever explosives it is carrying. Metal parts fly into the air along with the asphalt lifted from the road.

The blast leaves a twenty foot deep gaping hole in the street while apartment windows in the surrounding buildings are shattered. Parked cars near the truck burst into flames from the heat of the exploding truck's shrapnel penetrating their gasoline fuel tanks. A water main is ruptured and water is spouting upward like a geyser.

"Son of a bitch," Khara thought to herself. She forgot Viktor is an old KGB agent with high-level contacts and can obtain actual military grade weapons from anywhere in the world.

The two stopped cars begin to make a U-turn trying to distance them from the burning truck.

From parked vehicles with tinted windows on a side street, Olga's Special Forces men jump out running toward the escaping killers. The trained soldiers fire their Kalashnikov AK-47 automatic weapons at the cowboys sitting in their cars. None of the Texans are able to leave alive, and Khara is a witness to this slaughter.

In less than ten seconds the ambush is over.

The ex-Russian military gunmen disappear into the early morning mist and are gone from sight like ghosts. Only their spent shell casings are left on the black asphalt. The brass shells begin to shine in the morning dawn as the eastern rising sun hits them.

The window on the M3 is closed as she shifts into first gear, makes a U-turn driving away from the ambush, and the dead bodies. This time she doesn't want to be anywhere near this massacre. Too many questions she doesn't want to answer if she is ever associated with the shootings.

While she drives away she can pick up sirens wailing in the distance.

Tired and needing some rest Khara decides to check into a motel by Sheepshead Bay. Still not able to go to her apartment yet, believing Al is dead, and Johanna is now going to work riding a water ferry to Lower Manhattan all she wants is to go to sleep undisturbed. After checking in at the registration desk she leaves her car parked out front and goes to her room to lie down. Tired she takes off her jacket, placing her guns on the night table next to her pillow, turns off the ringer on her phone, and lies down exhausted.

***

Midafternoon her cell phone does not ring because she turned off the ringer. The vibrations rattle the phone on the nightstand next to her bed. Groggy she hears the light clattering but doesn't open her eyes to answer it. The caller must wait.

Again the smartphone continues to vibrate against the wood table top. Bleary-eyed and still tired she, at last, opens her eyes and turns the ringer back on. The screen on her cell shows she missed three calls.

Johanna is the first one listed who called her. Not knowing what she wants Khara presses the green call button, and returns her call.

"Hey Johanna its Khara, you wanted me?"

"Yes, this morning I am on my way to work when the department called me about a truck exploding near your apartment house. The precinct reports a number of dead Texas security men's bodies in two cars, and they are full of bullet holes. What happened? Were you involved?"

"No, this time I had nothing to do with any shooting. Remember I went to the explosion in Staten Island you asked me to investigate. From the ruins, I drove home, but I'll tell you about it when I meet you later if you want."

"Yes, I want to speak to you because for hours your phone is not picking up. Where are you?"

"Due to the police blockade of the street I couldn't enter my apartment so I crashed in a motel in Sheepshead Bay. Right now I'm in the room, I needed some rest because it is almost thirty hours since I slept, and I wanted to crash somewhere."

"Remember you can always come back to my place."

"Of course I am aware of your condo being available to me, but it was late, and I was too tired to drive to Jersey. My body needed to jump into the closest bed I could find to rest my head. In a little while, I'm going to try to go home to shower. Hope I'll be able to enter my building without too much trouble."

"Alright Khara, call me later, and I'll tell you where to meet me."

"Johanna I need about an hour or two before I will call you again, bye."

With the cobwebs still in her head, she sits up in bed and is annoyed due to a tiny streak of the afternoon sun shining through the blackout drapes by the window. The caller id when she presses down again on her phone shows Don also dialed her along with an unknown number, and he is the second person she calls back.

"Hi Don its Khara, you called me?"

"All morning I've been trying to call you. Are you okay? My immediate supervisor told me about the explosion and shooting by your apartment this morning. Somehow I figured you must be mixed up with it knowing you so well."

"Believe it or not I was not involved with it this time. I'm fine but exhausted. A few minutes ago I spoke to Johanna, and I'm meeting her later to speak about the incident with her. Where are you calling me from?"

"I'm back in Dallas. The FBI is investigating the Texas for Texans Foundation. The Bureau thinks there is a link to drug smuggling from Mexico."

"Yer no surprise there, I would bet money they are involved."

Khara did not want to tell him she knew as a fact they are guarding the real kingpin of the Ecru Cartel. In her mind, he is too honest a man, and although she likes him, as much as she can like anyone, she didn't want him enmeshed in the dark side of her life for his sake, and hers too.

"Well as long as you're not hurt. I worried about you because you did not answer your phone."

"To be honest with you I understand what you said Don, but I needed some shuteye since I went almost thirty hours without sleep, and collapsed dead tired in bed."

Not feeling it is necessary to tell him everything about the night before, or where she is at the moment, she decided to omit the details.

"Sometime soon I should be back in New York, and we can meet and go out for dinner" he said.

"Wonderful, I can't wait to be with you again, bye."

Again she glanced at the unknown number on her phone but resolved not to call back. The mystery caller can hold a while. Desperate to take a shower and a change of clothes she puts on her jacket, guns, and checks out of the motel to try and drive home.

Over eight hours passed since the incident by her building. The police are still investigating with the crime scene unit people marking, collecting and photographing the area. The block is still cordoned off to traffic. The city engineering department is present along with sanitation and asphalt trucks. No way can she come close to her building with her car.

Two young valets from her building are waving to her when she is approaching the corner of her street. The car stops alongside of them, and they took her car to park the M3 in Olga's private lot a block away. Now she will continue the rest of the way to her home on foot.

The dead men are taken away and only the white chalk outlines of their bodies remained on the black asphalt street. Flipping her badge out of her blouse she walked towards her apartment house, and a small circle of police department commanders standing and talking on the sidewalk in front of her building.

In the crowd milling around before her is the first deputy mayor, the Brooklyn borough president, the chief of police, the local captain and his area commander, the head of sanitation and the fire commissioner as well as the deputy commissioner for terrorism, Johanna. The cluster of people are discussing the devastation on the street in front of them when Khara walks by and waves hello to the chief of police. He knows her from the Ecru Cartel shootings in Times Square last year, as did the other top brass standing in the group. Upon seeing her all the law enforcement bigwigs sighed with resignation. The brass all know of her reputation, and if she is here they all believe somehow she is mixed up in this madness on the city streets, but they could not understand how.

Johanna excuses herself from the gathering and walks up to Khara.

"Khara please tell me you are not involved in this mess."

"Remember before on the phone I told you I investigated the blast in Staten Island you sent me to investigate. After I finished I drove home. The officers cordoned off my block, and I couldn't enter my apartment so I checked into a local motel to catch some sleep. Here is my receipt, see for yourself."

The date of the stub corroborates what she told Johanna, and she is satisfied. The local motel did not time stamp it, only a check-in and check out day.

"Don't worry Khara I'll tell the brass you were not involved in the killings. You were on assignment for me at the Staten Island explosion and stayed in a motel last night. At least I can verify your excuse to satisfy their interest in you. Remember, I have your back."

"Thanks, Johanna, I need to report back to my precinct tomorrow. Today I couldn't go to work, too much stuff happening at the Staten Island blast last night. Are you going to be around tonight if I call you?"

"No, I must attend a political black-tie dinner with the mayor in Gracie Mansion. After I am finished we can try to arrange something together for tomorrow?"

"Too early to know yet, if I can I will. A lot depends on what develops at work" Khara said.

"Call me if you are able to join me for a late dinner tomorrow. I am looking forward to spending some time with you."

The doorman is back at his post while she continues to the front of her building, and he smiles at her as he opens the damaged glass door for her to enter. In the lobby the concierge waves, hello, and hands Khara some mail he saved until she came in the main entrance foyer again. With the letters in her hand, she enters the elevator and pushes the button to her floor.

Khara unlocks her front door, and she stops in her tracks because a man is snoring in her bedroom. The only people who carry a key to her apartment beside herself are Olga and Viktor. The Sig Sauer from under her jacket is withdrawn as she flips the safety off, and proceeds into her bedroom with her gun drawn.

Walking into the room ready to shoot she stops in the doorway and is shocked because Al is sleeping in her bed. This upset her and she yells at him.

"Hey asshole, wake up! Everyone thought the Texans killed you in the explosion at the club. You couldn't call me?"

Startled, he wakes and sits up in her bed with his back against the headboard.

"Last night I tried to reach you Khara, but you didn't answer. A lot of shit went down yesterday evening, and I did try to call you. Unfortunately, I needed to use my burner phone so I couldn't be hacked."

"Oh... a number on my cell did come up but I didn't know who it is from. My body was so tired I fell into a deep sleep at a nearby motel, and I also turned off my ringer so I wouldn't be disturbed. If this helps any I'm glad to be here with you. How did you escape from the assassination attempt?" Khara asked.

"Remember the Mexican investigator from Dallas Texas you met at a rest stop in Pennsylvania on your way to Virginia? You told him to contact me with the signal I gave you. The congressman's campaign is paying him five hundred a day to follow you. In my office, I met with him and said I'll pay one thousand dollars a day for information on the Texans, and what they are up to. In detail I explained to him I understood they want to kill me, and if he tips me off in time he'll earn a twenty-five thousand dollar bonus, in cash. I wanted to make sure the offer is attractive for him to keep me informed."

"Yesterday about an hour before the blast he calls me from a restroom stall at a gas station somewhere. In a whisper, he said the one word I told him I wanted him to say if I am in danger. As quick as I could I emptied the facility, and ordered everyone home except for three of my men. The guys stayed out front and parked their vehicles next to my Cadillac so the place seems somewhat busy. Immediately I called off the bachelor party and sent the groom and his friends' home. Big Boy is in Brooklyn picking up the girls so he is safe. It took me almost a full hour to empty the place out. The shit head kid needed to be bribed so he and his friends would leave. The groom thinks I am going to pay for his wedding in the Caribbean because of this crap, screw him."

"The people left and I walked around the perimeter of the building to inspect the property, and saw only one car remaining parked in the side lot. The sticker on the windshield showed it is a rental car, and the plates are from Texas so I figured this car to be the one they are using to load with explosives. At my age, I ran as fast as I could, and I went around to the other side of the building. As I turned the corner on the far side of the club the car bomb went off, and I was able to dive behind the dumpster for protection. My men were blown about twenty feet away onto the front driveway. The men are a little shaken up, and with some cuts and bruises, but otherwise not hurt too bad. We are all lucky to be alive. After I sat a few seconds to get my bearings back I walked to my Cadillac. I did not hesitate to call Viktor and Olga to warn them the Texans will be coming after them tonight also" he concluded.

"You didn't call your son or Big Boy to tell them you are not dead?"

"No, I wanted everyone to think I died in the explosion. This gives me some breathing room to plan the Texan's death. I am fed up with this Ted Ferry bullshit, and I made up my mind he's going down, and hard."

"Well, at least you still employ the investigator working inside their operation for you."

"Well... I am not so certain about him anymore because I think he might be in one of the cars which went to Olga's last night. If he was, he's finished, and saves me a lot of money."

"Well, I it must suck to be him now. I need to shower, and I missed my coconut body wash. Want to join me?"

***

The time is late afternoon, and both of them are hungry. Al recommended they order in from the kosher delicatessen he went to with Khara and Olga a short time ago. After he suggested it he remembered the shootout on the sidewalk and the attempted assassination attempt on his life when he left the deli after lunch.

"Call downstairs to the concierge. Ask him to send someone to buy the food for us, because I can't begin to tell you how much I enjoyed the corn beef sandwich I ate there," he said.

"No... Let's hop out of bed, dress, and go ourselves, I want some fresh air."

He stared at her, and for a second hesitated getting dressed.

"You're being a pussy again Al. I'll protect you, come on let's go."

"Screw you Khara, you better take care of me. Let's put our clothes on, and get the hell out of here."

About a half hour later they are ready to leave her apartment. She opens her bottom dresser drawer and takes out a replacement hand grenade, and places it in her small over the shoulder sling pocketbook. "Think this is about everything I need at the moment, I'm all set now, let's go eat."

The two of them take the elevator down to the lobby, and she decides for a change to use the rear service entrance instead of the front door.

"Nervous Khara, is this why we are using the back entrance?"

"No, I think of this as a precaution. If possible I prefer to spot them first if anyone is out there waiting so they don't expect me and I have an edge, and the upper hand."

"Bullshit Khara. Who's the pussy now?"

"Shut up Al, and hold my left hand as we walk. I would like us to be seen as somewhat normal so we don't draw any undue attention."

"You're a pisser Khara. Here we are on the sidewalk in Brighton Beach Brooklyn, known as Little Odessa, filled with white Russian immigrants, and a black woman is walking holding hands with a white Italian man. And you don't want to attract attention, are you nuts?"

On the spur of the moment, Khara stops, turns to face him, puts her arms around his neck, and plants a big kiss right on his lips in the middle of the crowded sidewalk.

"Who am I to argue?" he said returning the affection with passion.

The deli is only a few blocks further down the street, and they arrive safe and sound. They enter the restaurant, and the counterman remembers her. Khara notices he has a small nervous smile on his face.

"Welcome back. Take a seat anywhere. The waitress will be with you soon."

Both go to the rear of the dining area and sit at the last table in the room, with her back to the wall as usual. Once she is seated she places her hand inside her jacket in a casual manner, lifts the pistol up a little to loosen it a bit, and flips the safety off on her gun.

The elderly white-haired waitress takes her time walking over to their table to take their order.

"Hey, it's good to see you again. Is this your boyfriend? He's a looker. Lucky for you he's too old for me." She tells them as she adjusts her slipping upper dentures. "What'll you have tonight?"

Khara orders for both of them. "Corn beef on rye with spicy mustard, two homemade round potato knishes, and four cans of Dr. Browns Black Cherry soda."

"You got it, sweetie, give a few minutes and I'll bring you the pickles. Did I ever tell you I like the all sour ones? The half and half pickles aren't strong enough for me, I like something which makes my lips pucker up." Smiling at the thought she walks away to go into the kitchen to pick up the sodas and pickles.

The counterman carries their food back to them himself after he plates it, and the waitress brings them their drinks and pickles. The aroma is strong, their taste buds are dancing in their mouths, and they eat their sandwiches in peace.

"Every bite I am enjoying, I must say this is good stuff Khara."

"Glad you like it. By the way, did you call Junior or Biggie yet to tell them you are alive?"

"Yes, when you started the water for the shower I sent them both a text on my burner phone. One word is all I needed for them to read. The two of them are cognizant I use a secret name which I arranged with them a long time ago, before the explosion, so they would know it's me. Remember I also gave you one before you left for Virginia?"

"Yer, let's finish and go back to my place. There is a lot of planning to do tonight. Wonder if Olga and Viktor are around, or did they skip out of town until things cooled off with the police crawling around everywhere today."

"As a matter of fact, I spoke to him earlier when he let me in your apartment. My larger boat is docked at Sheepshead Bay. Later we are going to meet them there around nine o'clock. My crew will take the cabin cruiser out to the Lower Bay by the Verrazano Bridge for a leisurely cruise. Nobody will be around, and we can talk undisturbed about what our plans are going to be to finish off those assholes once and for all."

"I knew you own the cabin cruiser Big Boy uses, but you also have a larger one?"

"Yes, I bought it...."

"Shush for a second Al. The sportscaster is reporting something about the Mets on the news I want to listen to what he is saying."

In silence, Khara listens and sits back in her seat smiling from ear to ear.

"What did you hear to which gave you a big smart ass grin?" he asked.

"The station announced the World Series MVP went to the Levy kid from Brooklyn. He plays second base for the Mets. Wow, I'm impressed. Next week there will be a ticker tape parade down Broadway, and I would like to go."

"Can't begin to tell you I'm so glad to hear the news, let's take the check and leave" Al said.

The waitress comes over and hands him the tab. Without looking at it he takes out a hundred dollar bill, and he gives the cash to her. "Keep the change" and stood to amble out the door with a full stomach.

With hunger abated they are walking to the front door when the elderly waitress calls out to Al. "Too bad you're so old if you were a little younger I would steal you from her."

With his right hand, he grips Khara by the arm, and they walk out of the restaurant to the sidewalk with her leading the way through the deli's entrance.

***

Back in her apartment, she brings out two beers. One beer is for him, one for her as they sit back on her sofa, and Khara turns on the television to kill some time. The clock says seven o'clock in the evening, and all the channels are broadcasting the day's news.

Every station is talking about the Brooklyn truck exploding, and the dead bodies found in the street shot full of bullets. The news broadcasters are saying this shooting is the result of a local gang war, and innocent people are being murdered. The Staten Island explosion is being attributed to a gas leak and is now old news since no dead people are discovered by the police lying on the pavement as they did in Brighton Beach.

After the broadcast ends he gets up and tells Khara they need to leave now for the boat because of the tides. This time they go through the main lobby walking past the two security men sitting on the sofa across from the building's concierge.

They stop by the concierge desk and Al asks if a taxi can be called for him. Parking on Emmons Avenue in Sheepshead Bay by the water is difficult at any time of day.

"Not a problem sir, I'll tell one of our guards to drive you there." In Russian, he says something and one of the men sitting stands up and walks out the door to wait outside. In a few minutes, a black Lincoln

Limousine drives up to the valet stand. The security man motions to them to come out, and sit in the car; he will be driving them to the dock.

The two of them are being driven to the docks as Khara is sitting next to him in the back seat.

"Amazing but I never rode in a limo before Al. Well, to be truthful I did for two seconds at the park two weeks ago, but I killed the driver. This is cool to be driven in style. I must thank Olga when I see her next."

"Yes this is a treat, we should be there is in few minutes so don't get too comfortable."

The limousine turns off Coney Island Avenue to Neptune Avenue, and it soon comes to the water. The car continues on Emmons Avenue along the sidewalk as they approach a large fifty-foot boat tied to the end of a long concrete dock. There are other large boats in the water getting ready to go out for their night fishing cruises. But this one is not a rental trawler; it is an ocean-going cabin cruiser with a Russian security man standing by the gangplank.

"Please stop by the green car parked over there, "AL said to the driver. The limousine stops, puts on its blinkers, and double parks while he and Khara step out. Needless to say, the traffic behind them begin blowing their horns in typical New York fashion, and tries to squeeze past them on the left.

Once they are out of the limo it pulls away. They start walking towards the boat, and she catches a glimpse of some men moving about on top by the bridge.

"How many crewmen do you have on board?

"There is a crew of two full-time, and on occasion, I'll add some more if needed. Tonight I added some men for security, a cook and a waiter. This evening we will be eating freshly made appetizers in the galley as we sail around New York Bay. Did you ever go on a nighttime excursion?"

"No, this will be a first for me, it sounds romantic."

"Tonight will be a pleasant cruise, and the water is calm, but this time we must talk business with Viktor and Olga."

Khara starts to walk up the gangplank ahead of him, and Big Boy is standing on the deck ready to greet her.

"Hi Biggie, good to see you again."

"Hey Khara, good to see you too."

Al walks on behind her and takes her by the hand to sit on the aft deck looking out at the small white caps as the sun is about to set behind them.

A few minutes later Olga and Viktor arrive with two of their security men holding a large manila envelope. Al calls out to them to join him and Khara, and enjoy a cold brew while the crew prepares to pull out of the dock. In only seconds they are in the center of the inlet heading out to the bay sipping a cold beer and enjoying the quiet night.

The boat makes the turn to head towards the bridge when they are called from below deck to come enjoy some hot appetizers. Earlier in the afternoon Al requested his Bensonhurst restaurant send one of their chefs with fresh supplies to prepare dinner for them aboard the boat after the finger food is finished. Then their late dinner will be served.

The chef prepared Chilean Sea Bass with mixed vegetables and a purée de pommes de terre [mashed potatoes]. Al brought his favorite imported white Italian wine to go along with dinner.

Finished eating the table top is cleared off, Viktor takes out the manila envelope he carried on with him, and spreads a topographic map of Booneville New York out flat as it unfurls. The flap is opened and he reaches in and brings out the faxed copies of the Texans plans Khara sent to him from Virginia.

"Olga, I was not told he faxed them to you," Khara said.

"I sent her a copy of the papers you faxed to me because I wanted to be sure they read everything also. Think of it as a kind of insurance policy in case something happened to me" Al said.

Hunched over the map, and looking through the stolen notes they decide on a plan, and date, to kill off the Texas for Texans at their training facility. Finished with their planning everybody goes up to the rear deck and takes a seat while enjoying the nighttime views of lower Manhattan, and the Statue of Liberty.

Later the boat returns to dock in Sheepshead Bay, and Viktor calls ahead for two cars to pick everyone up, and bring them back to the building.

In their limo, Khara asks him if he would like to spend the rest of the night with her. Reaching over he takes her hand in his and brings it up to his lips.

"What a silly question. Of course, I would."

Chapter Thirteen

The next morning Khara wakes, and dashes in the shower to be ready for work. The time is late and she must drive to Staten Island, and report to her precinct.

In the bathroom she grabs the coconut body wash, showers and dresses as quick as she can. Al awakes upon hearing her stirring around the apartment, decides to dress and go to his condo to change his clothes instead of sleeping any longer. Both are ready and they leave together. With a whole hand smash, Khara presses the elevator button and they take it down to the ground floor.

The concierge greets them as they enter the lobby, and asks if they would like their individual vehicles brought around, or are they going in one car.

"No, we need our own thanks," she said.

Both walk outside and stand by the front door, under the awning, waiting for their cars to be driven to the valet stand. The overhang extends about thirty feet to the street, giving cover to anyone standing under it in inclement weather or scorching sun.

The sidewalk is busy with people hustling to the train station, or the bus stop at Coney Island Avenue, on their way to work.

A red Cadillac driven by a valet turns on the block and heads for the yellow painted line by the road. Al spots it coming, kisses her goodbye, and walks to the curb waiting for his car to stop without a care in the world at the moment.

Next to the doorman biding her time Khara is standing and views a pedestrian start to approach Al. A man in the crowd is wearing cowboy boots and is approaching him, and she catches a clickity click of taps on the sidewalk.

Concentrating on his car coming to the valet stand he did not hear the sound of boot taps as it comes ever closer.

The group of pedestrians is now within ten feet of him, and the man with the boots reaches into his jacket with his right hand. Khara runs towards him with her Sig Sauer in plain view of everyone and yells out to get down. The volume of her screaming at the top of her lungs causes Al to turn and face her, and he catches sight of her running toward him with her service weapon out.

The man with the cowboy boots takes his hand out of his inner sports jacket pocket, and puts his sunglasses on his head, keeps on walking, and leaving Al standing and wondering what all the excitement is about.

"What is going on Khara?"

"False alarm, guess I overreacted when a man wearing western style boots came towards you. Sorry for the excitement I thought he might be from the Texans and here to kill you."

"Well, I understand. Glad you care about me, thanks, I'll call you later."

With her explanation finished he tips the valet, sits in the Cadillac, and is on his way to Bay Ridge.

The next car to drive up is her washed and polished black M3. Seems there are standing orders to wash her car if it needs it. The car washes are part of the rental deal Al negotiated with Viktor on her behalf.

The quick trip to Staten Island is a quiet one, and she arrives at the precinct in time for her shift to start. Matt is at his desk when a call comes in to investigate a felony in Eltingville.

He greets her at her cubicle and informs Khara they are going to a murder scene in a housing development. Once downstairs he tells her the keys to the unmarked car are in his pocket this time.

"Today I will drive Khara. Last two weeks I had a relaxing few days while you were away, and I would like to keep it this way. You do realize you drive like a crazy person."

"So you don't want a little excitement in your life?"

"Not this early in the morning, thank you."

Matt drives with care to the crime scene keeping the flashing lights off, and no siren blaring. The felony is already committed. No rush to arrive quickly, only to arrive. On the way, Khara asks where they are going, and she recognizes the address as the anger management doctor's home.

Eltingville is not too far a drive, and they pull up and park next to the two squad cars which are in front of the home. In no hurry to enter they walk to the open entrance door, and a uniformed officer directs them to the basement using the side stairway.

Upon entering the basement office a woman is seen handcuffed and sitting on the sofa. The doctor is on the floor covered in blood with a large carving knife protruding from her chest.

Matt bends down to take a closer once-over at the body while Khara wanders around, and inspects every nook and cranny in the room.

"Absolute no-brainer Matt, I would say one of her psycho patients did her in."

"Looks like it, go ask the woman on the sofa what she did."

Khara turns to the handcuffed woman and points to the body.

"Hey, you want to tell me what went on here?" To her, it is pretty obvious what went down, but she asks to make certain no deviation exists in her story.

The woman is sitting, and not saying anything. No tears, no remorse, only silence.

"Listen, Miss, I need you to tell me what happened to her. Otherwise, they are going to lock you up in a looney bin at the crazy people's ward in the hospital. So I'm not going to ask you again. Start talking." Khara said to her in a threatening tone of voice as she stood over the woman.

In a halting manner, she starts to speak with measured words. "I am a professor with a doctorate in history, and I was experiencing anger issues at work. The school is trying to force me to leave my teaching position. The chairman of the department is an asshole, and so is the president of the college. The doctor, I came to realize, is my last resort to stay employed. I don't understand why I killed her, she is a kind person, and would hypnotize me to try to calm me down. The only thing I remember is she said 'no' to me which is the last thing I can recall. Go look at her computer because she always digitally recorded our sessions."

The computer is on the desk as Khara starts it up, but it is password protected. A few guesses at a password opens the program. Khara last tried Anger and it worked.

"Can I listen to the recording of your last session here? It might help solve the murder, and even help you in court."

"Go ahead if you think it will help me," the woman said.

The recording starts and everyone in the room is listening to the doctor hypnotize the woman. After a minute or two, the doctor instructs the woman to react violently if someone says "no to you". Then the doctor goes on to instruct her to enjoy pain. Khara turns the recorder off after hearing what is said on it.

"Matt this doctor is a whacko. Now we have the answer as to why her patients killed people."

Looking around the room stacks of disks is on the upper shelf of a wall unit, and she goes over to them. The top one is taken off and she inspects the disk and finds out they are labeled with people's names. These are recordings of her sessions with clients as Khara informs the crime lab people to bag and save them, and let the district attorney decide how to use the evidence.

The morgue arrives and removes the body while the suspected killer is taken to a holding cell in the precinct.

"Matt lets search the house while we are here. You never can tell what will turn up, I'll take the master bedroom, and you take the other two smaller ones."

Back upstairs Khara opens the bedroom door, flips on the light switch, and enters inside. The room is empty except for a large round bed on a small platform in the center of the room. There are red sheets and pillowcases with a screaming true red comforter on the bed. The carpet is dark black as is the carpeted raised platform with the walls painted in a flat black color. The ceiling is mirrored from wall to wall with four high-intensity spotlights situated on each side wall and focused on the round bed. In the investigation she walks into the room, snooping around and spots two expensive video cameras hung over the transom of the door facing the bed.

"Hey, Matt you must come in here to understand what's in this master bedroom."

In a minute or two he comes into the room to find out what Khara is yelling about.

"What do you think Matt?"

"The recording makes sense now if you come with me to the middle bedroom right next to the bathroom."

Both go into the mid-sized room and are stunned to find chains hanging from the ceiling, whips, and on a table in the room are instruments which can only be described as unusual. Framed lithographs are on the walls of sadism, masochism, and bondage scenes. Left on a tipped over large wooden whiskey barrel are leather garments with chrome studs on them.

"This doctor is a true nutjob with a propensity for violence. How could she counsel anger management patients not to act out their feelings? To me it seems she couldn't control her own emotions" Khara said.

"Well, I guess one did, so much for her success rate."

"What I think, is she put a post-hypnotic suggestion in the minds of people with a propensity for violence. Problem is this time it came back to bite her fatally. Come on Matt let's get out of here. Include this stuff on our report, and I'll tell the crime lab, people, to take photographs of the rooms."

Matt is driving back to the precinct to write their event report when a new call comes in about a hostage being taken during a domestic dispute. The flashing lights are flicked on and the siren begins to wail as he speeds up trying to drive to the ongoing standoff. As they head to the Jersey Street projects the dispatcher on the police radio requests an ambulance be sent to the scene.

Soon they arrive, and there are squad cars stacked up outside the building. The structure is a low-slung city housing project. The officer by the entrance tells them the domestic disturbance in on the first floor on the left side of the hallway.

The wall of half-opened mailboxes, which seem to be pried open, is on their left side when they view uniformed officers gathered by the apartment's front door. With their gold shields hanging around their necks they ask an officer what is the situation.

The officer began to explain the current situation.

"About two weeks ago we visited this place and I remember we took a male resident into custody because he was naked and incoherent. A neighbor had called 911 and we responded. The city sent him to a hospital psych ward for observation. The doctors must have released the nut case because we are back again. The same person who dialed 911 for the second time could again listen to a woman screaming in his apartment."

A woman's screams are now penetrating through the door as they talk in the hallway.

'No don't, stop it, help, put the knife down, help."

Upon hearing the loud plea for aid the sergeant on scene ordered the door broken in to try to save the woman before she is killed. A battering ram is used, and the officers rush in the apartment one after the other. Khara peers into the apartment and a naked man is standing over the woman, who is lying on the floor bleeding from an abdominal wound as he holds a knife, and dripping blood off the tip of it.

"Drop the knife, drop the knife" an officer screams at him. The man continues to stand still, not moving nor dropping the blood soaked blade. Again he shouts out the last warning "drop the knife now." Still, the man does not obey, and he stares at the police gathered in his apartment with a blank expression on his face. The knife is held in both hands as he raises his arms high in the air and appears to Khara he is going to stab the woman again.

The two uniformed officers also in the apartment decide not to wait any longer and Taser him in the chest. The fifty thousand volts from each Taser sends him flying back to the floor. Moaning in anguish he thrashes around a little clinching his teeth. The officers stop sending the voltage and jump over the fallen woman to restrain the suspect.

An ambulance arrives, and one of the medical technicians bends down to help the woman and applies a compress to the wound. A stretcher is brought into the apartment and the medical techs take her to a hospital emergency room.

Matt takes a statement from the next door neighbor who called in the emergency. He closes his notepad when he finishes with the woman he calls Khara, and they walk out of the project to their car.

"I'm proud of you today Khara. No one died."

"Thanks, Matt, see sometimes I can show restraint."

***

"Almost lunch time McMann, where do you want to go to grab something?"

"One of the fellows in the precinct mentioned a new diner opened on Arthur Kill Road off Rossville Avenue near the water. The guy said the food is pretty good, and the prices are reasonable. What do you say?"

"Fine with me, let's try it, can't be too bad."

Matt turns the car around and heads for the place to eat lunch.

In the distance coming up fast is a small diner, and when they pull up the parking lot is almost filled.

Both leave the car and put their badges back in their shirts, and walk into sit at a table. A pert young hostess chewing gum with teased blond hair takes them to a booth by a window looking out at the water. The woman leaves two menus, tells them their waiter will be right with them and strolls away.

The menu is large. Matt decides to order a cheeseburger deluxe, it includes lettuce, tomato, pickle, fries and creamy coleslaw. "What are you going to eat Khara?"

"Think I'll order a Spanish omelet, but with yellow rice instead of home fries. Much healthier I think."

"Yer you're right on it being healthier, but I have a craving for a cheddar cheeseburger."

A young waiter comes to the table to take their lunch order, and Khara asks if they carry Dr. Brown's sodas. "No, I'm sorry we only sell Pepsi products.

"Can I order a black coffee instead of a soda please?"

"I'll drink a Diet Pepsi with lemon," Matt said.

The waiter leaves to input the order into the diner's computer system. Both Khara and Matt lower the volume on their radios since they called in for a thirty-minute break. If a hot call comes in they'll need to leave the diner. No calls come in, and things are quiet for a while so they can eat.

The food comes out fast and they start eating. Eggs or a burger are hard to kill. Finished they go to pay their check, and a young woman is at the register complaining to the owner she is not going to pay for her lunch. The complaint is the food served to her is not hot enough.

"Did the food come out cold when the waiter brought it to you?" the owner at the cash register asked.

'No it wasn't cold, but the fries were not hot, only lukewarm" she answered.

"Did you eat everything on your plate?"

"Of course I did, I was hungry, but the food was not hot."

In a stern voice, he told her "you need to pay for it, or I'm going to call the police and have you arrested."

Now standing next to the woman as she argued with the owner Khara overheard the conversation, and she is getting irritated waiting to pay her check.

With a short quick outburst she ran out of patience, flipped her badge out of her blouse, and told the woman "either pay the damn check, or I'll arrest you for theft."

The young woman turned to Khara, and with her forefinger poked her in the chest while spritzing her with saliva, and yelling "you ain't going to arrest anyone today bitch."

No sooner is the saliva, and her finger touching Khara the situation is over. The woman's hair is grabbed by the back of her head and Khara smashes her face forward, and down, on the granite countertop twice. A blood smear is left on the rock hard counter along with parts of the girl's front tooth. The stunned young woman's body lost its tension. Matt handcuffed and led her out of the diner gripping the girl by her arm.

"Asshole you don't attack a police officer," Khara told her.

The money for lunch is left by the register, and she tells the owner the tip is included. Both officers leave the diner to take the woman to a holding cell at their precinct.

On the way back to their office a call came over the radio about a shooting at the site of the burned out dance club Al owns. "Matt you must take me there now."

"In the back of the car we have a prisoner in custody Khara, and she needs medical attention."

"Screw her, and I realize the situation Matt, but I must go find out what happened. This is important to me. Later we can transfer her to a squad car when we arrive at the building. I need to go on this call."

Knowing her relationship with Al he acquiesces, turns on the flashing lights, the siren and heads to the back 440 highway and the club. Both of them are ignoring the moaning in the back seat as Khara jumps out of the car when it stops at the demolished building's driveway. The ambulance is on the way, and two squad cars from the local zone patrol are present.

Big Boy is standing next to a body lying on the ground draped in a blue construction tarp. With abandon, she is running at full speed towards him and shouts a lot of questions at him in rapid succession.

"Biggie what happened, who was shot, where is he?"

Khara noticed the big guy had tears cascading down his face. "Al is dead he had no chance, I am sorry Khara. The contractor is excavating his office, and he drove up to supervise how it is going. The red Cadillac is parked on the other side of the wooden fence. One of our Mexican day laborers is taking a cigarette break next to where Al parked his car. The door to his Cadillac opened, Al stood to stretch his legs, and the worker walked behind him and shot him in the head. The boss had no chance, no chance."

"Where is the shooter now Biggie?"

"The Mexican worker tried to run away but we caught him before the squad cars arrived, and he's still alive for the moment, but not for long. Al is more than a boss to me Khara, he is my trusted buddy. Back in the day, we grew up together on the streets of Brooklyn like brothers."

The question she asked him is not answered, and she asks it again. "Where is the Mexican? I need to speak to him about the shooting."

"The guys took him to the waterfront warehouse we use sometimes. Remember you were at the place before when we were questioning one of the cartel's men. Do you still remember the address at the warehouse district?"

"Yes, my GPS will get me there, but first I must go to the precinct for my car. Tell whoever is watching him you need him alive until I arrive at the warehouse."

"Will do, I'll call them now."

***

Matt transfers the woman to an ambulance on scene and drives back to the precinct with Khara to drop her off at the car. The M3 starts and she coasts along the twisting streets to the dock area situated a little before the ferry terminal to Manhattan.

Now remembering where it is she turns into the warehouse district, and parks near the building Big Boy had sent her previously. Two men are standing outside the door and she recognizes both of them. One is a valet from the club, and the other a member of Big Boy's crew.

The men wave to her to enter. Khara is brought back into the bowels of the old rotting wharf warehouse. At a slow pace she is walking with them and again can hear the waves whispering beneath her feet splashing against the wooden floorboards. The musty air is mixed with the fine mist of salt water from the shallow bay below.

The last large room of the decrepit wharf they enter. She spots a small man sitting tied up on a small wooden chair in the middle of the room with his hands secured behind his back. One last door is open at the far end of the room, and she sighted a familiar small cabin cruiser idling and waiting.

"Here is the creep who shot him," one of the men standing in front of chair said to her. Behind him were two very large and powerful overstuffed men. One of them is holding a rope in each hand to be used to garrote the prisoner.

Khara asked the men "do you know who he is?"

"No, he is a Mexican day laborer we picked up at the corner where they all hang out for work. The Mexican gets a hundred a day in cash like all the rest."

Approaching the tied man she asks him "do you speak English."

Yes, he nodded his head.

"Why did you shoot him?"

"A gringo said my family in Mexico would be sent money, and be set for life."

"Who told you they will send money?"

"A man from Laredo told me. Two years ago I crossed the border and did work for him each day when I was at his house. The gringo told me a famous Texan would take care of my wife and children if I came north, and shot a man with a red Cadillac. The man sent five hundred dollars to my wife and children in Mexico to show good faith. The man drove me up here and gave me a gun. Today they picked me up to work a job, and a big red Cadillac drives up, and I shoot him."

"You realize you will be killed now," Khara told him.

"Yes, I did it for my family, and I am ready to die so they can live a good life."

Standing in front of the man she stares at him in silence and begins to speak to him for the last time in Spanish.

"Your wife will not receive a penny more for what you did. You will die for nothing. They will never pay your family any more money. The only thing the gringo wanted is someone to kill the man you shot dead."

Upon hearing, Khara say this to him in his native language his eyes filled with tears.

Khara ignores his emotions, turns around, and leaves the warehouse back to her car knowing full well he will not last a minute longer in this life.

The road out of the warehouse district is twisting and close to the expressway entrance. Her mind is working overtime thinking how to tell Olga and Viktor what happened to Al. While driving she is wondering if Junior will take over Al's operations. The future now is a mystery to her, and she does not foresee what it will hold.

In the BMW on the expressway home, she calls Olga on her car phone to tell her of Al's death.

"Olga Khara, Al was shot today, and killed at the club."

"Do you know who did it?"

"Yes, a man who was hired by Ted Ferry's group. Now you and Viktor are the only ones left, and you are in their crosshairs."

Olga does not hesitate and is decisive. "We need to take action as fast as we can and implement the plan we all decided on last night when we rode on the boat. When is the funeral happening?"

"Don't know yet. Later I will contact Junior to find out, and I will inform you as soon as I am told the time and date."

"Okay Khara, thanks for calling me."

At the Bay Parkway exit, she turns off to go to Junior's funeral home for some more information about the arrangements. Parking in the rear lot she walks around to the front entrance and enters. A tall slender man with a pencil thin mustache, his jet black hair brushed back, and in a black suit again greets Khara, and asks if he can help her.

"Yes, I would like to speak to Junior. Tell him Detective Bennet is here to talk about his father's death."

"One moment please while I will try to page him, and you can take a seat in the chapel in the meantime.

The man turns and walks into a private office closing the door behind him. A moment later he comes out of the room and asks Khara to follow him. The staircase is not too long and he takes her to a room with a small desk and two chairs. Sitting behind the large mahogany desk talking on the phone is Junior, as he motions for her to sit on a chair while he finishes his conversation.

"This is a terrible day Khara. I can't believe my father is shot in the street like a dog. This is awful, and I'm going to kill every one of those bastards, and their whole families. I know it is Ted Ferry's group of asshole Texans. The whole bunch of them must be killed, you understand?"

"Let's go outside to talk," she said.

Junior looks puzzled, he seems to not apprehend why she wanted to leave the building. Khara thought he is still young and not as experienced in security measures as his father due to being involved in illegal activities for years.

"Why go outside?"

In no-nonsense tone of voice as she answers him. "Because I asked you to go outside with me, it should be enough of a reason."

Junior knows of her reputation and does not want to mess with her. The desk chair is pushed back, he stands and escorts her down the back staircase to the rear parking lot. The back entrance door is closed as

Khara turns around, and orders him to stretch his arms out.

"I don't feel comfortable in rooms I'm not familiar with, and I need to pat you down to find out if you are wearing a wire because I trust nobody."

Raising his arms out she pats him down, feeling his chest and back to ensure she didn't miss anything.

"Do you wear a tie clip?"

"No, I don't wear them" he answered.

With extreme care, she opened his suit jacket and felt the lining. Then she spoke to him in a frank and forthright manner.

"Here is what's going down. Last night your father met with another couple and me to plan to eliminate the Texas for Texans. The group is building a training facility upstate New York. We are going to go in the camp and wipe out all those racists, and I may need Big Boy and some of his crew to help me when I arrive there. Can you arrange it for me?"

"Not a problem. Tell me when you need them, and I'll send the guys with you."

"One more thing, when is Al's funeral? I would like to attend."

"In about two days from now, I am getting the body brought here when the medical examiner is finished with it. Figure I'll have the viewing in three days, and the burial in four. Don't worry I will be in touch."

Khara thanks him, and goes to her M3 to continue driving home.

At Brighton Beach, she drops off her car and decides to walk to the deli to get a sandwich to bring back to her apartment. Once she flips the key fob to the valet one of Olga's security men is there waiting for her. She is told Olga insists he escorts her if she is going anywhere in the neighborhood since the recent attack on the building.

Understanding the situation she does not protest, and they cross the street on the way to the kosher delicatessen. They are walking under the elevated tracks when a downdraft of air from a passing overhead train is felt against her face as it leaves the subway station. The thin sea mist is refreshing as Khara takes a deep breath trying to capture the tang of the ocean in her lungs. In a matter of a minute or so the salt air is replaced by the aroma of cooking brisket and pastrami emanating from the deli's open front door.

"Come in with me, this is where I am going. Want a sandwich? It will be my treat."

"Nyet, I am on duty. Thank you for asking."

The counterman recognizes her now as a steady customer.

"Want a corned beef and a knish today?"

"Yes please, and two Dr. Browns black cherry sodas, to go."

The elderly waitress spots Khara and slides behind the counter standing in front of her. "I'm going to wrap up some sour pickles for you sweetie, he never remembers to pack the pickles. How is the good-looking man you were with the other day, you remember I had my eyes on him."

"He died today."

"I am so sorry dear, my condolences."

"Thank you, I'll be back soon. Good night."

After paying for her order she heads back to her place to eat the sandwich in solitude and watch some television.

***

It is late now, and she sits down at her kitchen table and starts to enjoy her hot corn beef on rye. The phone rings and her caller ID reports it is her sister calling.

"Hi, Dixie Pearl, what's up?"

"Nothing much Khara I wanted to find out how you are doing, I am so happy I, at last, met you. Praise Jesus I can't begin to tell you my lifelong dream came true."

"Well, I am also pleased to find some family because I never knew any of my parent's relatives. How is your husband?"

"Fine thanks. After the fire and shootings at the convention center, he decided to retire. This week he is fresh water trout fishing in the mountains with his buddies."

"Glad he is doing some fishing, it must be relaxing for him."

"Yes, it is. Do you have any hobbies Khara?"

"I practice Krav Mega which is a form of hand to hand combat the Israeli Defense Force uses. Also, I go to the gym a few times a week, and shoot at least once a week at the range."

"Thanks sounds like you are pretty busy."

"Yes, I am. Sorry, I must hang up Dixie Pearl, but I sat down to eat a hot meal, I'll call you soon, bye."

Khara is not a person for small talk. Although it is a short conversation with her sister it is long enough for her.

One-half of the corn beef sandwich is finished when her phone rings again, and it is Johanna. This one she must answer.

"Hi, Johanna what do you need?"

"The Organized Crime Bureau in the department called to say a major drug crime boss in Staten Island was shot and killed today. Turns out he owned the club which was blown up the other day. Did you find out anything about it when you investigated the blast the other day?"

Even though she is intimate with Johanna she does not trust her enough to tell the real story about her relationship with Al. The truth is shaded, and Khara tells her enough information so she would be in the clear if the department had assigned an undercover internal affairs officer at the club snooping around and spotted her in the place.

"The truth is I somewhat knew him as I used to go dancing when I was off duty. The place made delicious steak sandwiches too, and I would stop in for lunch on occasion. The owner knew I am a cop, and a customer, so he would sometimes sit at my table and talk to me trying to pick me up. I do not go in the club too often."

"Glad you are not in the dance club too much because he is involved with drug smuggling from Mexico. The FBI's sources said a domestic terrorist group is attempting to kill him, and his partners. We do have our suspicions but we can't confirm anything yet."

"Johanna, are talking about the bigoted people who are setting up a training camp in Booneville New York?"

"I am glad we're on the same page Khara because I need you to go and snoop around to find out what they are doing. The state police took aerial photos of their site, and I understand the facility is completed, and ready to go live with recruits from all over the country."

"Can you send me a copy of the photographs Johanna before I go upstate?"

"Tomorrow I'll ask them to email copies over to my office. I will bring them home with me, and if you stop by we can eat dinner together."

Khara is talking and the phone rings again. Another incoming phone call is buzzing on her line.

"Let me check what my schedule is Johanna. I'll contact you later during the day, and call you back about dinner."

"Talk to you soon, bye."

She picks up the incoming call, and it is Don.

"Hi Khara, I'm in New York tonight. Are you in the mood for some company?"

"Sure Don come on by, I'll ring you in when you are in the lobby."

"Be there in a little while."

She puts her phone down, finishes her once hot sandwich, and potato knish.

Walking into her living room after cleaning up the kitchen she is thinking about how she is going to ask Don for a topographical map of the Booneville New York area. Through the FBI he has the connections to obtain one. The problem is she can't tip her hand to him about Al's plan. Maybe tomorrow when she contacts Johanna she'll be able to have one for her. She is well aware she'll need one for the attack on the campsite if the aerial photos are not good enough.

***

About forty minutes later Don is in the lobby, and the concierge calls upstairs announcing his arrival. "Thank you, send him up."

In a short time, her doorbell rings, and he is standing in the doorway holding a huge bouquet of flowers for her.

"These are for you Khara, and I want to say you are much prettier."

"Thanks, but I'm not much of a flower person. They are too prissy for me; I would prefer a box of ammo or a gym membership."

"How about I give you a kiss hello instead of the flowers?"

"Sounds good to me Don, come in."

Escorted to her living room he places the bouquet on her kitchen table and proceeds to sit on the sofa next to where Khara is now sitting.

"So what brings you to Brooklyn tonight Don?"

To her, it is a rhetorical question. She thinks she is cognizant of why he is here, and it is the same reason she believes she invited him to stop by when he called.

"There are two reasons I'm here. The first is I miss you and want to be with you. The second is my terrorist sources informed me the Mexican Secret Police are after their two drug partners in the United States. The Bureau said they knocked off one of the partners the other day. Some mob guy in Staten Island, are you aware of it?"

"Yes, Johanna asked me to investigate the explosion at the club he owned. In a coincidence, I used to go there to dance and blow off some energy, and I even met the owner a few times. Once or twice he bought me lunch."

There is no way she could tell him the truth about her relationship with Al. Don would leave and not come back. It is not because she loved him, and would miss him, but he is a stable influence on her when they are together. In the back of her mind her psychiatrist Eloise recommended, for a long time, she tries not to be as promiscuous as she had been in the past. The man sitting next to her is the psychological medicine Eloise said she needed. Khara is constantly told by her not to sport fuck anymore so she is now behaving herself more or less.

In conversation, he told her the FBI is informed the Texas for Texans Foundation "maintains ties to the

Mexican police, and the Foundation is a domestic terrorist organization."

"Guess I can tell you this Don. Johanna asked me to go to Booneville to investigate the training camp they built upstate, and I need a topographical map of the area. Can you send me one tomorrow?"

"Should not be a problem to obtain one for you. In the morning I will call Washington, and ask if they can hand deliver one to you here by evening."

"Wow, it will be great. Come join me, I want to take my nightly shower."

Chapter Fourteen

The next morning when she woke up she rushed into the shower and started the hot water. After finishing, and drying off she opened her medicine cabinet to grab her Chanel No.5 as is her routine, except this morning she spots a small black gift box on a glass shelf.

With her right hand, she reaches up and takes the box out of the cabinet, opens the lid, and finds a diamond engagement ring. Motionless, she is stunned. A big question pops into her mind. Did Al leave this here the other night when she slept with him or did Don place the ring in the cabinet last night after she went to bed? Which man gave the ring to her, the living one or the dead one?

The decision is made to play the situation in a cool way so she puts the diamond on her finger, and in a confident manner comes out of the bathroom seeing him sitting up in bed.

Now thinking to herself if he says what is the ring on her left hand Khara is going to say she bought the diamond herself to keep obnoxious guys from hitting on her.

He spots the glittering diamond on her finger when she saunters naked back into the bedroom. "So what do you say Khara? Want to keep the ring, or should I return it?"

Soon she is standing next to the bed, and she sits next to him on the mattress.

"Listen to me Don, I didn't expect this. Are you sure you want to marry me? There is a ton of emotional baggage I carry, and you are not aware of my problems" she said.

"To be truthful with you I am at the point in my life when I don't care about a lot of stuff anymore. Age is catching up with me, and I am getting too old to continue playing around with a lot of women. Would I like to settle down with you, yes I would. What do you say?"

"Yes, I will marry you, but you need to understand something. Many times I will be away for a while traveling for Johanna, and I won't be home for extended periods of time. Can you live with my being away from you?" The thought is going through her mind should she tell him she is bisexual but decided not to do so. In the future, if her sexual preferences come up she will. At this moment she decides to wait, and not give any explanations.

"Not an issue, I understand what you are saying because I also do a ton of travel for the FBI. No problem with me if you say yes."

"Come give your fiancé a big kiss good morning."

"Tonight we can set a date when we eat dinner later," Don said.

"Depends, if I can be home in time we will discuss a wedding date. Later today I am meeting Johanna to grab some papers from her. The arrangement we made yesterday is I meet her in Jersey City tonight at her condo after she gets home from work. If I am running late I might sleep over at her place, I'll let you know if I am coming home. Hard to say on where I need to be in the morning."

"Okay, I understand your position. I need to go to work now myself. Later, if I can, I will call you."

After they each dress and leave she drives to her precinct for the day shift. On the way, she gets a call from the funeral home.

"Hey Khara, this is Junior. The coroner's office notified me I'll be getting my father's body back late today. The viewing will be held tomorrow at noon."

"Thanks for calling me. I'll be at the wake."

For the first time while driving over the Verrazano she glances upward and realizes the sky is blue and the clouds are fluffy and white. In all her years of going on the bridge, she never viewed anything above the roadway before. In a flash her emotions are different, she is at peace with herself for the first time, and can't understand the sudden positive mood change.

On the Staten Island Expressway, she calls her psychiatrist on the car phone to make an appointment. This is a new experience for her, and she is not sure how to react to her feelings. The service picks up her call, and she explains to them she needs to talk to Eloise. Satisfied they will call her psychiatrist she expects a call back later so she continues on to her precinct.

In the main lobby, she meets Matt after arriving, parking in the side lot, and he informs Khara a young girl is in custody to interrogate for drug possession with intent to sell.

The pair takes the stairway downstairs to the basement holding cell, and they lock their guns in a wall safe and proceed to the holding area. The suspect is ordered to sit on the bench and place her hands behind her neck. Once her hands are interlocked they open the black iron door, enter and escort her to a room for an interview.

One of her arms is held by Matt as they walk down a hallway to a small room containing a desk and three chairs. After she reads the arresting report Khara asks the woman "why does a twenty-five year old carry over one hundred and fifty plastic bags of heroin in her possession?"

"I don't know, and I don't care either because what the cops found in a pocketbook is not my pocketbook" she answered.

The statement is ignored and she continues probing.

"The officer's event report states you and the driver are the only two people sitting in the car when they stopped the vehicle for a traffic infraction. Your wallet with your driver's license and identification is also found in the pocketbook. Did the drug fairy sprinkle pixie dust to make drugs appear?"

The woman shrugs her shoulders and doesn't answer.

At last Khara's patience runs out, and her good mood for the day disappears as she leans forward towards the girl in a menacing manner.

"Better listen to me bitch you are going to be charged with possession with intent to distribute. In New York, with this much shit on you, you might be looking to walk out of prison when you are eligible for social security. Why spend the rest of your crappy life behind fifty-foot concrete walls? Tell me who supplied you with the heroin. The girl is starting to become jittery, beads of perspiration are forming on her brow, her nose is running, and her eyes are watery and glazed.

"Matt she's high and will be going through withdrawal soon. Let's transfer her to the county jail and out of here before she begins throwing up all over the place. She will die in prison, we're finished here."

"Wait, can you help me?"

"Depends on what you tell us" Matt replied.

"My pimp gave the smack to me, and I became addicted. He did this so I wouldn't want to leave him, and go independent. He is the driver of the car the cop gave a ticket to when they stopped us."

"Matt I copied his name from the event report. The officer issued a citation, and the car was let go since they found the heroin in her pocketbook, and not on him. Let's go interview him, I wrote down his address in my pad" Khara said.

The girl is returned to the holding cell, their weapons are retrieved, and they walk upstairs and take an unmarked squad car to make the visit.

"Hand me the key Matt, I'll drive there."

With Khara behind the wheel, they arrive at a residential area off Hylan Boulevard in only ten minutes. The street is tree-lined and the houses are not much bigger than summer cottages turned to year around homes.

The police car parks in front of the house and they walk through the sagging chain-link gate. Matt knocks on the door and waits because the doorbell is missing from the front of the home. With a harder rap on the door, he bangs again, and the door opens creaking as the rusted hinges yield to its age.

A scruffy looking young girl swings the door wide open, and she appears to about fourteen years old. The girl is wearing a filthy unwashed tee shirt, soiled dirty jeans, and her hair is stringy and disheveled.

"How old are you? Matt asks.

The girl gives them the finger and slams the door shut in their faces.

In a sudden rage, Khara kicks the flimsy door open and storms in. The girl turns around and stands in front of Matt and tells them to leave her house before she calls the cops. In a defiant stance, the young girl is standing in the middle of the living room with her hands perched on her hips.

In a swift move, Khara grabs her by her shirt, bunches the filthy cloth in her fist, and throws the petite girl on the sofa.

"Don't screw with us you little piece of shit, we are the cops! Where are your parents? Who else is in this house?"

The young girl yells out her answer to Khara as loud as she can.

"Nobody else is here, only me!"

Matt points up, and they listen to some movement in the attic. The home is not a two story building so they realize someone is crawling around above their heads trying to hide. He takes the girl by her arm and handcuffs her to the exposed cast iron radiator.

Now they go from room to room looking for the opening in the ceiling so a person can climb up to the attic crawl space. The house contains only two small bedrooms besides a kitchen and Livingroom. In one bedroom closet, Khara finds a hatch in the ceiling with a chair beneath the square hole.

Below the opening, she is standing and yells up to the person crawling around in the attic. Either you come down now, or I'm going to set this place on fire, and you'll be burned to a crisp.

No response is given.

A quick walk to the kitchen and Khara takes a dish towel, turns on the stove and lights the corner of the fabric. The flaming cloth is thrown through the open hatch, and she yells out "I'm not kidding you. Next, I'm setting your sofa on fire. The whole damn building is going to go up in flames."

'No don't, I'm coming down.''

Outside of the closet, Khara waits until a man's pants descend from the opening, and tries to balance on the top of the chair he used to climb into the attic. With a sudden impulse, she kicks the chair away and pulls downward on the legs causing a man to fall out of the ceiling to the floor of the closet with a thud.

Now hearing a tumult coming from the bedroom Matt remains in the living room watching the handcuffed girl. From experience, he understands sometimes it is better if he does not see what is going on with Khara.

Still, in the closet, she takes one of his arms, twists the arm behind his back, and flips him on his stomach while grabbing a handful of his long hair in her other hand. "Do not even think of blinking or I am going to break your arm right off your body."

"No, no don't."

"Tell me who your supplier is?"

"This is police brutality, I am aware of my rights, and I am not telling you shit" he screams.

"Oops what is a nasty fall you took from the ceiling" as she slams his face on the floor. "Hope your nose isn't broken."

The man is now moaning as blood starts to flow from his nostrils.

"Better listen to what I am going to tell you, someone once told me people break their legs when they fall from a distance, do you think you broke any bones? How is your leg?"

"No more, no more. In Park Slope Brooklyn I buy my smack from a Spanish biker gang. The bikers bring the stuff up from Laredo on their bikes."

For a moment the thought flashes in her mind about the irony of the situation. Here she is arresting someone for selling the drugs her dead boyfriend is importing into the country. The big problem is as a psychopathic person she is not capable of remorse or feelings towards the victims of the drug trade.

Matt walks into the bedroom and helps Khara secure the man to send him and the girl to the precinct to be booked and further interrogated. The police send a van to escort them to the holding cell.

More squad cars arrive and the officer in charge secures a warrant. The officers tear the house apart from wall to wall looking for illegal drugs, which they do find. The drug detail smashes the toilet with a sledgehammer searching for opiates. Water starts to flood the house. No one is turning off any water valves, and when they go the whole house is left flooded. The water is continuing to run and takes about an hour for the interior of the house to be in ruins when they leave.

***

Finishing the paperwork Khara leaves for the day and heads home to change her clothes. Later she will call Johanna to find out if she acquired the aerial photos she wanted. First, she must shower and dress before she leaves to go to the wake for Al.

After grabbing something to eat she will go to the funeral home and hope she will still be able to head for Jersey City to meet with her before the time gets too late.

Khara drops off her car with the valet at her building and strolls into the main lobby when the concierge asks her to wait a moment. "Olga would like to speak to you, she will be right down."

The elevator bell rings as she is standing in the lobby and Olga strolls out. With a hand wave, she motions for Khara to go up with her. In a moment she is entering behind her watching Olga press the penthouse floor where she lives. The front door opens as they walk inside, and she asks Khara to please take a seat at the dining room table.

"This afternoon a messenger hand-delivered a topographical map for you and our concierge signed for the package. In a minute Viktor will be out of the shower, and he'll explain to you how he plans to attack the Texans in Booneville."

Mail addressed to her is held behind the desk in the lobby, and she is cognizant letters are being opened and resealed, but Khara says nothing. Any personal letters she receives is sent to a UPS mailbox she rents so opening her mail doesn't bother her. This confirms she needs to be careful what papers or items she leaves in her apartment. In this building, no privacy exists for any tenant.

"Do you need the aerial pictures? The photographs might make this easier so we are certain where they will be situated" Khara said.

"Yes, but we can study them later. Now we need to learn the terrain so we can plan how we are going to approach their training camp."

The sound of the shower stops and in a few minutes Viktor walks out of the bathroom wearing a large blue terry cloth robe with a red sash tied around his waist and rubbing his hair dry with a towel.

"Good evening Khara I'm glad you stopped by tonight. Here is the address of their training camp from the papers Al sent Olga. The facility is located east of Booneville in a thick and desolate wooded area. From Google Earth, I obtained the coordinates to pinpoint where the facility is, and I coordinated the street address to the map we obtained today. Sit over here I want to show you what I think is the best way to attack them" Viktor said.

"What is the plan of attack?"

"In the morning we will travel to the Utica area then up route 12 and shoot off to route 28. The vehicles will pull off, and search for a spot to park when we arrive at Moose Road. From the staging point, we go on foot since they are located between the two roads. From my sources I ordered some Russian RPG-7D paratrooper rocket-propelled grenades and launchers. The RPG's breakdown for easier carrying. The cars and van will park before dawn and go by foot through the woods to their camp. After we surround them during the night, at daybreak when our visibility is better, we attack them on three sides before they wake up. Anyone who manages to run out of a building will be shot and killed on the spot."

"Sounds good Viktor, how many men is Olga bringing?"

"I'm not sure yet. All the men who will be going with you and Olga are retired Russian Special Forces. There won't be a need for too many, they are elite soldiers."

"Well, everything seems good to me. Late today I will obtain the aerial shots and drop them off at the front desk when I come back."

The plan is finished being discussed so Viktor goes back to his bedroom to dress for dinner.

With the plans explained, Khara stands, and Olga escorts her to the door.

"Sleep well tonight Khara because we are going to finish them off. I don't need those idiots trying to blow us up in our own home. Are you going to the wake?"

"Yes after I change and eat I'm going to run up to Junior's, and pay my respects."

"Later Viktor and I will attend, there is a chance we will meet you at the funeral home."

"Tomorrow I will be ready bright and early, goodnight Olga."

***

After cleaning up and finishing a light meal Khara puts on a clean pair of jeans, a different blouse, and is ready to drive to Bensonhurst to the wake. The valet signals for her car when she comes out of the building, and in a moment one of the men brings the car to the yellow curb.

On Bay Parkway going to the wake, she becomes aware of a car parked on a side street across from the funeral home's driveway. The vehicle is a nondescript dark-colored sedan with two white men sitting inside.

Under normal conditions, this would not arouse her suspicion, but they are holding a camera and taking pictures of visitors as they enter the front door to the facility. The fact she is given an excuse from Johanna to be investigating the explosion does not change her preference she does not want to be photographed, less explaining to do if asked. So she parks near the rear entrance and phones Big Boy to open the back service door for her. In a minute the door is opened and Big Boy waves her inside.

Together they walk up the back staircase to the first floor and enter the viewing room. About thirty people are sitting and talking, and only a short queue is in front of the open casket. Khara and Big Boy go to the back of the line and waited their turn.

The room is overflowing with floral wreaths and sprays hanging on a stand, except for the rear of the room flowers blanket every wall. The florist next door always arranges the flowers which are being sent for funerals. Big Boy said, "Al's cousin runs the flower shop, and Al owned the floral business also."

Big Boy went first, knelt on the footstool, and crossed himself before standing. To the right of the body stood Junior, and he is next to a more mature looking woman Khara thought must be Junior's mother. Big Boy is standing in front of the son and both of their eyes filled with tears as Biggie wrapped his massive arms around him and they hugged in sorrow. Now turning to the woman next to Junior Big Boy hugs and kisses her on the cheek, and said he wished he, not Al, is in the casket. Tears crept down her face, and she raised her hand, and with apparent empathy stroked Big Boy's cheeks with a soft touch. Big Boy turned and stands next to her while waiting for Khara to move up in the line.

In front of the massive brass and chrome casket, Khara stood, and glances down in silence. An atheist she did not kneel or make the sign of a cross. With the soft lighting of the room he seems so serene to her with his blue suit and tie pressed, and no gunshot markings are visible on his head. Motionless she views his still body and turns to face Junior. Khara hugged him, and he whispered in her ear "I want you to realize you made my father happier than he has been in years, thank you."

He stepped back next to his mother as Khara turned to face the widow.

Big Boy did the introductions. "This is Detective Khara Bennet who worked part-time with Al on security issues at the club, and this is Al's widow Maria."

"My condolences, I am so sorry for your loss," Khara told her as she took Maria's hand in hers, and held it for a moment. The two women stared at each other for a few seconds in silence

"Thank you, Detective. Next month we would be married twenty-nine years."

The awkward silent moment passed, she let go of her hand, and Khara walked to the rear of the room where she sat on a standard sized gold colored upholstered chair. Big Boy followed and sat next to her using two chairs to accommodate himself.

"Hey Biggie, Al never told me he is married. To be honest, if I knew it would not make much of a difference to me."

"You realize I can't answer for him Khara, but I think you understand why he said he is married. All I can tell you is he was crazy about you and loved being with you. Of all the girls he dated you made him happiest, and you also scared the shit out of him when you are driving your car with him sitting in the passenger seat."

A smile crossed her face when Big Boy said it to her.

Khara's left wrist is turned a little so she can eyeball her wristwatch and told Big Boy she needed to go.

Johanna would be expecting her to call. Ready to leave she taps Big Boy on the knee as she stood to go, and Khara told him she'll call tomorrow.

On the way out Khara stopped in front of the ladies room, and entered. A short stocky girl is walking in the restroom right behind her. A sudden feeling comes over her the woman is following too close for comfort.

Once inside the room, Khara turns around, stares at her, and is struck by the girl not wear a lot of gold jewelry or the black teased hair the girls in Bensonhurst most often wear. A sense something is not right starts her adrenalin flowing. This woman is a blond with straight hair, blue eyes, and is wearing western styled boots with pointed toes.

Face to face Khara's gut tells her this is going to be trouble, and she takes one step back away from the girl in a defensive move. Not one to fade away Khara now confronts the girl in a confident and angry tone of voice.

"What's your problem?"

"Ever since Virginia I am following you. You went in the ladies restroom at the convention center with my sister, and I witnessed you run out seconds before the explosion killed her. My father arranged for your boyfriend to be shot, and now, you black bitch, you're going to die."

The hefty girl flips open her pocketbook and reaches into withdraw a pistol from a small hip holster secured inside the bag. In a flash, Khara leaps forward grabbing the hand by the wrist which is holding the gun. With her other hand, Khara grasps the girl by the throat. The muscles in her fingers tighten as she squeezes with all her strength on her windpipe. The assailant's eyes start to bulge open. In a life or death struggle, the stocky girl reaches back and throws a left hook with her free hand to the side of Khara's face. The clinched fist lands with such fury the punch loosen the firm grip on the girl's throat. Khara, slightly dazed, she still continues to hold the girl's wrist.

The blow causes Khara to fall back to the ground. Still grasping the girl's wrist Khara drags the girl down with her and uses her leg strength to flip her over her head, and she lands on top of the young woman after doing a backward somersault.

Once both are on the tile bathroom floor Khara swings her lower body upwards, and with her legs pins the girl in a choke hold between her knees. Struggling to breathe the girl begins to turn her wrist, and point the pistol at Khara. The struggle becomes a matter of brute strength. The girl is pointing her pistol towards Khara's head when a deafening shot rings out, and the struggle is over.

The girl's body goes limp, her brain matter splatters on the floor, but the shot is not from the younger sister's gun which went off.

On her stomach, she glances up from the floor in the bathroom, and Khara stares at Maria standing in front of a stall in the ladies room holding a Glock .45.

"Screw her, I stood in a stall, and I overheard everything. How her father killed my husband. This piece of Texas trailer trash isn't going to hurt my husband's girlfriend. I am well informed about you Khara. You gave him what I couldn't give him anymore due to my illness. Al and I enjoyed an open marriage for many years, and I am okay with his mistresses. Do not be embarrassed, I am aware he had feelings for you, and I'm glad you kept him acting young. Now leave as fast as you can, and I'll cover for you. Junior will need you in the future."

"What about the body. What are you going to say to the police?"

"The cops will never find her body. Junior uses a special coffin in cases like this. She will be placed on the bottom, and someone else in his refrigerator will be over her. They will never be able to find the girl. Now leave at once."

With one hand on the floor, she presses down, bends her knees, and stands while straightening out her leather jacket. With her composure returned after the fight she walks out of the ladies room and leaves the building.

***

Once in her car, she calls Johanna to confirm she is home with the State Police photographs.

"Yes, Khara I'm home. The water ferry dropped me off a few minutes ago, and I acquired the pictures you need. Come up, I'll be waiting for you."

"I'm on my way, bye."

First, she needs to go back to her apartment to put on a clean pair of jeans. Maria's gunshot splattered the girl's blood all over her pants legs. After the clean clothes are put on she will drive the M3 heading for Staten Island.

The BMW is speeding over the Verrazano and Bayonne bridges with its lights flashing and siren on Khara is on the back 440 highway in Bayonne, and at Johanna's in record time. The parking lot is almost full so she pulls into her reserved space to park.

Upstairs Johanna opens her door and takes Khara by both hands pulling her into herself. A kiss on the lips says hello. While holding Khara's hands she feels the engagement ring on her finger.

Puzzled she peeks down at the ring.

"May I assume Don asked you to marry him?"

"Yes, he did this morning after I woke up. My psychologist wants me to settle down, and stop sleeping with many different men. For my mental health, she told me I need stability in my life."

"Stability I can appreciate Khara. Where does your commitment to him leave me?"

With her right hand, she reaches out to hold Johanna's. "Don't worry, unless you are a strange man, I don't think a problem exists. Guess we can still be close friends with each other as far as steadiness is concerned. What do you think Johanna?"

The two embrace, and kiss.

"Come sit down I think we should eat dinner before the food gets cold," Johanna said.

After finishing their meal Johanna takes out the aerial photos, and she goes over them with Khara at the kitchen table.

"The schedule you gave me from the briefcase stated the Texans will be in Booneville soon. The pictures are clear and show the camp is complete, and they should be traveling to the facility as we talk."

Khara is informed of the plans with Viktor and Olga, but Johanna is not. The plan now needs a diversion to keep the New York State Police planes away from the area taking photographs while they attack the Texans in their training camp.

In the kitchen sitting next to her at the small round table, Khara leans in and kisses her on the lips. "Please Johanna do not ask me why, but I need the state police to search for the Texans in Buffalo instead of Booneville next week."

Nothing more is said about upstate New York as they stand, and walk to the bedroom.

***

The next morning Johanna leaves before Khara wakes up and a hot pot of coffee is on the stove waiting for her. A cheese Danish with cherries is sliced in half on a plate, and covered with a clear plastic wrap on the counter for her breakfast.

After Khara showers, she is fresh and invigorated because Johanna remembered to buy her favorite coconut body wash, and a bottle of Chanel No.5 for her to use. Finished drying off, and before she goes back into the bedroom to dress Khara dials Olga to tell her she will be at her place with the pictures in an hour or so.

In her car, she is leaving Jersey City and hops over the Bayonne Bridge. On the way, she stops by her precinct in Staten Island to speak to Matt. At work, she goes upstairs, and he is in his cubicle when she asks him to come outside to talk with her. This only happens when Khara is going to do to something important, or illegal, and after years of being her partner, he knows all her habits.

Once standing by the cars out front they are between two parked squad cars.

"Wanted to tell you, Matt, I'm going to be away on a mission for Johanna which is my cover. I will tell the captain, but I wanted to be honest with you. Soon I am going after the Texans and the remnants of the cartel. I am tired of them coming after me."

What Khara didn't tell him is she is also going to try to kill the presidential candidate too if she can.

Finished with Matt she goes into inform her captain she will be on assignment, and away for a week. The commanding officer is well aware of the unspoken knowledge in the precinct of people dying, or injured when Khara is out on a case. The captain in not so many words is happy to let her go. Less violent statistics in his district is good for him.

Back in the M3 she soon arrives in Brooklyn to join Olga. The two women meet in the penthouse and are sitting at the dining table looking at the aerial photographs Johanna obtained.

"Tomorrow, Saturday, I am going up to Utica with two cars together with my men. A van carrying our weapons for us will be driving between our two vehicles. Early in the morning, I would like you to come also."

A second before Khara can answer Olga's phone rings and the concierge downstairs asks her to put on the television. An important news story is breaking, and he thought she should turn on the report.

The television remote is on a table as Olga grabs a controller and turns on a political right-wing station. The reporter is standing in front of Congressman Ted Ferry's home in Texas. A representative of his is saying a picture surfaced in New York with the congressman in a compromising position with a young girl. The girl appears to be underage, and Mexican. The television camera turns to show many satellite media trucks gathered in front of the home waiting for a public relations person to come out and make a statement.

"Did you involve yourself with anything to do with this Khara?"

"No Olga, Junior must be the one who sent the picture to the news media as revenge for Ted having his father killed. This is the only explanation I can think of for the media running the story which makes sense to me."

The television cameras on the scene show a blond, thin woman, walk out of the house and stand next to him. The reporter introduces her as the congressman's new campaign manager. The camera turns to her and does a close-up as she starts to address the press.

"Good evening from Austin Texas. Congressman Ted Ferry categorically denies having anything to do with this doctored photograph which is being floated around the media as real. The congressman is a religious person of faith and is one of the founders of the Family Values Movement in America. This picture is not in any way authentic and is a slur on the ethical beliefs Americans hold close to their hearts. The congressman would also like to say, at the request of the mayor of the City of New York Mister Ted Ferry will be at City Hall next Wednesday to receive an endorsement. The presidential candidate will be standing beside the mayor who announced yesterday he will support him on the historic front steps in his run for the presidency, and to denounce this humiliating falsehood in person. Thank you."

With an intense interest, they listened as the press representative finished, and turns back into the house behind her without answering any questions from reporters who gathered in front of the home.

"What do you think Khara?"

"This affirms he is another political asshole from Texas. At least we are aware his schedule is changed, and he'll be in the city next Wednesday. This change of events makes things easier for me to kill him."

The news report now over Khara turns back to the photos and begins to memorize the layout of the buildings. Satisfied with her information she stands to leave as Olga walks her to the door. "In the morning we are leaving early, meet you by the curb."

"I'm going to ask Big Boy to follow me with a few of his crew. Is that a problem?"

"Not at all, see you then."

The elevator carries her down to her apartment, she locks the door once inside and starts to pack for the short trip. The first thing she does is clean her MP7 submachine gun, and make sure the spare clips are loaded. Next, her two pistols are cleaned, and she takes out a few hand grenades from the bottom drawer of her dresser and places them on top by her mirror.

Nothing will be left to chance.

Chapter Fifteen

The sun hasn't come up yet when Khara walks out of her building with two small duffle bags and wearing her backpack. The valet ordered her car be brought around to the front for her. In the haste to pack she forgot to call Junior to send Big Boy with her.

Only a block from the ocean she can inhale the salt air floating in with the morning mist while standing on the sidewalk under the overhang. Early predawn Saturday morning in Brighton Beach is quiet. No one is rushing to catch a train to work. Only a few automobiles are on the road, and the area is peaceful.

The M3 turns the corner and drives up to the awning as she spots the car coming to her. To her satisfaction, the car is washed, and with a full fuel tank due to Olga's orders for today. The valet pops the trunk for Khara, helps her place her bags in the car, and he goes around to the side, opens the door for her to enter, and wishes her a good day.

In the driver's seat, she depresses the clutch and is shifting into first gear ready to leave when in her rearview mirror two cars pull up behind her. Olga and a group of men walk out of the building and wave to Khara as she drives off.

The New York State Thruway is boring to her.

Once out of the metropolitan area low-slung mountains scattered small farms, and miles of nothing but trees are in view while she is cruising along. With a finger, she presses a button and turns on her car radio. The smartphone in her pocket plays her personal mix through the car's speakers. Her favorite Stones album is now playing, and a smile crosses her face as the highway drones on mile after mile.

When she reaches the Patterson rest stop she pulls in and waits for Olga to meet her. Time goes quick and it is not too long until the two cars and a van reaches her and park in the rear lot next to her M3.

Everyone goes inside except for two men in the van who stay and guard the contents. Olga buys lunch and drinks for the group and sends some food out to the men outside. Khara is now informed where they made reservations to establish a staging base. The area is a secluded home in Old Forge New York in the woods away from prying eyes where they can stage their assault on the training camp.

Finished eating all head out and drive to the rental property to set up and be ready. In a few hours, they will arrive at the house, and supplies will be unpacked.

Arriving at the base they park and start to get ready.

In the house, Olga and Khara talk over the plan again and decide to case the roads around the Texan's training facility. Plenty of daylight is still left so they drive out to the site.

They find a spot north of the camp where they can leave the cars before going into the primal forest to make their advance the next morning. The clearing is off a winding desolate country road, and if anyone comes along they will think the vehicles belong to hunters.

Arriving back in Old Forge they all gather for dinner at a nearby restaurant and afterward return to the house when they are finished. Olga takes out the maps and photographs and goes over everything with her men again. The plan is to arrive at the training camp before dawn, and attack from three sides.

Satisfied everyone understands what to do before they retire for the evening they now can relax for the night .

***

Early the next morning before sunlight they arise and load the cars heading off to the remote clearing Olga scouted the afternoon before. The men pull off on a gravel road leading into the woods and a small grassy area. They break into teams of three plus Khara. The forest begins where the cars are parked, and they head south towards the camp.

The moon is full giving off some extra light while the underbrush is not too bad as they make their way using a compass and night vision goggles worn by the point man. The soldiers are in combat fatigues and boots. Khara is wearing jeans, a tight dark blue wool NYPD sweater, her black boots and carrying her MP7 in a sling over her shoulder ready to use in a split second.

Upon reaching the site the point man signals for the groups to fan out.

Three large tents are built on wooden foundations off the ground. Khara thinks they must contain a lot of bunk beds in them. Set apart, and to the side of the others is one smaller tent building with a Texas flag printed on the side of the canvas. She figures it must be the Foundation leader's bunk.

Still in the woods, and standing next to Olga, she signals with her hands she is going into the leader's tent herself.

Olga waits till Khara runs to the leader's structure, opens the screen door, and enters while holding a knife in her right hand. She gives the signal of three short shrill whistles, and the attack begins. Multiple RPG"S are shot into the structures causing massive explosions and starting the canvas fabric on top to catch fire. Without hesitation, a second round of RPG's are fired at the buildings.

Screams are heard emanating from the burning tents as Olga's Russian Special Forces start shooting into the bunks at anything backlit from the flames, and trying to stand. The soldiers approach the buildings to peer into the fire better, and shoot at anyone still alive and moving.

The loud military assault starts. The Texan's leader is jolted upright in bed only to be surprised Khara is standing at his bedside with a sharp blade to his throat. He stares up at her, and with no vacillation, he recognizes who she is.

"You black bitch you're going to die today. My men will be in here any second." He is solely focused only on her blocking out all the noise outside his tent. He did not realize the explosions and gunshots are his men being slaughtered.

Khara responded "I don't think so. I'm going to kill you like I killed your two asshole daughters."

After she spoke he attempted to stand to fight her, but Khara's quick reflexes enabled her to plunge the knife into his rib cage. The blade slid between his bones and the sharp point plunged into his heart. The leader fell on his knees to the floor. In a blink of an eye, Khara raised her left leg, swung her foot around, and kicked him in the chest. Now on his back, he stared up at her with the knowledge he is dying. The knife is sticking straight up, and he is struggling to take a breath. With his teeth gritting he picked up his fist a little while raising his middle finger at her. Upon seeing him give her the bird she is incensed.

The MP7 is swung around from her shoulder and lowered toward him. Khara sends a short burst of bullets into his head and chest scattering his brains and blood all over on the wooden floor. The flames from the other tents spread to his canvas tent top, and she is aware little time is left to leave the tent.

Seeing her men standing in the middle of the compound Olga is satisfied everyone is accounted for and the militiamen are all dead. It is time to head back to the cars and Brooklyn.

***

The drive back on Sunday morning seemed quicker to Khara for some unknown reason. Her music mix is blaring Janis Joplin as she tooled south on the New York State Thruway back to the city. No one called and bothered her on the phone, and time seemed to fly by.

Khara arrived at her building and the valet took her M3, and one of the security men inside came out to help with her bags. At last in her apartment, she double locks the door and places a shim under the door to prevent the door from opening. Tired from this morning's long drive and excitement she walks to the bathroom to shower, clean up, and rest.

Early Sunday afternoon Don calls her and asked to come over to her apartment. He enjoys walking on the boardwalk and breathing in the fresh sea air. Khara tells him to come about six, and they can go out for dinner.

After putting the phone down she thinks about calling Eloise on her private number and telling her she is engaged. Instead, she contacts the service and leaves a message she wants an appointment to meet with her. Khara would rather speak to her face to face than over the telephone.

In the kitchen, she opens the refrigerator, takes out a cold beer, and sits on the sofa to pass time. The late news will be on television by the time Don comes, and she will turn the news off. Midway during the broadcast, she receives a call.

"Hello is this Detective Bennet?"

"Yes, can I help you?"

"Junior is calling from the Fattachie Funeral Home, and he would like to speak to you. Please hold a moment."

For a few seconds, there is silence on the line until he picks up the telephone.

"Hi Khara, how are you today?"

"Fine thanks, what can I do for you?"

"I'm sorry you encountered a problem in the ladies room last week. My crew cleaned up the mess, and everything is gone. To the point of the call, I would like to speak to you in private. How about we meet tomorrow morning for breakfast?"

"The morning is good for me," she said

"Meet me at the diner on Nostrand Avenue by the bay. I'll be in a booth by nine."

"I will be at the diner by nine tomorrow, thanks."

The short conversation is finished so she hangs up the phone, sits back, and starts to think of why he would want to see her.

The concierge calls Khara to inform her Don is waiting downstairs.

"Please tell him I'll be right down.

The elevator opens on the ground floor and she enters the lobby with him waiting for her.

"What do you feel like eating tonight Khara?"

"Some of the guys in the building told me some good things about a steakhouse on Emmons Avenue, and the place is not too far from here. Want to try eating there?"

"Sounds good, I can always go for a delicious steak."

Khara turns to the concierge and asks him to call a taxi for them. Instead, he calls out to one of the security men sitting on a nearby sofa in the lobby. "My man will drive you where you need to go, Miss Bennet. Please give me a minute while I arrange for a car to be brought around."

"Thank you," Khara said.

Once in the black Lincoln limousine, only minutes pass before they are in the restaurant and seated.

The menu is filled with delicious options when Khara decides she will order the pan-seared filet minion with roasted vegetables and twice baked potato. Don likes the rib eye with grilled carrots. The waiter suggests a red wine and they buy a bottle to go along with the meal.

After the waitress takes their order Don places Khara's hand in his.

"Are you thinking of any particular date you would like to be married on Khara?"

"To be honest with you I married my husband in June and the marriage didn't work out so well. So any month except June is fine with me. How about next winter we say our vows in the Caribbean on an island, or even maybe Bermuda? The ceremony can be on a beach."

"Sounds good to me, next week I will inquire into a destination wedding."

After eating they walk to the bay, and view the docked charter boats. Walking hand in hand with the water to their left he turns to Khara, and asks if she ever "thought of retiring?" They stop walking and she leans back against the round steel fence by the water's edge.

"I never thought about retiring, although I did put enough years in, but not the age. Guess I could, but I never gave retirement any thought. Why do you ask?"

"The FBI wants to move me up to a supervisor level in the Midwest. If I take the promotion this would mean we would need to move. I can't take a new position knowing you would be unhappy living somewhere else."

"No family is holding me here, I guess I could. Did they give you any idea where they would transfer you?"

"The human resources people told me the two openings are in St Louis and Omaha, but either place can be the one where I am moved."

"To be truthful I would need to think about moving Don. Today I'll say I will think about moving with you, and I'm not saying no to you. But I need time to think about it"

"Yes, I realize it. The bureau gave me two weeks to tell them if I accept the promotion. The position will be a big raise for me."

What Khara does not tell him is she is clinically diagnosed as a psychopath and is a self-centered person. In a short time, she must decide about moving, and marriage.

Don hails a cab to take them back to Khara's apartment where they spend the night.

***

The next morning she wakes up early, decides to go running leaving him sleeping in bed, and places a note she is jogging on the kitchen counter.

Monday morning commuters are on their way to the train station as she runs past them heading for the boardwalk. Khara thinks there is enough time to exercise before she goes to meet Junior.

Johanna gave her plenty of cover time wise so she is not in a hurry to report back to her yet. When finished with her jog she showers and gets dressed. He is up now and showering before leaving for work. The bathroom door opens and she calls into him she is going to work. With time to spare, she goes downstairs to bring her car around and drives to her meeting.

Parked in the back of the diner Big Boy is sitting behind the wheel in Junior's black Cadillac. The BMW parks next to Big Boy, and she walks over to talk to him. "Hey Biggie, do you know what he wants to speak to me about?"

"Nope, but he was told what you are capable of doing, and also by some of the fellas who worked for Al. Guess you will need to talk to him yourself. Good luck with him."

"Okay thanks, later."

She goes to the front of the diner leaving Big Boy in the rear lot on Nostrand Avenue and walks up to a short flight of stairs.

Inside Junior is sitting in a large booth on one side of the diner, and nobody is eating in the booths on either side. He tipped the maître d to arrange they stay empty while he is at this table.

"Good morning Khara. How are you do-in today?"

"I'm fine." You wanted to talk to me about something?"

"Would you like some breakfast first? At the moment I am in no rush."

He waves for the waitress to come to the table and take his order.

"I would like two eggs over easy with home fries, bacon well done, and dry toast. What would you like to eat Khara?"

"This morning I want a black coffee and a toasted English muffin please, and no butter on the muffin."

"Is this all you are going to eat? It's my treat."

"Thank you Junior, but this is my usual breakfast. So why am I here today?"

"It is common knowledge around the organization you are my father's gumar, and he was crazy about you. Also I know you were a valuable asset while you worked for him. My family values loyalty and certain abilities. I would like to offer you work on an as-needed basis. This can be a financially rewarding situation for you."

"Listen, I'll be on the level with you Junior. What I did for your father was in my best interests. A Mexican drug cartel tried to kill me many times. I helped your father out, and he helped me out with those bastards. I didn't do any of this for money. I did what I did for self-preservation. And yes your father treated me well, with finances too, and I also enjoyed being with him. I am not for hire. If you are in trouble in the future let Biggie contact me, and I'll decide if I can help you out. But there are no promises. Also, I might be moving to the Midwest soon, and I'll be out of New York for good. I'm just informing you, nothing else."

"I understand what you're saying, but I learned a long time ago never say never."

"As long as we see eye to eye there is no problem here," Khara said.

Junior did not to push her too hard because he is told by many people she can be a volatile person. They finished their breakfast and left together, and he picked up the check. He walked her to the back parking lot to her car where she said goodbye to Big Boy.

Done at the diner she drove back to her apartment. Once inside she opened her closet, lifted up a backpack, and took out her Remington C.S.R. sniper rifle. With precision and care, she places the rifle on her kitchen table and proceeds to oil and clean the weapon

Tomorrow she is going to need the gun to be in excellent working condition.

When she has finished Olga calls and asks if she is available in an hour for a meeting with her and Viktor. Khara did not intend to go to work today so she said yes, and would come upstairs at eleven.

At eleven she rang Olga's doorbell and Viktor opened the front door to welcome her into the living room.

"Take a seat Khara. We want to speak to you about something."

Not knowing what they wanted to speak to her about she felt no choice but to sit and listen.

"Olga and I want you to know we like having you as a tenant. Al paid one year's rent for your apartment in advance. We would like you to stay here, and help us out on occasion instead of paying us to live here."

"What kind of helping you out did you think I would be good for?"

"We do a lot of international work, and a little in the states too. Sometimes we need someone with a certain skill set, and we appreciate the fact you possess the tools we on occasion do need. If you like traveling you can think of this as a paid vacation. Travel expenses are covered in full plus bonus money for you when the job is completed. Your police work in terrorism can be your cover while you also work for us. And no rent will be charged on your apartment either. Does anything we said sound interesting?"

"Yes everything does, I'll tell you soon because I need a day or two to mull this over. Thank you for thinking of me, and I am interested."

Nothing is mentioned of her moving to the Midwest because she thought this is too early in the conversation.

She is thinking to herself on the elevator ride down to her floor.

Knowing Al is gone, and she cannot afford to live in this ultra-secure and expensive luxury building without him paying the rent she is serious about considering their offer. In all the time she is living in the apartment it never dawned on her he is covering all the expenses for her. She thought this is a mutual deal between two partners helping each other out.

Could she live a bucolic lifestyle in the Midwest? In her mind, she harbors real doubts about the quiet life since she is an adrenaline junkie.

Not receiving a return call back from Eloise she calls the service again. An operator answers and Khara tells her she is recalling for an appointment. Earlier she called in but Eloise did not return a call back yet. "We are sorry about her not returning your call Miss Bennet, but she is in the hospital. Yesterday she suffered a heart attack, and is in the critical care unit at Mount Sinai."

The operator hangs up.

Khara calls the hospital, but they will not release any information on a patient.

A decision must be made about moving and marrying Don. This is the first time she is experiencing an urgent need to speak to Eloise, and she is not available. Khara is inundated with too many options, and she must talk to someone about them.

Her psychiatrist always helped her to make a decision. Most of the time her life is straightforward and her gut reactions guided her, but now this is different. Khara senses she is lost without her emotional crutch.

The last thing she does before leaving her apartment is pack her rifle, a few bullets, and drove to Manhattan to visit Eloise in the ICU.

The parking lot is near Mt. Sinai and she takes the stub and walks to the hospital. She enters the hospital lobby, and flashing her detective's badge to security is able to go up to the critical care unit. At the nurse's station, she inquired about Eloise, is told she is resting and in stable condition. "She will be fine. She must be sent for some rehab but otherwise, she will recover" the attending nurse told her.

"Can I stay with her? I am her significant other" she said.

Upon seeing Khara's gold detective badge and shoulder holster the floor supervisor allowed her to sit in the room. Later in the day Eloise woke up and saw Khara sitting next to her bed. Upon seeing Khara she smiled and waved for her to come close.

"Kiss me," Eloise said.

Khara stood next to her bed, leaned over, and kissed her on the lips.

"I love you Khara."

"You are going to be fine. I spoke to the head nurse. You need to rest, and you will be better soon."

Incapable of true love Khara could not respond to the statement of affection with a quick reply. She held Eloise's hand and waited for a moment. Khara bent forward to be close to her, and whispered in her ear she loved her too. The affirmation of love is a lie, and Eloise knew it too. After twenty years of being her psychiatrist, and lover, she is aware this is the best she would ever receive from a psychopathic killer.

The floor nurse asked her to turn her cell phone off when Khara inquired if she could stay with her through the night shift. All night she slept in a chair next to her bed till morning, except for going downstairs for a quick bite to eat.

The next morning she kissed Eloise goodbye, put on her backpack, and headed downtown to City Hall by subway.

Congressman Ted Ferry is scheduled to give a political speech denouncing the picture of him, and the young Mexican girl as a fake. The large obnoxious and obese mayor, who ran a robust and aggressive primary campaign against him for president, is supporting him now in the hopes of being named the vice presidential pick at the coming convention, or after the election the Attorney General of the country.

Khara bounds off the subway at the City Hall station and scurries up to the parking lot in front of City

Hall Park. From the top step by the building's entrance, she gazes south towards the Battery and can make out a tall building at the corner of Fulton Street and Broadway. There is a clear view of the City Hall steps. Yet the structure is far enough away nobody standing by the podium will be able to spot her.

The walk is only a few minutes, and she enters the office building on Fulton Street. The doors open and she takes the elevator to the highest floor where she gets off and searches for a way to the roof. The stairway she is searching for is situated around a corner at the end of a long hall.

Climbing the steps to the top the stairway is two flights in one. At the highest step, she pushes the panic bar on the door open, and the door is not alarmed or locked from the inside. Stepping out on the flat tar paper roof she places a strip of duct tape over the tongue of the door to keep it from shutting and locking on her. A scarf is pulled up around her face before she leaves the stairwell, puts a Mets baseball hat on her head, and flips her hoodie up and over her hat to hide her face.

With a casual walk so as not to attract attention she goes to the corner of the roof and glances down at City Hall Park. The trees are not too high, and she can visualize a clear shot. With a turn of her head, she glances up at the office buildings across from her and realizes she will need about five seconds and only one quick attempt before anyone will view her standing on the roof.

Her wristwatch informs her the time is ten in the morning, and the offices in lower Manhattan are filled with people. The speech at City Hall is supposed to start at eleven, and she must now kill one hour.

Going back inside the stairway Khara sits on the top step, begins to think about Don and Viktor, and what her options are.

Should she marry and move to the Midwest? Or stay and work for the Russian syndicate and Junior? Or retire, and go live near her sister Dixie Pearl in Virginia? Now more than ever she must speak to Eloise to help her make a decision, but she is not available.

With fifteen minutes to go, she opens her backpack and assembles the rifle. Screwing on the noise suppressor she loads a bullet into the chamber and closes the bolt action. With the stairway door open she spots a flagpole on top of a building across the street. Still inside the stairwell, and sitting on the last step she aims at the gold metallic eagle is perched on the pole to test the scope. One quiet shot is all she needs, and a small four-inch wing flies off the bird. Satisfied as to accuracy she is ready and reloads the chamber.

At eleven o'clock on the nose, she begins to walk to the corner of the silver painted tar-papered roof with the rifle hidden inside her leather jacket and hiding the weapon as best she can. The gun is held close to her body trying to conceal the weapon from being seen by anyone in another building. At the edge of the roof, she stops at the parapet. Looking north she can distinguish a large crowd gathering by City Hall. The speech is starting.

With a careful and steady quickness, she sets her arms in a stable triangular position on top of the concrete wall and uses a small binocular to see what is happening on the front steps.

The candidate moves toward the podium and brushes his willowy comb-over blond hair back off his forehead.

Khara estimates the distance and wind direction as she lifts up the sniper rifle from under her jacket, sets, and takes aim.

One second passes.

The scope focuses in on the target.

Congressman Ted Ferry starts to speak. His amplified voice echoes off the office buildings.

Two seconds pass.

Assured in her mind she adjusted for everything, and the target is in her sights she squeezes the trigger while exhaling.

The bullet streaks across city streets and whistles over City Hall Park seeking its destiny. With unbelievable force, it hits the congressman a little to the side of a red tie he is wearing. Tearing a deadly hole through the front and back of his heart, and exploding out the back of his suit chipping a stone step behind him, Ted Ferry falls to the ground.

The End

www.CreativeFiction.net